LOVE'S ENDURING HOPE

June Masters Bacher

HARVEST HOUSE PUBLISHERS
Eugene, Oregon 97402

Scripture quotatioı
Bible.

LOVE'S ENDURI

Copyright © 1990 by
Eugene, Oregon 974

Bacher, June Masters
Love's enduri
ISBN 0-89081
I. Title.
PS3552.A257L68
813'.54—dc20

Printed in the Unit

Contents

1. Descending 7
2. Home Is Where the Heart Is 11
3. Changes 13
4. Introductions and Interruptions 23
5. Comfort in Time of Affliction 27
6. "I Will Not Leave You Comfortless..." 31
7. Evil's Bright Lining 36
8. Decisions 43
9. The Letter 47
10. "Where Is God?" 50
11. Doubt Is Out! 57
12. Goodbyes Without Tears 63
13. The Twain Shall Meet 71
14. The Light of the First Day 79
15. And Then the Dark 87
16. The Return of O'Higgin 95
17. Understanding—and Lack of It 101
18. Midgie's Letter 107
19. "Mica, Mica, Parva Stella..." 112
20. Quiet—and Then the Storm 117
21. Death March 121
22. Turning Point 128
23. Revelations, Uncertainties—
and a Promise! 133
24. A Most Amazing Christmas 142
25. Aftershocks 148
26. What Christmas Is All About 155
27. Life Must Go On 161
28. End of a Silver Silence 169

29. Calm Before the Storm 173
30. The Smell of Blood 177
31. Warning—Unheeded 184
32. The Legend of True North 187
33. "Starbright" 194
34. Volunteers for Jesus 200
35. Some Went, Others Stayed 203
36. The Outside World 207
37. Crossroads 214
38. "Whither Thou Goest..." 219

Known unto God are all his works from the beginning of the world.

—Acts 15:18

Decision of character will often give an inferior mind command over a superior.

—W. Wirt

1

Descending

In that mystical time of day when gray light precedes the coming dawn, the world held a wraithlike look. Smoke spiraling from chimneys of early-rising farmers looked black against the billows of white clouds, which (like the vine-maple leaves) blushed with just the right amount of pink to whisper the change of seasons. Like a wheel at the top of its climb, there was a breathless pause before summer yielded to fall, and then the world would be white with winter. Inside the cozy cabins, fires would blaze as they hissed happily on the diet of pine-resin logs; and hominy grits, swimming in lakes of melted butter, would replace the garden greens of summer-gone. People drew close to nature, God, and neighbors.

Like the wheel, the rented buggy had reached its apex—as had True's heart. The beauty spread before her and Young Wil brought a lump to her throat. It was too much to digest. One could only look, remember, anticipate. And then would come the descending...

"Happy?" Young Wil drew the horse to a halt.

"Of course I'm happy—I'm with you, am I not?"

"And 'whither thou goest...'? There needs to be more than that."

True cast a quick look at her husband's face. His eyes were darkly luminous in the soft light which was beginning to flood the world with morning. Was *he* having doubts? His plans had always been to return to the Valley, finish his internship with his uncle, and then doctor back to health the people he loved so dearly. It was a dream which, though interrupted briefly, was about to resume.

"There *doesn't* have to be more than that!" True said with heartfelt conviction, resuming their conversation. "Your people are my people already. But even if they weren't—"

"I know, darling—I know. You would follow me to the ends of the earth, regardless, just as you did when we gave up a year to see Marty and Midgie through that crisis." His voice grew husky with emotion.

"I loved it!" she said lightly, reaching for his hand. "It's going to be wonderful to get back, though, Dr. North."

"Not quite yet," he smiled. All the same, he patted his vest pocket with pride. In it was his temporary license. "There's the year to put in with my uncle, the senior doctor, which I'll enjoy and appreciate. It's just that—"

"You feel a little queasy. Very natural, Doctor."

Young Wil grinned. "Thank you for diagnosing my case for me, an indication that you have the same symptoms. With test scores like yours, how could you doubt yourself?"

As usual, she had been transparent in his presence. He was wrong in what he read into her mood, however. It was something she herself was unable to understand, so why try to explain? "Test scores are one thing, but standing before a roomful of proceed-with-caution young eyes is quite another. So I can understand how you tremble at the thought of deciding if the patient's tummyache is appendicitis or indigestion from eating green apples. So how *can* you tell?"

"Very elementary," Young Wil answered in mock seriousness. "Just look for peelings under the bed."

"Very good. And if you find a saddle instead?"

"He ate horseflesh, of course!"

"Wil North, you are destined to be a quack!"

Together they laughed. *Please, Lord, I love this man You gave me; let me sustain him forever with a merry heart*, True's own heart whispered.

Aloud she said: "You will be a wonderful doctor—one who will crash through every obstacle and win out by sheer persistence and—" her voice lowered as she looked at the handsome man beside her, so clean-souled, so massive in spirit—"you will win confidence with your gentle manner. But you may be a shade too good-looking. Women have a way of falling in love with their doctors, so I may have to pull hair—"

He stopped her with a kiss.

The human mind moves swiftly. In the short time there on the rise overlooking the dewy Valley, True's mind did a quick review, beginning with the most recent chapter and thumbing backward. The landscape between a rapidly growing Centerville and Portland was unchanged—verdant, mysterious, inviting while the larger city remained impersonal, almost uncaring, so filled was it with newcomers . . . ambitious businessmen with flowing ties, sharp of eye and alert of ear in search of new clients. Yet the elderly man with neatly trimmed goatee and resonant voice had appeared sincere as he monitored their tests. Used to be a doctor, he said, and was Mr. North sure? Well, all right then . . . To True, the good man's wife had some words of caution, he said. But seeing their youthful enthusiasm and determination, he shrugged and handed them the forms.

It was hard to concentrate. The monitor kept waving blue smoke from a fat cigar their direction in the poorly ventilated room, while noise below the second-story window was deafening . . . street vendors' voices trying to screech out the quality of their wares above the cheers, jeers, and shrieks as men hand-cranked Portland's first backfiring automobiles. City life was not for them, True had said. That was good to know, Young Wil had replied after giving the matter some thought. At the moment she had supposed that he agreed wholeheartedly. But did he?

True drew a deep breath, trying to clear her lungs of the stifling memory and to dispel doubt. They loved the countryside—all of it.

Her mind went back to the Double N, its surprises and its victories. Marty and Midgie would manage. Of course, now that they had the baby, they must give thought to schools. And there should be a church. How strangely the lives of the four young Norths paralleled those of the generation ahead of them . . . Angel Mother and her love for Daddy Wil . . . Aunt Chrissy and hers for dear Brother Joe. How mysteriously God worked, holding them together, binding their hearts with ropes of love, when the Grim Reaper, life's last enemy, stole away Angel Mother and Uncle Joe. The brokenhearted spouses had found solace in their mutual grief, had married, and had held together the bewildered children . . . nourishing their faith and preparing them for service in their beloved Valley, but never making them quite understand their strange relationship.

"Would you believe," True asked suddenly, "that Jerome asked me just what 'kin' he is to you and me? I guess he wants to be called 'Jerry,' saying that the new minister thinks a new name's in order after baptism."

Unabashed by her out-of-context question, Young Wil answered with a grin of amusement. "I'd believe anything of that pair! Kearby told me how much she loved honeymoons—and when could we have another?"

"*Another?* If we ever have a *first* one I'll be surprised! Imagine an entire family's invasion—oh, well, it was fun! You know, Wil, they've grown up thinking of me as a sibling instead of as a cousin on their mother's side. Same for you: on their father's side, Marty an adopted brother . . . but we loved them, 'kin' making no difference."

"You're wonderful—let's go home!" Surely the mountain stream, darting in and out between laurel thickets and ferns, sang a welcome song as they descended.

2

Home Is Where the Heart Is

The "Big House," Daddy Wil's family home, came into view in spite of Aunt Chrissy's flowers' efforts to obscure it. There was the gnarled old apple tree which had served so faithfully as a shade for Angel Mother's beehives, still intact just as she had left them. True's throat tightened, so caught up was she with tender memories . . . her mother's singing lullabies beneath the tree . . . Daddy Wil's building swings for her and Marty . . . Young Wil's tree house . . . the fat apple pies from the tree's fruit.

One could tell the seasons by that tree—its pink pouting buds whispering spring, then bursting forth with fragrant Hallelujahs on Easter morn (*always* then, in her memory). The leaves served as umbrellas to shield the infant green apples, which blushed with promise of summer as the season marched on. And no matter how many of the forbidden fruits she, Young Wil (who was old enough to know better, said his uncle-turned-doctor), and Marty ate with salt (even though the green fruit put their teeth on edge), there were always ample left for pies, cobblers, dumplings, and the best jelly in the world. Come fall, the leaves warned of winter. There had been no more than three months of real school, since starting was postponed until harvest was over. Closing came when it was "plowing time"—with countless closures between due to inclement weather and flu epidemics . . .

It would be wonderful getting home. But if anybody had told her she would feel like this, True supposed she would have disbelieved it. Why, she was homesick (not quite the word, but she could think of no better) for the lonely, formless landscape, the vastness seemingly blotting out time and space as it stretched on and on into infinity. The land they had feared and near-hated and grown to love now laid claim on their hearts . . . the faultless summer skies . . . the beauty of sudden storms—awesome and humbling as blue-white lightning clawed at the sky's ceiling as if seeking a means of escape—and, yes, even somber winters that bandaged their small world, forbidding movement. She would, True thought with a small smile of surprise at the idea, even miss the strange winds which whimpered, sometimes sobbed, as if in pain. Here the wind gossiped among the pines during the languid days and hummed her to sleep with nighttime lullabies.

Unknowingly she sighed. Perhaps the foreign thoughts came from the incomparable beauty of this Valley: mountains and more mountains, some bonneted with snow which refused to recognize the seasons which the old apple tree foretold, others waving wispy clouds like white flags floating from the tallest peaks, so gently did the autumn zephyrs unfurl them.

"Come, come! Who but you could smile like Mona Lisa while wearing such a pensive expression? Wake up, my precious, we're home—and from where I sit, we are about to come under seige!"

How true—with the leggy twins, barking dogs, and mass of adults charging upon them! There was Aunt Chrissy in a starched apron smelling of sunshine and sourdough, Daddy Wil pointing with pride at the sign proclaiming NORTH & NORTH, M.D.'S., Grandma Mollie ordering breathing room for her "babies" in order to gain right-of-way, and O'Higgin's mellow voice singing the doxology: ". . . as it is now and ever shall be . . ." True could only think of Angel Mother's sampler HOME IS WHERE THE HEART IS.

3

Changes

During the following week, True saw little of her husband except at mealtime. And even then, although Aunt Chrissy had gone all-out to prepare his favorite dishes, he might as well have been eating day-old corn pone and drinking unsweetened juice of wild grapes plucked from the vine before ripened. She understood, as did her aunt and (she supposed) the wives of all other doctors, particularly rural ones. Daddy Wil must catch his nephew up on the condition of patients, what they could afford to pay (and when), which ones were housebound, and which could make office calls. They went through mountains of files, discussed medical terms and new findings, and arranged a filing system which "the women can help set up."

Chris Beth smiled patiently and turned her palms up. The gesture, so characteristic of her, said: "Oh, sure, sure! All we have to do is loaf around here anyway—cooking, mending, keeping an eye on two unbroken coltish adolescents, and, of course, teaching! Bring on the files!"

True giggled. Aunt Chrissy loved every minute of it—and so did she! Besides, the two of them needed time to do some planning. And, to her aunt's obvious delight, True wanted to renew her acquaintance with every square inch of her childhood home—the old mill, the yards, the gardens, but most of all the cabin that she and Young Wil would call home. So she only half-heard Daddy Wil say that Young

Wil's book was still popular. (Needed some updating to increase royalties, of course.)

The mill was still, but the footlog which connected the two houses was still intact. Mossy but showing no signs of age, the log, anchored securely between head-high clumps of sword ferns, lay in contentment—seemingly unbothered by the silver-tongued prattle of the gossipy stream it spanned. One day they would rebuild the bridge which the flood washed away, but True resolved that she would never permit removal of the log. It would be like carving away a part of her heart, for the mossy log represented the magical rainbow-arch which had catapulted her from childhood to maidenhood—quickly, so quickly. One day she and Marty were outrunning Young Wil, their adored but sometimes strict keeper. The next day Wil had joined their play in a game of fox-and-hound chase. True had slowed (purposely, although this she would never admit). As planned, Young Wil caught her while the unsuspecting Marty dashed on in triumph. Triumph? It was she who won! Her adored Wil, pinning her arms to her sides in victory, stared at her with a new fire in his eyes. That same fire ringed her heart.

"You're my prisoner!" His eyes still burned into hers.

"Yes," she said. "And, yes, I will."

"Will what?"

"Marry you, of course."

"Now, listen, brat—"

True had laughed up into his face brazenly. Even now the thrill of awakening came back . . . the thrill of knowing that she had won by losing. They would marry and live happily ever after. And they had.

"Still daydreaming?" Chris Beth laughed like a young girl. "The place always brings back memories for me, too. Just wait until you see 'Honeymoon Cottage.' Uncle Joe and I spent our honeymoon days there, too—" her voice trailed off sadly. "The heart remembers—come on, my darling," she said, her eyes brightening with second bloom. "Love has many faces."

True could only gasp when they entered the cabin, inhaling so deeply that it hurt her chest, then exhaling in a ragged gasp. Was she dreaming? One could never relive the past. Yet Aunt Chrissy's bringing all of Angel Mother's beloved furniture back (even rearranging it as her sister would have done) brought back memories so sacred and so real that the years between melted away. She felt small again, as if she must stand on tiptoe to see the top of the fruitwood highboy where her mother kept the monogrammed silver hairbrush and hand mirror, great bouquets of flowers (always flowers), and her precious diary which kept the memories alive forever. The walls were a riot of color—needlepoint pastoral scenes, dainty pastel petit point baskets of fruit and kittens in quaint tent stitch, embroidery...punch-work...appliqué—all the work of Angel Mother's slender, childlike hands.

With a lump in her throat, True turned to the marble-topped washstand where her mother had placed the hand-painted china basin and giant pitcher, the mirror above it lowered so that a child could comb her golden curls, admire them, then experiment with her still-new face, twisting it into sordid shapes. How her mother had laughed! Maybe, in a way, she had never grown up. Certainly she had never grown old. There had been no time.

Tears stinging her eyes, True reached to stroke the highly polished spool-and-spindle bedposts, then let her fingers trace the outlines of the double-wedding-ring design of the quilt that Angel Mother had stitched lovingly in remembrance of the ceremony at Turn-Around Inn, uniting her and Daddy Wil, Aunt Chrissy and Uncle Joe. And then...

"Isn't this the bed—" True began, then choked back a sob, remembering...

Chris Beth nodded. And then they cried together, sharing their loss.

"Thank you—oh, thank you," True said a few moments later. "I am at home here in every way. I love you all so much—"

When the sun waved scarves of golden mist against the sky, too blue to be real, Chris Beth suggested that they turn home. Days were shortening, she said, even though summer's warmth remained. True agreed reluctantly. Time, she needed more time—time to drink in the beauty of her beloved Valley. With her remained the conviction that every twig, every blade of grass, every bush and tree was a jewel in disguise. Actually each was a precious stone—a sapphire, diamond, turquoise, or amethyst that must be protected from The Forty Thieves! But evenings were shorter here than in the flatlands of the Double N. So she quickened her footsteps to keep pace with her aunt, wondering if she had answered the millions of questions hurled at her this afternoon. There was plenty of time, of course. Why then did she feel a sense of urgency—a hurrying to tie events of the past year together? To make herself understood?

"I hope I am doing a fair job of putting the 12 months into words, helping you see the changes in the hearts of Marty, Midgie, Young Wil, and me. All the time I was there, I kept thinking of how I would relate it all—make you *see* it, *feel* it. And now I find myself tongue-tied, wondering if all is truth—or if words trip me up, forcing me into the realm of imagination, confusing facts with Maud Muller's 'might have beens.' "

Aunt Chrissy understood. "Don't I know and love you all enough to read between every unspoken line? Words are always like that—often baffling the speaker. I guess only God understands our prayers when our mouths utter one thing and our hearts whisper another—and," she sighed, "our spirits try to approach His throne while our minds gather daisies or wonder what we are going to have for dinner. Speaking of which—"

Laughing, "mother" and daughter linked hands and ran through the goldenrods, reaching home just as the sun dipped behind the hills rimming the valley.

Twilight had darkened the livingroom, but neither of the men had bothered to light a lamp. Would they always be this engrossed? Probably. They always had been.

"Wilson North, you are ruining your eyes—and you a doctor!"

The senior doctor did not look up, but the corner of his mouth went up appreciatively, a characteristic his nephew had inherited. True tried to remember which the two doctors thought more important—heredity or environment. Did the apostle Paul know anything about this thing called "genes" when he spoke of nurturing one's gifts?

"I still think of taking more courses in nursing," True said as she set the table for four. But before Aunt Chrissy could answer, she spied Young Wil's favorite cake. "Snow on the Mountain," she called it—a towering devil's food cake topped with swirls of feather-light frosting, often tracked with small fingers that could not wait. But now the cake reminded her to look high up the peak of Mount Hood. Yes, snow still topped it, lines waving here and there by the fingers of nature. She had missed that mountain. And the cake. *Oh, thank You, Lord, again for family, love—and home.*

"You will get plenty of practical experience in nursing in school," Chris Beth assured her as she rescued a cast-iron pan of cornbread sticks from the oven, "as well as helping your husband here."

True nodded. "Will I find things changed, Aunt Chrissy—the people, the church, the school?"

"Very. But I will let you find that out soon enough. I had planned a little shopping trip tomorrow—then church Sunday..."

True was surprised to see the sign: ABE SOLOMON'S MODERN STORE. Somehow she had supposed the Solomons to be retired. They were here, she recalled, when Aunt Chrissy and Angel Mother came to the frontier from Atlanta so many years ago.

She was surprised again at the inside of the department store. It was more like two stores, the old and the new. One side of the enlarged building was indeed modern—some of the merchandise rivaling that shown in the finer stores in Portland. But the other side held a strange fascination, perhaps from recollections of the Caswells' store in Slippery

Elm, a trip into the past and a store whose proprietors had become dear to her heart. But that too was a part of the past...

The Solomons had not greeted them. Instead, they were greeted by remembered smells: food (strong hoop cheese, bacon fat, and the pungent fermented odor of pickles in barrels); mixed leathers of harness (probably there since stagecoach days, as the bridles were gaudily tasseled and cowhide-bottomed); and straight chairs clustered around the same old bumper stove she remembered since childhood.

An even shorter, stooped Abe attempted to straighten from the sliding door leading to a rounded glass display case where he had been arranging spools of colored thread. As, with hands to his back, he continued the struggle, Abe said: "Hep yersef t'coffee brewin' on th' back burner. Bertie, come hep—*Bertie!*" the word came out in excitement when his watery eyes caught sight of True. "Miz Vangie!"

"Vangie's daughter," Chris Beth reminded him gently. "You remember True—and, yes, the resemblance is striking."

"Oh, yes—yes, or course. Th' ole noodle ain't quite what it once was. Can th' two doctors in yer family do much fer heads?"

Bertie Solomon bustled briskly from the back room. "As I live and die, she *does* look like her dear departed mother. I would've supposed 'twas a figment of Abe's mind—come, darlin', let me feast my eyes!"

After the inspection, True wandered into the "Better Dress" department and was surprised to find how expensive fiesta dresses were. Why, Mariah could make a fortune here! Not that she would move, though...

True forced her mind back to the present, fingering feathered bonnets and partially opening parasols. (Not opening them enough to admire the designs, of course. Mrs. Solomon would suffer a grand mal. *Everybody* knew it was bad luck to open an umbrella inside a building. Worse than breaking a mirror. That brought only seven years of misfortunes, but an open parasol—that could strike a body dead!)

Amid True's mental wandering, snatches of conversation between Chris Beth and Bertie reached her ears. How was Maggie? Mention of Bertie's daughter set the woman's tongue loose at both ends. Maggie was in the pink in every way. A real jewel, that girl. Took her time about growing up, but now she had the world's best husband ... was the world's best wife ... and kept the world's cleanest house. The Lord had forgiven her one transgression ...

Actually there had been several, according to Angel Mother's diary—mostly those of casting verbal stones. True further remembered that Aunt Chrissy had felt a pang of jealousy of what Grandma Mollie called the "town harlot, even drest in red befittin' her profession—why, Wilson North wouldn' spit on her likes, jest pray fer her soul! Twarn't even reasonable entertainin' that green-eyed monster th' devil created an' named 'Jealousy' whilst Adam 'n Eve wuz namin' th' animals!" True smiled, recalling that she too had played hostess to the same sin of jealousy. How *could* she have suspected Young Wil of turning his affections to Midgie (of all people!) when she herself was in Atlanta? All women were geared for the unsaintly emotion, she supposed, when another woman came between them and the men they loved (real or imagined).

"... and *so*—we're right glad to be welcomin' you and Young Wil back Sunday," Bertie Solomon was saying, leading True to believe her talk had never stopped. "I guess you had a good doctor over yonder, else you'd never have left. Young Wil bein' a young deacon almost from cradle days led most Valley folks to speculate he'd be a preacher like his Uncle Joe, rest his dear soul. Old one or young?"

Minister, True supposed Mrs. Solomon meant, and answered accordingly. "Neither. There is only a minister who visits periodically—the community being—well, different than our Valley." True paused, something warning her to choose her words, as the woman enjoyed tidbits of gossip. "The hub is hardly a town at all, and houses are far apart, since the ranches are widely separated. Or," she stopped suddenly when it occurred to her that Bertie probably meant a resident doctor, "if you meant physician, we have—*had* none at all."

Mrs. Solomon clucked her tongue, eyebrows arched in question marks. Thank goodness, Aunt Chrissy came to the rescue. "I have a list here, Bertie, and, yes, we will all be in church." She handed a scrap of lined paper to the news-hungry saleslady. "True and Young Wil came back just as we have planned all along. Now, about the list—"

Another customer came in, forcing an end to the conversation. True did not know him, but was to learn later that he was the minister of the church now called "Centerville Community Church." Her impression was that he was a man of great height. Or was that because Abe Solomon was attempting to rise again, unfolding himself like a jackknife, to match the stranger's six-feet-plus? The result would have been ludicrous had True's heart not gone out to the older man. *Why do we try to be what we are not, Lord?* her heart whispered. *Teach me to be more thankful for what I am and to use it for Your glory.*

Shopping completed, Chris Beth waited as Abe Solomon counted each penny twice, then prepared to pick up the flavorings, spices, and coal oil. True hurried to assist her independent aunt—only to have another stranger reach out a work-hardened masculine hand to cork the spout of the fuel container by expertly clamping a raw potato over it. "Keep it from spillin', Miss—yuh must be th' new teacher, a pilgrim hereabouts. Welcome—here, hand me th' bundle an' I'll be obliged to heist 'em all in th' buggy. Guess yuh got no man fer this."

There was no time to answer the well-meaning stranger in the linsey-woolsey shirt that was buttoned to his Adam's apple and topped by a suit coat badly in need of pressing. He must be smothering! He hurried out with the parcels, stumbling over an untied bootlace, and disappeared down the alley of the long street—much longer than True realized.

Before the young man reappeared, Mr. Solomon brought "Brother Prescott" for an introduction. "Brother" made him sound older to True than his facial features indicated. The face was arresting. She almost smiled at the silly description which crossed her mind when their eyes met. The Reverend William Prescott's patrician nose, delicately drawn (but firm) mouth, and deep-set eyes glinting like hardened quartz took him from the beginning of the twentieth century and changed him into one of Robin Hood's men. His eyebrows arched with interest.

"So this is the new teacher? How do you do, Miss North—how nice that you will be working alongside your mother here."

It was a perfectly natural mistake, his addressing her as Miss, one which Mrs. Solomon did not ignore (or wait for True to correct), adding every detail of the family relationship to her captive audience.

The minister apologized and then they spoke of church matters.

"I'm sure the congregation has grown as everything else has?"

"Not really," William Prescott admitted. "There are so many denominations. We've come a long way since the Lee and Whitman missions. Other Protestant churches keep springing up—Baptist, Congregational, Episcopal, Methodist . . . then the splinter churches . . . and Catholic—"

"Splinter churches?" True questioned with interest.

"Actually, we embrace all," the minister said with a certain degree of pride. "Some original members remained, and new people join us by letter."

True felt a tug of concern. "What about—persons not knowing the Lord? I know they are welcomed. But—well—I find myself wondering if," she smiled, "we address Christians only, as Paul spoke to churches?"

The question hung in midair. William Prescott appeared to be considering the role of the church while True was remembering needs which the circuit-riding Randy Randall had met in the wide valley around Double N.

Their conversation terminated when a customer needed a hundred-pound sack of sugar for preserving late-ripening pears. Too heavy for Abe, so would Brother William give him a hand? True tried to manage a departure, but not before Bertie had wedged in "a word of caution." Young women had to be careful—surely True had seen the interest the stranger showed. And, well, even ministers were *men*!

True felt strangely relieved to be starting home, the late-afternoon sun suddenly thrusting its fire through the horizon ahead. *Home*, her haven, an island floating in the world's immense sphere of sky. An escape? *Had* she found things different? Yes—and no. True felt, momentarily, like a stranger. A confused one, with a forced smile.

4

Introductions and Interruptions

The church was smaller than True would have supposed. What happened to the plans for a building so large and expansive that it could accommodate "the saved" (converts who formed the congregation) and "the unsaved" (newcomers, as well as wayfaring strangers who had never met God personally)? The latter Nate Goldsmith described as folks "knowin' Somebody with a Mind put this Valley together but got no inklin' they're akin to 'im?" True wondered again if the growing population found what they were looking for in the other churches.

And then her eyes (and mind) wandered over the worshipers. The Norths had arrived late because one of the horses developed a sudden leg cramp which the two doctors (serving as veterinarians when the need arose) had to attend to. Jerking the cramped back leg into place by means of a rope took time, then more time as they soothed the frightened animal. How gentle the two men were, Aunt Chrissy pointed out in misty-eyed pride. And how patient their wives must learn to be. How did Aunt Chrissy manage? Chris Beth laughed at the question. "It takes time, faith, prayer—and understanding," she said as if sorting words carefully. "Remember, I've been a wife to both a minister and a doctor. Qualifications are about the same." Still, True was on the verge of saying that women (if anybody at all) should be called the "*Very* Reverends" when bedlam broke loose upstairs.

The twins!

Thank goodness style dictated that skirts were two inches shorter this fall, else Chris Beth and True would never have made it up the stairs before one twin slaughtered the other. Even so, both tripped near the top. Breathless, they were forced to be spectators of an ugly but comical scene. Kearby had cut herself some irregular bangs, the yellow fringe standing in peaks where the cowlick sprang. Their mother had tried in vain to explain to her brother that it was natural for a girl on the brink of young womanhood to pay attention to her appearance. Today, however, she had upset Jerry's cologne (tucked behind a photograph of Grandfather Somebody). Chris Beth's reasoning furnished the enraged Jerry verbal fuel. Grabbing her cork-bodied doll (joints allowing it to "walk"), the boy was dancing wildly around the hall, forcing the jointed legs to bend out crazily and singing:

> Down in the meadow where the green grass
> grows
> Sat little Kearby as fair as a rose!
> She sang and she sang—she sang so sweet,
> Along came her feller 'n kissed her on the
> cheek—

Furiously, Kearby wiped up the spilled cologne with her handkerchief. Waving it like a banner back and forth, she made a somewhat successful attempt to drown out his voice:

> Jerry's mad 'n I am glad
> for I know what'll please him:
> A bottle of ink to make him stink
> and I-know-who to squeeze him.

"Stop this silliness—*right now*, both of you!" Aunt Chrissy ordered in her best schoolteacher voice. "Open that window, Jerry, and give that cheap-smelling stuff some air! Kearby, True can even those bangs tomorrow. We will settle this later—and don't give me that I'm-not-going look, either of you."

Well, here they were in church, even though True wished they could have been in a more worshipful mood. The men undoubtedly were remembering the chestnut mare's leg (fortunately for the twins, who were still sulking). Aunt Chrissy, obviously still concerned, leaned over to whisper that she was glad True and Young Wil were here. They would be a leveling influence . . . and she jerked her head toward Kearby and Jerome.

True had nodded mindlessly, her eyes wandering. No new fall clothes—too warm. The ladies were still in their summer voiles or lawns, and so many folding fans waved back and forth that a small breeze stirred in the airless room. They wore, she noted, strands of ivory beads she had seen at Solomons'. And turban-style or roll-front "Cheyenne Effect" hats (so popular last year) had for the most part replaced sunbonnets, except for the few very elderly ladies and the wives of the Disciples with their carefully stitched white skullcaps.

Brother William prepared to go forward to occupy the pulpit. His face reddened and True could almost hear his grunt as he folded his giant frame to lace one shoe, methodically crossing and tying the strings. Rising to his full height, he carefully buttoned his suit coat and tightened his tie. He would choke when the fanning stopped.

Which it did when the congregation rose for the first hymn. Folding their fans, the ladies placed them in the racks ahead of them alongside the Christian publishing house advertisements, an assortment of combs and tortoise-shell hairpins—and, alas, wads of hurriedly stashed-away gum garnered from children's mouths.

The brief message was more of a testimonial. William Prescott had been a farmer, a progressive one, he said. But there came a call plain as day: "Come over and help us today—like the old hymn says." He had no choice but to stop plowing and say, "Here am I, Lord, send me." His "assignment" had been the Western frontier. On the way from Kansas he met the love of his life, a dedicated Shaker lady—

True's ears picked up the word, hoping the man would tell more about the dedicated woman he would have married had fever not struck her down. But he moved to family relationships: husband-to-wife, wife-to-husband, children-to-parents . . . and, finally, Christian fellowship. *Amens* filled the church, so True supposed that the members were satisfied. She was not. She wished that the minister had delved into the gospel story with as much enthusiasm and passion as his "feeling the call," as much live-forever love as his mention of his mate-to-be . . . Didn't giving one's heart to God come before walking in His tracks?

True's wandering thoughts came to a halt. A commotion similar to that which the twins had created earlier erupted with a squeaky opening of the church door, followed by a din of frenzied male voices. "Is there a doctor in the house? Quick! We gotta have hep—*now*! Waylaid by hoodlums—er Injuns—on th' way t'th' Bab-Baptis' church over yonder—wimmen, chil'drens are—gonna be kilt—doctor, doctor! Runaway horses—hep us find a doctor, Parson—'n the rest be prayin'—HEP!"

The two Dr. Norths were at the doorway, asking questions tersely of a man who was calmer than the others before the unnecessary details were finished. Number in party? Which direction? True could hear no more right now; Young Wil would tell her on their way. Her husband was all doctor, racing out the door without her as if whisked away by a whirlwind. No invitation, no goodbye—just a quick stop to pick up the inevitable black bag, trademark of his profession, and he was gone.

A growing heaviness encircled True's heart. It was hard to pin down—similar to (but strangely different from) an emotion she had felt back when . . . oh, that was it, *jealousy*! Pure, green-eyed jealousy. Another woman she could cope with, wrestle to the ground if need be! But how did one grapple with a man's work? *We have to talk, Lord . . .*

Brother William tried in vain to restore order. They must pray, he reminded them . . . and he wanted to introduce the new teacher. But people were filing out. All but the stranger who had answered questions. He was making his way to her. And then recognition came . . .

5

Comfort in Time of Affliction

With her usual briskness, Mollie Malone O'Higgin began herding the confused and frightened women into a corner of the church. "On your knees now, all of you. Know what it would feel like if 'twas your own out there? We're safe—our families are safe—we're in th' house of th' Lord. What better place for prayin' 'bout th' matter? With this many surroundin' th' throne, how can we fail? Git t' th' heart of th' problem, them out there in that runaway wagon—no mealy-mouthin'—"

Nate Goldsmith took issue with the words. "Now, be hearin' me, Miss Mollie! Prayin's fine fer women, but us men got a bigger job t'do—"

"Bigger than prayer?" True watched in awe, her own heart throbbing beneath the frilled lace jabot of her blouse as Grandma Mollie wilted her challenger with words. "I'm s'posin' yer all set fer formin' a posse, takin' th' law into your own hands. And on th' Sabbath—shame on you! Now, best you follow my man's example," she continued, pointing to where the big Irishman was already squatting beneath a giant Douglas fir. "You know th' Good Book tells us t'comfort one another in time of affliction. *O'Higgin!*" The three-octave rise in his wife's voice brought O'Higgin to his feet. "Nate 'n th' others'll be joinin' you. See that they make it!"

Without further ado, a low chorus of prayers began.

"What a vital woman!"

The words were whispered, but True sensed their source. The man whose face she recognized was from the settlement just east of the Double N. Why he was here and why he sought her out she had no idea. And surely this was no time to inquire.

She could only nod to the Shaker and whisper in reply that they would talk later. Right now there was a greater need.

He understood. "A new breed," he whispered as if to himself, "a woman who braves hardship and danger to serve where she is needed."

"We all try to—here—"

"And elsewhere. Later—Mrs. North. God go with you."

The tall, sober-faced man covered the distance between himself and the kneeling men in two or three long strides. True dropped to her knees, overwhelmingly tempted to pray for her husband and Daddy Wil. But the others came first. The men she loved had put them there...

The sound of hoofbeats did not disturb the concentration of the women inside the church. The voices had reached a low, near-moaning chant while outside the men's ears were alerted. Generations of vigilance had entrenched in them the awfulness of truth. What happened elsewhere could happen here.

The stranger in their midst was equally conditioned. True sensed it. Dedicated to peace, he nevertheless faced reality. Evil existed; it was how one faced it that counted. She sensed as well that he had left the other men and knelt beside her. His inquiring glance spoke of his philosophy as his eyes locked with True's when she lifted her head slightly. Without words the two of them communicated as he reached a hand of assistance. As she rose soundlessly, True surveyed his face. It was younger than she had thought in their brief encounters at the few circuit-rider services near the Double N. The flourishing mustache that came to a point near his sunk-in middle, only to part divergently and curl upward in opposite directions, added maturity and proclaimed fundamentalism. But nothing in the gentle countenance resembled a holier-than-thou attitude—just acceptance of God's will.

He motioned her to the door, away from the other men, who—although prayers had stopped—watched the road and trails in silence. Unnoticed, the two of them stepped to the opposite side of the building.

"Begging your pardon, Ma'am. 'Twas blatant of me to approach thee without permission." When True waved away his explanation, he continued: "I have not met thee formally, so may I be presenting myself as a God-fearing man on whom He has laid the burden of maintaining peace—one of the Brethren, Jeremiah of the Tribe of Benjamin. Jeremiah Dykeman be my earthly name. I salute thee in the name of Jehovah—knowing thou art my friend."

Although the introduction was lengthy, Jeremiah Dykeman did not seem to hurry. Neither did he do so in explaining his mission. He had led a group of "pilgrims"—no, he didn't know their name—over the hills and this far in their journey to Portland. Brutal, the trip had been brutal—ill-fated since the pack of mysterious riders had stalked them all the way from the community. Oh, how things had changed back there—but best keep on the story at hand.

"It makes no sense—it be so unnecessary—even before the volley of gunfire which sent the horses running out of control, I set the people doubting—disbelieving the Word I promised would guide us." The gentleman's mouth tightened. Breaking out of his amiable, sympathetic character for the first time, Jeremiah appeared to be wrestling for an answer within himself. "When God would have me demonstrate His faithfulness, I be leading them astray—milling, complaining, proclaiming life to be unfair, unpredictable, cruelly senseless—"

Sometimes it *can* be—or seem so, True wanted to say. Instead, she hastened to get back to the reason for the man's need to share with her in particular. "What happened on the way?" she asked.

"They demanded all our goods—and I be surrendering them instead of standing firm. 'Twas to save lives—only wouldst thou believe the peaceful gesture served only to arouse their ire? The sinful men fired on my people, killing a lad of 13—an innocent lamb—"

His voice broke. *A broken spirit. A contrite heart.* The phrases came unbidden. But what happened was not this man's fault. And the words were not intended to make such a dedicated man feel guilty.

"They would have fired anyway," True said helplessly. She stifled a sob and shook her head resignedly. "Some things are unexplainable. But," lifting her head, "whatever happened was not your fault—the important thing is that *you* have not lost faith." Lifting her head determinedly, and wondering where the words came from, she consoled, "You will bring them back together. Perhaps that is God's mission after all."

"Bless thee. We buried the lad along the trail—and I must be burying the past, preparing for the news ahead. Thou art thankful surely for law and order here, something we be lacking—although it be shameful that man be compelled to rely on any save God's law. We be obliged to the Norths, His servants—which be reminding me—"

The sound of hoofbeats came closer, then blended with wagon wheels. And then there were voices. Weeping. Wailing. Moaning. All told the story of tragedy. There were low words of consolation and encouragement, promises of justice, a reminder that already the culprits were in custody. Nate Goldsmith's voice rose threateningly, almost as if he hoped other would-be assassins were slinking in the brush. True was occupied with straining her ears for the sound of her husband's voice—so busy that she took little heed as Jeremiah handed her a sealed envelope...

6

"I Will Not Leave You Comfortless..."

"True!"

Young Wil—oh, praise the Lord! And Daddy Wil assisting with lifting the injured from a rickety wagon pulled by a pair of scrawny mules.

"Darling—dearest—" True's words were lost in the deafening confusion of everybody's trying to talk at once. She lifted her skirts to keep from tripping and ran into her husband's arms. He embraced her briefly. Then, "I need you."

I need you. Three beautiful words amid all this horror. Mechanically, True ran to the buggy, opened the box on back, and pulled out bandages and extra bottles of medication that he always carried in addition to sterilized instruments in his black kit.

Around them swam a sea of faces, ghostly and congealed in silence, eyes blank and expressionless with shock, or else angry and menacing in their grief. The latter ones, hysteria their master, were beside themselves, spitting out rash words, some punctuated with oaths, verbally shaking their fists in the face of God. But True, like Aunt Chrissy who had joined them, was scarcely aware. Fragmented conversation reached her subconscious—enough to communicate death. But the job at hand was to minister to the living. True blotted out all sights except the broken bodies in need of repair, all thoughts except assisting the doctors—and all voices except that of Young Wil's low-pitched voice ordering supplies or actual assistance as he set broken bones and splinted them, or stopped the flow of blood and bandaged the open wounds. Surely these must be the most rugged souls on earth, gritting their teeth and bearing up when the painkilling drugs ran low.

"Keep talking to them. They need reassurance. The commotion out there's doing them no good," Young Wil whispered at one point.

In a white haze of single-mindedness, True said words she would never recall, soothed feverish foreheads, and held cold compresses to parched lips. Thank goodness, Nate had quieted down, and—hoping the Lord would forgive her if her befuddled thinking was wrong—True felt it was to Pastor Prescott's credit that he sensed this was no time to chastise the angry mob out there for irrational behavior or to force unwanted prayers. Instead, he followed Jeremiah's example and moved among them quietly, letting his calm presence be enough for now.

True was dimly aware of the passage of time. Fatigue was taking its toll. "How many casualties?" she asked wearily at one point, unrolling another bandage and cutting her finger as she snipped a length from the roll.

"Here—get some antiseptic on that," Young Wil said as he wound the gauze around a child's hand, held the cloth with his teeth, and secured the wrapping as True obeyed his order. "There you are, my brave little lad," he soothed, and to True: "almost finished—all ways—"

A movement close by caught True's eye, bringing her back to a fully conscious state. A second look brought eye contact with Aunt Chrissy, who was standing to stretch. True followed her lead, feeling as if a strong irritant had been rubbed into live, but wounded flesh all over her body. It was almost good to feel again—feel anything. "Are you all right, darling?" Young Wil's voice came from a long way.

True nodded, managing a smile. "My head feels like somebody had bored holes in it to let the devils out—"

"Now, where on earth did you hear about that?" Looking on the verge of collapse, he too managed a tired smile—

tired but exhilarated, an emotion she too was experiencing.

"Something I read in one of your old medical books. 'Bleed, blister, purge, and other appalling techniques,' it advised doctors."

"Grisly, dangerous, and painful, I'll wager. They stopped such quackery in the Dark Ages. 'Counter-irritation' I think they called it. The more excruciatingly painful, the more sure the cure—like some preachers of today!"

Together they laughed—and the world came back into focus again. There was still work to do. But they had worked together—a man-and-wife team—serving. Rising above fear, she had attended to the needs of others. And the result was surely what the Lord intended: True North had slain the green dragon of jealousy. She understood her husband's calling. The exhilaration rose within her even as she surveyed the bodies swathed in bandages around her. Now to cover them in case of delayed shock . . . Young Wil was rummaging in his bag for a disinfectant.

"Fatalities?" True asked as he poured the stinging liquid over her extended hands. "Ouch! That stuff's pure firewater—how many?"

Young Wil blotted her hands gently and kissed the bruised and blistered palms before handing the bottle to her and holding out his own hands. True gasped, "Oh, darling, you're a mess! Even your body's bleeding!"

"The blood's from others, sweetheart," he replied soberly. "There was one elderly lady, a mother and her new baby—and one of the attackers. Uncle Wil and I did what we could—and there was interference all the way. Grief-stricken men not trusting our methods—and—Ouch! that stuff *does* sting—there was real trouble when we medically treated the murderer. There were threats that we would swing from that gesture, so crazed were the men. There's no explaining to an angry mob that doctors are under oath to treat saint and sinner without discrimination."

"But the man died—" she said pensively.

"With an oath on his lips." The words tore at his throat, stinging far more, she knew, than the medication on his open wounds.

"I guess God deals with life in His own way. He looks after His own—bringing you and Daddy Wil back, and saving the others—"

"I've no sure answer for that, little nurse of mine. I only know that all of you prayed—and there is no greater earthly power."

It was a sacred moment between them, one that True regretted must be broken. Reluctantly she inquired about the bodies of the dead.

"We persuaded the survivors to remove them to Helwig's Funeral Parlor in preparation for tomorrow's burial—here in the cemetery."

True nodded, then mused aloud: "Why, *why*, Wil—why the slaughter?"

"It's insane—and these were not the only casualties. They looted and killed all the way from Slippery Elm—you were aware that they came from there, newcomers?" When she nodded, he went on: "They killed about a dozen fellow emigrants along the trail—shot one man in the back as he sat working on his harness. Paid looters, some say—"

Young Wil was busily picking up his dwindling supplies and handing blankets to True when the awful possibility occurred to her. "Wil!" she gasped, "what about Marty and Midgie—and the baby?"

His arm was around her when Jeremiah Dykeman joined them. "Oh, this is Jeremiah Dykeman, Wil. My husband—"

"I recall," they said in unison and shook hands.

"I be remembering thy kindnesses past," Jeremiah said warmly, "and see that the Good Lord be using thy skill and loving here as well. May I be posing a question? There is unrest, doubt, and fear in my flock, a need for reassurance that the transgressors are—are—punished."

"Apprehended," Young Wil assured him. "And we, in turn, need an answer to our concern. Our brother's family—are they—?"

"The letter will explain all. Mrs. North will tell you. As I be explaining to thy wife, 'tis a dangerous territory—uncivilized. But, yes, your family is under God's wing—in spite of all that has happened to them—begging your pardon. There be a need for my help in moving thy patients into the church with thy permission. Plans be that they will remain, some of the bereaved going to Turn-Around Inn, others elsewhere. Brother Prescott will lay the dead to rest come the morrow."

The funeral service was simple. The bereaved, in control now but with fury still roiling inside (judging by the tightened lips and clenched, white-knuckled fists), requested a common grave. No ceremony—just a hymn and a few words from the Good Book at the graveside.

William Prescott chose a passage from the Gospel of John. As he read, rain-darkened clouds appeared from nowhere, almost immediately releasing a deluge. Children scampered into the church. Adults covered their heads with whatever protection they could find—coats, blankets, hymnals. Grandma Mollie produced an enormous umbrella as black as the churning sky and held it over the head of the young minister as loudly he intoned the words in an attempt to make them audible above the whine of the wind.

Even so, only fragments reached the ears of those huddled together trying to hold a tarp over the little knot of mourners. The scene could not have been gloomier as the intended words of comfort faded in and out: "Verily, verily . . . I go unto the Father . . . I will not leave you comfortless, I will come to you . . . yet a little while, and the world seeth me no more . . ." Oh, dear friends, Jesus *will* send you a Comforter, and because He lived, these dear ones shall live . . ."

The clouds dispersed and the sun reappeared—comfortingly . . .

7

Evil's Bright Lining

The next day was brilliant, the air rarefied by the rain. It was as if nature, having wrung the clouds dry before pinning them back against the blue, willed their bright lining to portend a message of hope. Little had remained of the night when Daddy Wil and Aunt Chrissy sent True and Young Wil home. Daddy Wil would take the first watch. The younger Norths were to get a bit of rest, have some food, and relieve the older couple in care of the wounded temporarily "hospitalized" in the church. They hadn't followed orders, of course. Dawn was ready to climb the silent hills; and there were preparations to make for patients which Daddy Wil and Aunt Chrissy undoubtedly would recommend moving to the Big House. The cabin, ready for their occupancy, could serve to house some of the overflow.

There had been no time for talk between True and Young Wil. Too, they were unnecessarily quiet in order to let the twins, shocked to silence, rest. As far as True knew, neither of the twins had spoken a word since the frightening episode began. It was their first encounter with disaster, cruelty, and sudden death. Western and Central Oregon were no longer "wildernesses." Only the vast area beyond the mountain chain to the East remained untamed. And that is where it all began...

Young Wil, his face still ashen with fatigue, helped True from the buggy—laden with fresh supplies and enough nourishing broth to hold body and soul together for the wounded until other arrangements could be made. They needed to hurry in, but True's eyes and then her footsteps were drawn to the single burial mound, washed flat by the rain. A retinue of shadows crisscrossed the single pine board which identified those who had perished. Head bowed, hands folded, True's heart murmured a silent prayer without checking the names of the interred, a single family.

She squeezed her eyes shut. This must never happen again, *never.* And then, behind stinging eyelids, came a nightmarish vision . . . charred ruins of cabins which the crazed night riders had torched . . . emigrant houses reduced to black rubble, perhaps with the remains of the owners still inside.

True shuddered, the faces of Marty, Midgie, and the baby floating before her horrified eyes. And then she felt the comforting arm of her husband around her. She faced him. He held her close. And just as quickly the horrible scene dissolved. Jeremiah had said they were all right . . . the letter would verify that . . . and that God needed her and her doctor-husband here for now. And once again she saw the world through the clear, crystal screen of yesterday's rain. The Comforter was with her . . .

"In some mysterious way, known only to God, perhaps some good will come of this," True whispered as they started toward the church.

"Oh, my darling—" Young Wil's voice broke with emotion too deep for expression. "I wonder about the name—" but True did not hear.

There were some very positive outcomes of the tragedy, but they unfolded gradually, as well they should. Who felt like seeing—even looking for—the good in time of unrequited grief? For now, the problems at hand must be taken a step at a time, "each day sufficient unto itself."

Although True was unaware of it at the time, the disaster brought the Beltrans back into the full fellowship of the church. The Basque family from the high meadows (Rube and Rachel, son Burtie, and Watch, their giant shepherd dog) once tended the sheep in the higher elevations, undisturbed. Then had come the war between cattlemen and sheep-raisers.

"All bein' hardheaded, there wuz no reasonin'," Grandma Mollie had said. "The Beltrans drifted from one denomination t' th' other—finally despairin' with us all. Our deacons called, but th' timin' was all wrong," Miss Mollie sighed. "Keep hopin' th' Lord'll speak t'them—"

He did. How else could one explain their sudden appearance at a time when they were needed most? Young Wil was checking the condition of the patients inside the church while True followed, taking notes, answering questions, reassuring, soothing, offering a prayer when asked.

"We'll check for those needing hospitalization—" he began, only to be surprised by loud outcries of protest. Fear ran rampant and, deciding he had made a mistake, Dr. North began a retraction. He had his hands full until twin shadows, short of stature, blocked the light of the window.

"Welcome home, Miz North! Wife here 'n me bin thinkin' a talk with the Lord might do no harm. Seemed like a voice from up yonder tole us th' day."

"Mr. Beltran!" True sprang to her feet.

"Th' same." The Basque were people of few words, and so it surprised True that Rube Beltran looked around him and gasped, then turned her direction and gasped again. "Good people, folks like you we need—and purtier'n a cowslip—all growed up 'n filled out." Embarrassed, he stopped and lowered his voice. "Terrible thing. *Wife*, we got vittles?"

"We allus got vittles, Husband," she replied with simple dignity.

True turned to Rachel. "Thank you, Mrs. Beltran," she said, automatically reaching out to embrace the woman who was old enough to be her grandmother. The plain face of the other woman lighted with joy as if this were her first embrace for a long, long time.

Young Wil had risen to his feet. "God bless you both—we can do with some help. But first that prayer."

The four of them joined hands and, knowing the ways of the Basque people, the young Norths stood with them in a circle of silent prayer for a full minute. "Amen!" It was Rube Beltran who broke the silence. "Now, Wife, you be goin' home t'make ready, spreadin' th' news as you go. Steer clear o'them victorias—could cause a runaway."

That was the beginning of getting the wounded housed until the two doctors could declare their recovery complete. There would have to be decisions made, True was sure. But for now—she would take no heed of the morrow.

"What's a victoria?" she asked instead, swabbing a stab wound with iodine, then blowing on it to stop the sting.

"Used to be a four-wheeled pleasure carriage for the well-to-do—now another name for an automobile, the open passenger type."

"These automobiles," True mused aloud, as she recorded a temperature reading her husband gave her, "will they ever take the place of buggies and wagons—be practical for—"

"Doctors?" Young Wil grinned. "Not until there are roads—and that looks a long way off—here, clip this thread and we're finished."

The sound of wagon wheels said that the settlement had rallied in time of need as always. Some faces True recognized, others she did not. She only knew that for the first time she felt *completely* at home with these capable men in shirts that needed boiling or flowing beards in need of a barber (or were young and fuzzy-faced, like overripe peaches). One man, a stranger to her, was barking orders as if he had treed a squirrel, his bald head gleaming (her tired mind thought foolishly) like polished marble. Even on a dark night she could see to write a letter by its glow. *A letter* . . . yes, she must read the one delivered by Jeremiah. *But for now, O Lord, let the others take over* . . .

Busy days followed. Dog days, bridging late summer and early fall, brought sultry heat. A view from the dormer-windowed structure (considered a "must" on the upstairs roofs of the better houses in the East, in the preceding century) was about all Young Wil and True's temporary quarters in the attic afforded. Although True declared she would never be able to stand upright again for fear of bumping her head on a rafter, and Young Wil's shins were barked to the bone from stumbling over old trunks, the situation gave them a much-needed cause for laughter as well as a sense of satisfaction that the Big House was doing what life expected of it—housing the homeless downstairs.

It was from one of the windows of the houselike structure that True spotted the chokeberries along the stream separating the Big House from the cabin. Somehow, she supposed, she or Aunt Chrissy would make time for jelling them—if she could coax the twins to pick the fruit without a fight ending up with a basket emptied over the top of one or the other's head.

Then True saw Kearby and a girl about the same age, ragged and palefaced (Clarice Somebody, wasn't that the name?). The two had become inseparable; and Kearby, who was a good two inches the taller of the two, had asked permission to go through her wardrobe and share last year's school dresses with the young survivor of the tragedy. "The hems have been let out twice and some are faced—please, may I?" she asked True.

Aunt Chrissy must decide, but True agreed that it was a good idea. In anticipation of a "permission granted" from her mother, Kearby was helping Clarice into a gingham gimp when True confronted them about the berries.

"Oh, surely!" Kearby surprised her by saying. "Isn't this blue pretty on Clarry?"

"Lovely," True responded, glancing at the watch pinned on her starched white cotton dress, the closest thing she owned resembling a nurse's uniform. "I have some ribbons about that color—if you would like your hair braided—"

"Oh, yes!" The gangling girl's face changed, her marvelously large eyes lighting the world and inviting all to admire the new image she envisioned in herself. "I never had my hair fixed—Granny, she's the one I—I lost—had crooked fingers. But," Clarice lifted her head high, "she always wanted me to look pretty—stop hiding—said I was as withdrawn and sociable as a scarecrow." The childish voice caught in her throat.

"You're very brave," True replied with admiration. "I think it would please your grandmother to see you standing tall."

Clarice took the words literally. With a lift of the thin shoulders still higher, she walked gracefully across the diningroom. "Where can we find a bucket?"

True handed her the granite one which the family had used for storing drinking water until a leak sprang in the bottom. Murmuring a polite "Thank you," Clarice marched ahead of Kearby, her mind obviously crowded with hopes and dreams never divulged. True hoped she would open up to Kearby; it would be good for them both. Then, to her surprise, Kearby turned and winked, the first sign of the old romping coltishness inside that True had seen since returning to the Valley. The girl was herself—yet different.

The next surprise came when Jerry whistled. "Hey, you two! Need some help? There are bears galore along that creek. And there's nothing they like better than berries—unless it's girls for munching!"

Kearby and Clarice stopped dead in their tracks. Then he also turned and winked. Jerry too was back, but with a change for the better, called maturity!

It was no surprise at all when Young Wil called (life was shaping up): "I need to go into Centerville, darling. Uncle Wil and Aunt Chrissy have things under control here, and we need medical supplies. Also (he inhaled deeply) I want to talk with one of the law officials—about Slippery Elm—"

True changed quickly into a skirt of bright floral material draped simply over a slip of plain color. She felt festive, ready to get away from the ordeal they had undergone. The pointed bodice was reminiscent of Dickens' *Dolly Verden*, so with a smile she bent up one side of the burnt-straw sunhat and pinned it with an artificial rose.

Downstairs, Young Wil whistled a signal for departure. The whistle turned to one of admiration as True hurried out to meet him. "You look as if you stepped right out of *Baraby Rudge*," he said, helping her into the buggy. Somehow she was glad he remembered the book they had read together—so glad that she abandoned the plan to read aloud the letter Jeremiah had delivered, enjoying instead the sun-warmed fields of goldenrod and the few bright leaves that floated down around them in the wooded silence...

"I've arranged for military escorts for those returning with Jeremiah," Young Wil told her on the way back. "The militia wants to check out conditions in Slippery Elm—the name stuck in spite of efforts to change it. People say it deserves no better—getting worse by the day."

"But the families who came here—why would they go back there?"

Young Wil inhaled deeply. "I looked around and there's simply nothing for them here. All the land's taken and nobody wants to sell—even if any of them had a dollar to call their own. As for jobs, there are none—seems the *good* times are over, a sort of depression in store. The poor souls would be lucky to find work for a quarter a day—and they couldn't survive. It's amazing what the money-grabbers will do when opportunity knocks—they'd charge 35 cents a night for a coyote hole. Don't look so remorseful, sweetheart. Jeremiah has a plan—"

They were home, his sentence unfinished. And the letter unread.

But something wonderful had happened! A sobbing Kearby ran to throw her arms about them both. "Clarice opened up—said the boy buried on the trail was her brother—" Kearby choked. "Oh, I'll never quarrel with Jerry again—no matter how impossible he is—I promised God—"

The sinking sun cast brilliant linings on the dark clouds of evil. God felt very near.

8

Decisions

Ten days winged past, long days for the two doctors and their outwardly tireless wives. Grandma Mollie was equally busy, planning every detail for meals and carrying each out systematically. "Me Mollie-gal never did she waste a movement that I be knowin' 'bout," O'Higgin began. "Me—I be tryin' t'give 'er a hand 'n she sez, 'Git out from underfoot!' Ye lassies puzzle us men, but here be Irish stew she knows be me favorite. Fer th' sick, she sez, but me, I be findin' they's a-plenty still brewin'."

True smiled, accepted the enormous kettle, and brushed the red-bearded cheek with an affectionate kiss. "You two have a perfect understanding and you know it."

"Sure 'n we do," O'Higgin said with emotion. "Sometimes bein' apart 'as its advantages—clears up th' mind. A man's got nobody but 'is shavin' mirror 'n th' Almighty t'be answerin' to. Nobody but meself t'pat on th' back fer successes—iffen I could be reachin' me back anymore. Only problem bein' I had nobody t'blame fer me failure, either. What I truly need bein' alone fer—in short little spurts, mind ye—is meditatin' on the greatness of me Lord 'n Master. Praise be fer all them He be savin' from th' womb t'th' tomb. He brung through them what survived fer a purpose, jest as He be addin' to me years. They's purpose in guidin' us stumblers down life's twistin' path. He be testin' us—that's what! So I best be goin'—hafta hep them what'll be makin' decisions 'bout leavin'. Got me some idees, somewhat like Jeremiah's, 'bout th' future. Wilson here 'n Young Wil's a-gonna heal bodies, but th' Lord'll 'ave His 'ands full healin' th' broken spirits. Them attackers was all beast. They be bound t'pay fer ever' humiliation 'n revoltin' act—not t'mention th' lives they be takin'. But we gotta pray fer 'em—'n pray just as hard fer healin' th' others."

Winded, O'Higgin stopped, grinned, doffed his hat, and left singing an Irish folk song, his melodious tenor voice all but shaking the needles of the surrounding firs. True wondered fleetingly why he had made no effort to visit the "March Hare," young Christian Joseph Martin North. Or, for that matter, why the proud parents had waited so long to bring him to meet the rest of the family. But, with a frown, she concluded that the answer lay undoubtedly in such harrowing experiences as the senseless attack.

Thank goodness, the injured gave welcome indication of recovering rapidly. True attributed the recovery to her uncle and husband's skill. Grandma Mollie said it was the good food, seasoned with heaping scoops of love. Could be their association with "decent folks," as Nate Goldsmith claimed. But on one thing they all agreed: God's power was at work through whatever medium He chose.

Virgil Adamson concerned True. His broken arm was healed and the splint was already off, since it was only a hairline fracture. However, his eyes looked vacant, and he wandered around, engaging in disjointed monologue.

"Give him time," Young Wil said, carefully masking any concern he might harbor. True often wished that doctors would stop writing in their confidential black books and would instead discuss their patients openly. But with pride she realized that this was her husband's fatal attraction—his holding the Hippocratic oath with near-sacredness, second only to the Bible.

"But what will happen to Clarice, his stepdaughter? He's all she has by way of family, now that her grandmother's gone. And she lost her brother along the trail. You know," she said, breaking the train of thought, "we owe a lot to that girl—called Clarry by her grandmother."

They talked about the positive reaction which the twins—Kearby, anyway—had had to Clarice's loss. But Wil had some news of his own.

"That accounts for Jerry's behavior," he said with a grin. "I approached the overdue subject of the constant bickering, only to be stopped when I tried explaining about changes as we grow up. 'Now, don't go telling me about the birds and the bees,' he said, his tone implying that he knew more about the subject than I do."

"Probably does, too, the way the younger generation talks now." The words were out—words that True found embarrassing. How did one go about *unsaying* something?

"Hey, thanks a heap, brat! I'm glad you have the grace to blush."

"I'm not blushing!"

"You are so!" Young Wil mimicked the twins. And without preliminaries, he reached out and drew her to him. She was sputtering mild protests and scattering records they'd been updating when Aunt Chrissy appeared at the office door.

"I should have knocked," she said with her still-beautiful ripe-olive dark eyes twinkling. "Another time might be better—"

"Yes!" Young Wil's dark eyes teased, too.

"No!" True gasped, trying to retain her dignity. Then, picking up the clutter to hide her pink face, she related the part of the conversation having to do with the children.

It surprised them both that Chris Beth said calmly that she believed Jerry was discovering girls, that he had eyes for Clarice.

"Oh, no—they're too young—"

"Now, now, True, don't go mothering Jerry as you did Marty," Young Wil said with authority. True made no effort to defend herself.

"The poor child will have her hands full taking care of Virgil," Chris Beth said, returning to Clarice. "He lost his wife and new baby. His first wife died when Clarice was born. She was in a family way and desperate. That was after the father was killed—and I suppose Virgil felt incapable of taking on two stepchildren when he married Clarice's aunt the very same day of the funeral. Anyway, the grandmother begged for her daughter's children."

True realized then that she had no idea what the girl's last name was. She had supposed it to be Adamson. Somehow it seemed important. Just how important time would tell.

The matter of Clarice and Virgil's relationship nagged at True's thinking. He seemed to see her as his anchor, who made him feel safe, no longer vulnerable. He was the child, she the mother. But Clarice was no more able to protect him than a fledgling could protect its parents. Although the grandmother had taught her well what Clarice referred to as the "three R's of reading, writing, and *religion*," she had held the child in the nest instead of teaching her to fly. Consequently, Clarice could make no decisions without consulting Kearby—even the simplest ones, regarding the clothing which Chris Beth had applauded her daughter for sharing. What should she wear? What went with which garment? Clarice accepted Kearby's opinion about trimming her hair and curling the bangs without question. Going against Grandma had been wrong, and going against the world amounted to the same thing. Virgil and Clarice's facing the "out there" was courting chaos. They needed roots . . . family . . .

Time was rocking on. There was talk of decisions to be reached. And all the while True became more troubled. Something half-remembered . . .

"What's your friend's last name?" she finally asked Kearby.

"Clarice? Hancock. Clarice Hancock. *Clarry*, she wants to be called."

Hancock . . . Hancock . . . where—? Of course! Anna-Lee Hancock, the Shaker lady back in Slippery Elm. And—the name on the pine shingle in the cemetery had been Hancock. Not Adamson!

9

The Letter

Nate Goldsmith called at the Big House shortly after True made the startling discovery about what surely must be a discrepancy in names on the pine-board marker serving as a headstone in the cemetery. He too had noticed the variance, a fact which disturbed the little man as much as the October heat that plastered his shirt to his chest, giving it the comical appearance of a bird cage.

Mopping the few remaining strands of hair across his balding skull, the deacon, president of the school board, and town crier panted out the news. "Sumpin' ain't right—I kin smell it," he declared. "First this Virgil man ain't havin' nothin' t'do with that purdy stepdaughter, 'n now he's clingin' like a leech. This stupor he's in is jes plain faked, if you ask me!"

"Nobody did," Grandma Mollie reminded him calmly. She had brought over some partially completed dresses for Kearby. "That was plum nice of you, chile, sharin' thataway with Clarry, pore little thang. So," she smiled in a conspiratory manner, "I up 'n felt justified in copying th' latest styles from Solomon's Ready-t'-Wear fer yourself."

"That's stealin'!" Nate said triumphantly, then leaped in to resume his discussion of them Adamsons, Hancocks, or goodness-knows-who from the post office's "Most Wanted" list. Course, some'd call him judgmental.

Mollie O'Higgin bit off a thread and spit it out as if it were dusty. "Stuff's rotten as dirt—probably been in stock 50-odd years."

"Like I wuz saying', ole Virge is puttin' on—"

"It could be shock, Mr. Goldsmith." True spoke for the first time. Noting Chris Beth's nod of approval, she told the story of the Caswells back in Slippery Elm. How Tillie, having lost her niece in the flood—Marty's mother—Mrs. Caswell lost touch with reality. "Even yet she confessed to Young Wil that she feared sleep because in her dreams the baby had drowned along with his parents."

Nate was taken aback, but only temporarily. "We jest ain't got no more room in th' school—even considerin' them whut's leavin' fer them denom'national academies 'n that farmin' college in Corvallis. Course there's that orphants' school. But this here's public, 'n as president of th' board, I consider it's my bounden duty t'keep it free from opin'inated meddlers. Still 'n all, th' gova'ment's stingy—ain't givin' us no more less'n we want more taxes—and there's folks a'plenty feelin' tax money oughta build roads. Gotta give th' matter lotsa thought—my job's a big un, one I wouldn't 'spect yuh women t'understand—least of all *teachers*."

"Lay off, Nate!" Miss Mollie bit off the word as she had bitten off the thread.

Nate Goldsmith cringed. But in a wavering voice he was determined to make a last-ditch stand. "Jest thought y'ud welcome my 'pinion 'bout this man claimin' t'be in a stupor—how 'bout it, Doc?"

Nobody had seen Wilson North, the senior doctor, enter. "You know I can't discuss the case with you, Nate—even if I knew. Let's stick to school affairs. Have you set an opening date?"

Nate's face brightened with self-importance. "I'm a-takin' census now. Crops is most in, but I gotta come up with figgers. You women—uh, *ladies*—got 'bout time t'brush up on th' lates' in that Normal School—queer name, ain't it now?—in Mammoth—er, Monmouth, guess it goes by since 'twas lib'rated from zealots—"

"I'd hardly call them that, Mr. Goldsmith!" Chris Beth objected with a flash of her dark eyes. "Churches have been responsible for the establishment of our schools. And, as for zealots, we all have to be careful, don't we? Zeal is fine; but it's the people *within* the church—and there are some in our very own Centerville Community Church—who become fanatics and cause friction. It's the same with the schools."

"Amen!" Miss Mollie said loudly. "Seems t'me you'd oughta be concentratin' on gettin' set up fer school 'stead of stirrin' up talk." At that point she threw back her head and gave a hearty laugh. "Sorry, but it's so ridiculous—your askin' Chris Beth 'n True here t'go back t'school. No matter what th' latest fashions are in learnin', cain't y'git it through that thick head what they've been through aidin' their men bring back t'life these unfortunates who's passed through hell on earth? You heerd what True tole 'bout that relation of Marty's 'n her with no doctor or preacher t'hep undo th' damage—"

True heard no more. Her own mention of Tillie Caswell had stirred the ashes of something near-forgotten. Overlooked, at least. And now Grandma Mollie's referring to it uncovered a live coal of memory.

The letter.

Mumbling an excuse, she hurried out of the room and up the stairs to the attic that she and Young Wil were still compelled to call home. She had given up attempts to keep their belongings in any kind of order, so it took several minutes to find the sealed envelope. How could she have postponed opening it? She knew the answer, or course. But what came first in life? Only the Lord knew what her priorities should be. And for now the letter was her top priority. With shaking fingers she clawed at the flap of the envelope, tearing off a corner of the single-page message that was signed by Midgie's childishly careful hand. She had known it would be...

10

"Where Is God?"

True scanned Midgie's letter, her eyes glazed with horror, then let it flutter from nerveless fingers. The dormer window above a battered trunk framed the setting sun, the only ornament embossing a cloudless sky, its fading light draping barren fields that proclaimed harvest was indeed over. Somehow the dying light shrouding the distant hills, defiling them with black shadows, portended evil. Or was it the lurid, shocking pictures that Midgie painted?

"Relax," she commanded her rigid, shuddering body. When she regained a measure of control, True wiped away beads of perspiration that glistened on her face. Then she recovered the letter and reread its shocking contents. Again. And again. Even then she was unable to absorb the words. For the first time in her life, True North wanted to escape life...run away...no, cower in a corner like a beaten child.

"Where is God?" she whispered helplessly, the courage inherited from her aunt and demonstrated all her young life now dwindling.

"If you don't know the answer to that, guess who's changed addresses?" Her husband's voice—strong and reassuring, even as it gently chided—brought True back to earth and into his arms.

"Cry it out, darling, then tell me about it."

Cry she did, as well as babble. "I want to leave...go

away, just you and me . . . you can establish a clientele anywhere . . . with me helping . . . I'd rather be your nurse than a—a—teacher anyway . . . *oh, please . . .*"

He could have chided her, patronized her, or even reasoned with her. Being Young Wil, wonderful man that he was, however, he came to her rescue slowly. Rather than pulling her back when she moved from the circle of his arms, he made no attempt to impose himself into her private world.

Instead, wisely and patiently the doctor worked his way slowly back into the conversation as if her thoughts made sense. "Where would we go?"

"Anywhere—even though I'm far removed from my mother's generation—and the ones that came long, long ahead—I know now that we never should have tried to adjust to this—this jungle of madness—called a frontier. It—it's not in my—what's the word, *genes*? A part of me's begging to go home—"

"Where's home, my darling?"

True, feeling as if she were coming out of a trance, hesitated. "Boston, maybe—back to a genteel society—or Atlanta—"

Atlanta. That was it. No, *Boston.* It was farther away . . .

"No!" Fully alert now, True found the thought repugnant. "I mean, oh Wil, I don't know. I—I just know I'm no coward. Running away settles nothing—we—have to take a stand, don't we? Against man's inhumanity to man—oh, pray that God will forgive me for my weakness. I've seen so much—and now this—but I should have been strong—"

Young Wil embraced her then. "I'm sure He understands, but—" with a feeble attempt at a smile, "I'm not sure I do—oh, is this the culprit? May I see it—or would you like a glass of water before we talk?"

"I'm all right—for now," True said, surrendering the letter when his hand reached out tentatively. "We'll find a way—as long as we're together—"

"And that's forever," he said tenderly. Then he began reading the letter.

For a fleeting second the letter was a knife thrust before Young Wil, daring him to make use of it. So fleeting was the expression that True might just have imagined it. Sensitive and caring, he always knew instinctively how to handle any situation. Right now, he recognized, was a critical moment in her own recovery. He would be careful. His nature and profession dictated that. But it would be foolish to deny his own emotion. All this showed in his face.

"Incredible," he said quietly, shaking his head in disbelief. "I understand how you feel—how *they* feel. Let's see if we can shed more light on Midgie's letter the second time around. Here, darling, come sit by me."

Young Wil shifted his long legs and moved from his sitting place on the bed toward the windows, careful not to bump his head where the rafters slanted above him. He patted the place beside him. True sat down, some faraway corner comforted by the warmth he had left behind. Unable to speak, she slipped a cold hand into his.

"My dear, dear True," he began uncertainly. The remainder he read without emotion:

> I don't know how to begin. I keep hoping I will wake up and find the past months have been a nightmare. We've tried so hard, and I am so proud of Marty. We should be so happy with the March Hare fat and healthy—and we would be if the Devil hisself—see, I can't remember how to say words proper? But the Deluder somehow found us all here, hid (hidden?) away—and he just up and set to work. If he was visible I'd shoot him—Daddy taught me to use a gun. But I guess I'd have to stand in line, wouldn't I? Oh, True, you'll know how to break all the awful news. Won't you say it with good words?

Things had changed, Midgie repeated Jeremiah's words as she plunged into the terrible story in her own way. Lots of people had come from Appalachia . . . good country folks but in need of everything from money to "learning." No ideas how to protect themselves—too used to old-time-religion preachers saying fear was evil. Then came the hoodlums—must've followed, demanding everything—

everything—heirlooms, food, *women!* In their ignorance, Midgie went on, the misguided immigrants tried to live by some well-meaning preacher's interpretation of the Bible... see no evil... hear no evil... speak no evil... just surrender and "be led to slaughter without a bleat."

Would it have mattered anyway? Midgie wondered.

> The cut-throats took from the ones who tried to protect their families anyway—busted into the Goldish house, shattered a bottle over Billy Joe's head and—you know the rest. Poor, helpless Mariah. It's happened before—and this awful treatment brought it all back. Mariah's not normal, hardly speaks, and what she says makes no sense. And them innocent little boys saw it! No preacher... no doctor... and I don't know enough of her language to make her understand we love her... and that some way, somehow God will send help...
>
> Tillie Caswell (the baby's "Grandy") could've helped but—

Some of the words were hard to make out at this point, giving a clue to Midgie's own deep wounds. But Marty had not known, being too busy in the fall harvests (*so* bountiful). Then one of the hands went into town for supplies... heard the awful news and hurried home like Paul Revere, spreading the news... and picking up some news in return. There was going to be a turkey shoot that night... and the poor innocents saw no wrong in that kind of gambling... no danger either. So bad as they needed food, they were bound on going, all being good shots. Marty knew there'd be trouble, felt it in his bones, took the ranch hands and went... but the bandits beat them there, got tired of shooting in the match and shot the lights out... yelled, "It's a stickup!" and shot one Appalachian in the back... and laughed! Aimed at Mr. Caswell and shot before he could open the safe. Marty tried to protect Curly... but got his shoulder shattered by a bullet (not to worry, he would be all right now). "And they still killed Mr. Caswell—shot him clean through the heart. So now 'Grandy' ain't right either—sometimes 'sane-like sometimes not, keeps switching. Normal 'round Martin. Otherwise addled..."

"Hang on, all of you, we'll help." Young Wil said the words as if the helpless victims were in the room. Then he added, "when we can."

He turned to True then. "As if these were the only enemies—but there are others—rustling, dragging sacks of seed to do fall planting, only to have it eaten by worms before it germinates—if starving wolves don't beat them to it—"

"Hadn't we better go?"

"You know we can't, True. School's opening next week. Nate said so after you left the room—and our practice here—"

"—is more important than our brother?"

Young Wil sighed. "You know better than that! But think darling, what could we do at this point? And we are needed here—all of us. Thank goodness, Jeremiah met with the survivors here, and they all but accepted his invitation to share from their common storehouse. What will tilt the scale is your willingness to share that you are reasonably sure that some of them—Clarry, at least—belong to the Hancock family. Nobody listens to Nate, but you know the background—"

True wondered what her answer would have been had Aunt Chrissy not called to say that dinner was waiting. *Dinner*—sweet normalcy of the word...

Outside was cooler than inside the house. The men found it bearable in their stuffy office, but True felt as if her chest were caving in for lack of air. She felt hemmed in from all sides, making her realize that Aunt Chrissy was probably right in saying the situation was responsible—decisions from all sides. The two of them were sitting in the porch swing, its motion making True a little sick.

"We've talked these things over—and everywhere I run into a road that ends abruptly above a steep cliff with no way to turn back. I can understand how little Clarry feels,"

True said slowly, fanning the heat from her legs with the tiers of her gingham skirt.

"Mmmm?"

"Unable to reach a decision—and her past, like her future, hanging overhead, like twin ghosts over Scrooge in Dickens' Christmas Carol."

Chris Beth plucked a pungent leaf from a hanging pot of herbs. "Since so much depends on Clarry's attitude—at least, it *might* help these confused people—let's concentrate on her first. It might be easier for you to talk to Jerry. He and Kearby think you and Young Wil know a lot more about life than we parents." She sighed and bit into the mint leaf in concentration. "Then if he would talk with her—she opens up like a flower for him, is his friendly ear, hanging onto every word about his botany experiments. I guess this is what a boy his age needs, as Miss Mollie puts it, 'a somebody he can spark to.'"

True was unconvinced—at least, that so young a boy should be forming relationships. But Aunt Chrissy was much wiser than she...and his talking to Clarry sounded like a good idea.

It was. And a conversation True and Chris Beth overheard between their doctor-husbands explained why—as well as the *whys* of other matters.

Their own conversation had lulled, each buried in private thoughts, when the men's words floated out the window. Young Wil was talking in a troubled voice. A voice sounding tired, so tired.

"Yes—yes, I *do* hesitate to encourage another change for Clarry—risk her trying to adjust to strangers again. I'd guess by nature the girl is timid and irresolute. Then the horrifying experience coupled with this stepfather—if he *is* that—caused her to further withdraw. But you know, Uncle Wil, there's something buried deeper. Even when she's with Jerry, she trembles at an innocently raised voice, flinches at a moving shadow, and near-jumps out of her young skin at distant thunder. It's more than her jumpiness, though. It's as if Clarry is so afraid of the world that she can't live with its ordinary sounds. True dropped something in the kitchen this morning and the child ran to hide behind the door—" his voice trailed off helplessly.

"Did our children notice anything irregular?"

True had a mental picture of Daddy Wil leaning back in his easy chair, arms lifted, hands laced together to pillow his head, while his nephew sat tensely on the edge of his own chair, brown eyes burning with such concern that they all but glowed in the dark.

"Notice? Yes, they noticed—but not the way an adult would. Or else they are excellent actors—or see something we miss altogether—" Young Wil stopped as if the words expressed a new thought.

"Meaning?"

"I'm not sure—Jerry and Kearby, during a truce, exhibit good manners and—well, sensitivity. They could have been trying to save Clarry from embarrassment—or, could it be that they see something's not right? Anyway, they turned Clarry's hiding into a game—"

"Which it is, more or less, a kind of hide-and-seek of the mind to blot out reality. Is that what you're saying? Cause for concern, yep—like this Mariah person—and Marty's Aunt Tillie, but—" his voice went with hands spread out in despair, "we've not come far—no powder I know will help the workings of the mind."

The air was charged. True and Chris Beth could feel it, as one feels electricity building just before a storm. But Young Wil's voice, while vibrant with excitement, was low and controlled when he spoke: "There's something out there—a connection between the body and the mind. I'd like to do some post-grad work—for my book—go to Portland—"

Where was God? With Young Wil, of course. As his mate would be!

11

Doubt Is Out!

The best way to spread the news that Clarry (and perhaps some of the other members who were struggling with the decision of where to relocate and start anew) probably carried the Hancock blood in their veins was to tell the Solomons. Their store had a wider circulation than *The Oregonian.* In any case, the newspaper was slow at best in reaching the Valley.

True and Jeremiah made a trip to Centerville, and when they returned, Abe and Bertie both listened—Abe somewhat passively and Bertie with ears actually appearing pointed like a bird dog's. She "just knew" there was something strange about "that girl." She "just knew" there was something unnaturallike about her relationship with "that man" calling himself a stepfather. Best get them all out of here before they "poisoned the minds of our young folks." Take the North twins—

True quietly but firmly interrupted. "We know nothing about them, Mrs. Solomon. Let's not be judgmental. Clarry is welcome in our house. But," she paused, "if she has family—"

"Right! That would serve the purpose for hurrying their exodus—" Bertie Solomon stopped short, her face reddening. "What I'm meanin' is that those Shakers, Quakers, Breth'ern—whatever they are—could prove helpful. And," she raised her shoulders as if adjusting what she called "the full armor," "it's our Christian duty to give these folks a proper send-off. I'll volunteer spreading the news. Abe here can let Nate know. No time to do a lot. Still, we could send some wagons about the Valley collecting—you know, like we do when they's a fire."

Eyes aglow now, Bertie Solomon went into action. After all, wasn't this a brilliant idea? And it was hers! Abe here could pass the word to Nate Goldsmith. Depend on Nate to alert all the committees he appointed himself to chair, well as the Board of Deacons and the Board of Education. Folks didn't need cash money. Take those Basque folks—still shearing woollies, dyeing, carding, spinning, and weaving. Just look at the warm clothes other womenfolks could knit in a hurry for that cold country "over there"! Her tone located the eastern portion of Oregon somewhere across the ocean.

"Now, Abraham, git th' mules hitched and git goin'!" Bertie Solomon's command to her husband ended her soliloquy. "Apt as not news'll carry to Salem and Portland. Glad them mule critters won't have to be goin' into th' city. Even blinders don't help their skittishness of trolley cars—it bein' all th' clangin' 'n zingin' that scares 'em outta what few wits God allowed 'em, not that a body can blame 'em—me, I'm not partial to trolleyin', all them sparks flyin' from wires. Wonder if it won't be one of them contraptions that starts the fire that consumes this wicked world!"

True smiled. "I doubt it," she reassured Mrs. Solomon. "Thank you for all the wonderful ideas—"

"Which we will implement." Jeremiah, finished with his purchase of a few essentials, paid Mrs. Solomon, her husband having begun his mission. "I can add to the list of items most needed for thee—dried fruit and beans, some staples—and a few learning books. Knowest thou that there is no school and that the Tribe of Benjamin teaches their own? Should we hope that Portland's State Board of Education will share?"

"They will," Mrs. Solomon responded, and went on planning with Jeremiah.

True's mind had gone back in time, remembering a similar situation as recorded in Angel Mother's diary. It was *this* valley which was in its early stage of development then.

And the miracle of response, her mother had recorded, "enlarged like the enlargement of their hearts." It would happen again...

Her train of thought shifted. Was this the time to share the contents of that sacred diary with Kearby? And what about Jerry? Saying goodbye to Clarry would hurt him, followed by Kearby herself, providing she chose to attend the Wilbur Academy for Girls that True had overheard her mention to Aunt Chrissy. Having "silly girls" underfoot was one thing, but being parted from them was another...

But, no, this was not the time. Opening the diary too soon would be like entering an empty tomb—no spirit. The timing must meet a specific need, answer a near-to-the-heart question. God would know when...

The die was cast. Once Jeremiah convinced the North family that Clarry was in all likelihood Clarice Hancock, and once Jerry communicated the news to the girl, it was she who—taking strength from her idol—found courage to suggest returning with Jeremiah. And once the Solomons picked up the message, news spread like wildfire, gathering momentum as it traveled. There should be—there *must* be—a proper send-off.

"Sorta like 'The Little Red Hen' story," Grandma Mollie smiled indulgently to True later. "Who would bake the ham? *I will.* Who would roast the hens? *I will.* The same with salt-risin' bread, corn pone, an' sugar-spice cookies. After all, these folks hafta do more'n fill their bellies one night. There's gotta be leftovers fer sandwiches that stick t'th' ribs. No question, of course, *where* the feast is a-gonna be—"

"Turn-Around Inn?"

"Shore as shootin'! A kinda celebration—jest between us homefolks. Meanin' th' mortgage's paid—'n things is all right 'twixt me 'n my man agin, thanks t'you, Young Wil, Marty, 'n Midgie. By the way, you been hearin' from them? Guess no news is good new—" Miss Mollie paused to wipe her hands on the generous folds of her Mother Hubbard apron.

"But I *have* heard," True said, feeling a twinge of guilt that life had kept her too busy to share the frightening message in Midgie's letter. She blurted out the contents in one run-on sentence without stopping.

Grandma Mollie kept nodding her near-white mountain of hair as she rolled out pie crust with expertise that required no directions. Watching her twirl the pan on one finger, pricking the bottom with a fork as it completed a single orbit, True thought how representative it was of this wonderful woman's life: no recipe, no waiting around for a Daniel Boone or a Davy Crockett to step from the pages of some book. Life was real. One learned by listening, learning, practicing. God was her leaven.

"Write her," the older woman suggested. "Here, scratch my nose," she said, twisting her face and holding up flour-dusted hands. "Thank you, sweetie—yes, send it by Jeremiah. I've a hunch he'll beat th' locomotive—serve t'git 'em all acquainted, too."

Of course! She would explain everything to her sister-in-law. And, yes, she must write to Tillie Caswell. Oh, if only she could go with this band, be the shoulder they so needed, hold them close and reassure them what they already knew but may have forgotten in the terrible crisis—that hope springs eternal . . . that love endures all things, hoping—*knowing*—that God will deliver them from the wilderness of despair. Like Grandma's pastry, hope needed no recipe—just practice . . . the only essential ingredient being love that endured.

The letters were difficult to write; words wouldn't come. Then True's busy mind piled them up extravagantly, only to find that they said nothing. After chewing her pencil, crossing out, and erasing, True finished bulky (though in her mind meaningless) letters and gave them to Jeremiah. His report would explain matters better.

"We should be there, but . . ." "We will be there when . . ." Young Wil's words echoed in True's mind: *when*? But this was the life of a doctor's wife, her tired mind said—more in acceptance than bitterness. This was where they belonged.

Or was it with Marty and Midgie, their own kin, in time of trouble? Yes, they had "Grandy," but Marty's aunt needed more comfort than the young Norths. As backbones of the troubled community, none of them dared allow themselves to break down. They were the hope of Slippery Elm. They needed support—*now*. Not a year from now, when Young Wil's internship was completed...

It occurred to True then that, according to the conversation between the two doctors, it was her husband's wish to pursue the revolutionary relationship between the mind and the body. Biting her underlip, True felt her eyes fill with tears. *Forgive me, Lord.*

For it was as if He had spoken to her. What more appropriate timing could there be, what greater mission? So it took another year? And another? Maybe it was God's will that her husband discover ways to help people overcome those vague disorders loosely labeled "hysteria." Tillie Caswell, whose mind had taken in more than it could hold and overflowed with heartbreak, had retreated into a world of unreality. Would she, without professional help, recover a second time? And how about Midgie? Could little Midgie, with her insecurities and her hurts, remain strong in her newfound faith in God's love—and Marty's?

A sudden excitement tingled along her spine. What a challenge! True could hardly wait to see her husband, to tell him that she understood. Oh, praise the Lord, she understood! Why, right here were dozens of examples. Clarry—timid, shy, irresolute, afraid to fall asleep for fear of dreaming of the hell on earth she had undergone. If some medical key could help her unlock the torturous journeying into her past, perhaps she could overcome her fears of men. Men? True realized suddenly that the child *was* afraid of the man who called himself her stepfather. But he was in need too, else why would he cling to Clarry as he did? Shaking her head, True found herself wondering why the idea had never occurred to her. And now examples, as if in the flesh, paraded across the threshold of her own mind: Zeck McDaniel, who resorted to a wheelchair only when he felt neglected; Lizzie Talissman, who "mouthed off" (Grandma Mollie's word), then developed hiccups that went on for days...

"Who hath known the mind of God?" Without realizing she was speaking aloud, True—wide awake now with revelations she had never known before—continued to quote at random from Paul's messages to the Romans. "We have the mind of Christ . . . neither be of doubtful mind . . . fully persuaded in his own mind . . ." *Doubtful, persuaded, doubtful—*

Back and forth zigzagged the shining thoughts, upward like the nuptial flight of a queen bee, then coming back for a soft landing. *As a man thinketh, so is he.*

"Doubt is out!" The words came out joyously—just as the loving arms of her doctor-husband enfolded her. Understanding without words.

12

Goodbyes Without Tears

The entire Valley must have shown up to see the ill-fated immigrants well-fed and well-stocked for the journey back to the part of Oregon in which they had stopped only briefly. Not a-tall surprising, Grandma Mollie said with a cluck of her tongue. Bertie done her work well. Never done anything by halves, that woman. Her tongue was her worst enemy, less'n its bridle was given a jerk in the right direction. Bertie Solomon could be nosy, git under a body's cuticles. "Still 'n all, she allus comes through in a crisis, as I explained to your Aunt Chrissy when, as a girl with a heart broke in half, she come to us. One o'God's miracles, that's what—and He's apt t'be turnin' out another from these poor souls. Jest you wait and see."

"He already has," True said, and then could have bitten her tongue.

Mollie O'Higgin chuckled as she motioned her husband to her for setting up picnic tables. "You've got that faraway look in them beautiful violet eyes—so like your Angel Mother's, except for th' look that closes a matter. O'Hig-*gin*!"

Fugitive bars of a song that her doll-like mother used to sing to the bees flickered across the screen of True's memory unfocused, then righted themselves:

> But to every man there stretcheth
> A high road and a low;
> And every man decideth
> The way his soul should go.

The matter was settled. Her soul had taken wing.

It was the sunset hour when the group sat down to eat. Little heat waves, reluctant to let go of summer, pulsed along the foothills. Above the little flurries, the still-brilliant rays of the sun painted the evergreen of the firs brick-red.

"I will lift up mine eyes unto the hills, from whence cometh my help." O'Higgin's musical voice, still burred with Scotch-Irish, boomed above the singing of the little streams victoriously cutting through the ridges at near-right angles to form miniature emerald-green valleys of their own. The big, God-fearing Irishman repeated the passage.

The Appalachians clung to his every word, identifying with the brogue if not always understanding his words. He made "horse sense" to them. But where, True wondered, was the minister? In fact, where had William Prescott been all along? She had hardly caught a glimpse of him. How could a dedicated minister declare a "hands-off" policy?

Irish O'Higgin read the remainder of Psalm 121, then repeated: "I will lift up mine eyes unto the hills..."

True allowed her eyes to travel higher and higher up the hills until they loomed to mountains, where the green-garbed forests had never paid toll to the woodsman's axe. There the snowy peaks, still bright with sunshine, bared their jagged-rock fangs in defiance of the persistent remnants of the past season. Somewhere through those hills lay a gap through which tonight this group must pass. It threatened, while beckoning, in the mysterious silence.

In the distance a coyote howled. Then, closer, a gopher—rare for these parts—darted True's direction, quickly stealing a breadcrumb, then with Jack-in-the-box speed did a disappearing act. But not before True saw the yellowed teeth (bearing a startling resemblance to the jagged fangs of the gap) clamped down on the morsel in a death-grip. Thank goodness, the militia would be traveling with this group—although it puzzled her as to why they should make the trip at night...

After Jeremiah's prayer, with its *Thee's* and *Thou's*, passing of the food, mountains of it, began. The children, while obviously awed, shook their heads and waited with downcast eyes. Only once did a thin-faced lad speak. His single word was a question: "So'gum?"

"Sogum?" True asked gently.

"'Lasses—sirp." His head went down again.

Of course! sorghum syrup, dipped in cornbread, as she recalled. But before she could answer, a bonneted lady whose face was hidden by its dusty brim scolded in an embarrassed whisper, "Got none, Jasper! Shet yo' mouth 'n take yore pot-likker!"

Silently the mother ladeled a soupy substance drained from a black pot of overcooked cabbage onto a wooden plate and set it before the boy. "Want some?" she asked True.

How could anybody want *that*? The night air reeked sickeningly with its smell.

But Aunt Chrissy had taught her that it was an insult to refuse to partake of whatever was set before her. Well, she would just have to ask the Lord to forgive her for this whopper. "Certainly!" she said, knowing that she was about to be sick.

"Hit's fittin'," the faceless woman said defensively. "I been cookin' hit all day—only way hit's safe. Hast t'turn red." Then she saved the moment for True by replacing the tin plate serving as a lid.

"I let these folks browse in my garden," Nate Goldsmith's voice, with ill-concealed piety, announced from the far end of the table. "But, now, chil'ern, you'd best be eatin' our foodstuff as well."

The children nodded eagerly and the mountains of food shrank.

From that point on the woman and children remained silent. The men kept up a lively conversation. Planning perhaps for the journey? It was hard to tell, as their speech was so quaintly peppered with strange expressions that it might as well have been in a foreign tongue: "afeared... aidge o'dark... blatherskite wimmen... sunball." These phrases sounded innocent enough, but what followed did not: "Man hadda right fer settlin' whut matters shore 'nuf wid a gun—nat'rul as a-wearin' pants. Hadda right fer hidin' a still fer likker...hadda right fer takin' keer o' 'is fambly. Hadda right fer marryin' like he chosen, cousins 'n all—better'n furriners. Long ez he did'n vi'late th' Good Book—er fornicate outsiders..."

Truly ill now, True laid down her half-finished ham sandwich, excused herself quietly, and slipped away. She was sure nobody noticed.

One moment the world was tinted with rose-pink memories of sunset, and the next a gray-purple twilight had settled over the Valley like a bird readying for the night. A new-phase moon offered little light, making it impossible for True to make out the identity of shapes of a few strollers along the several narrow trails. She stopped, not wishing to disturb them. And then she was rendered unable to move. Darkness could not blot out the identity of the voices, mingled though they were above the wail of fiddles in sad-sweet farewell... their only goodbye.

Jerry—Jerry and *Clarry!*

"I don't want to leave you!" Clarry's little-girl voice carried a telltale sound of tears.

"And I don't want you to go," Jerry choked, his voice breaking embarrassingly as he changed octaves from childhood to adolescence. "You don't belong with them, do you Clarry? I mean you've not always—"

"Lived among the mountaineers? No—he—uh, they—*we* have been from place—oh, Jerry, don't ask me any more—I *have* to forget what I—I—can't explain to you or myself. But I'll keep this forever—"

The musty scent of late-blooming roses reached True's nostrils, as shapeless as the horrifying suspicion that gnawed at her heart.

"I must take you back," Jerry said with more maturity than True knew the boy possessed. The girl, openly sobbing now, and promising to write, clung to his hand as they passed within inches of where True stood gripping the body of a towering fir that graciously pulled her into its shadows.

The snap of a twig alerted her to the fact that she was not alone. The gopher? She shuddered. Another snap!

"Who's there?" Her voice trembled.

"'Tis I, the big, bad wolf."

"Wil—oh, Wil darling—" True clung to her husband with such force that her own muscles ached.

"Hey, I should do this more often! I saw the youngsters leave and was wondering if they should wander out here alone—then you—"

"How long have you been here?" Still clinging to him while accepting his handkerchief, she dabbed at her eyes. "What did you hear?"

"Everything. But my suspicions needed no confirmation, darling. Surely you put two and two together, knew that they are tasting first love—and remembering how sweet it is, especially when it endures—"

It was a beautifully romantic moment, one for which she had longed as time robbed them of togetherness. But the timing was wrong. As sweet as Young Wil's gestures were, his voice was light-years away.

True nodded against his shoulder—remembering. "I love you—I love you—but, oh, Wil, what about Clarry? Is she a prisoner? Has she—?"

"Been violated? Yes darling, I am sure of it—"

"You mean—?" True was unable to speak the words.

"I mean," he said softly, yet in a tone that betrayed unleashed fury, "*used*, molested, and left an emotional cripple. Incest is common—not against their code."

"By that beast—that terrible man claiming to be her stepfather—"

"We don't know that for sure."

The slight pause said he suspected it. "With a little encouragement I could hate Virgil Adamson—if that's his name," True said with uncharacteristic fierceness. "I could. I could. And," thoughtfully, "why was he so eager to remarry, right into the same family?"

Young Wil drew a ragged breath. "This only time will tell, darling. But dismiss bitterness until the facts are in. All our friends in and around Slippery Elm will be on the lookout. Then O'Higgin—"

"He's going?"

Young Wil nodded. "Sort of under the pretense of looking in on the Double N. Of course, he's dying to see the March Hare—"

"As am I! And as are Aunt Chrissy and Daddy Wil. Oh, Wil, why can't we—? But, of course, I know why a visit's out now."

Reaching up, Young Wil pulled a twig from the closest fir bough and plucked off the needles one by one as if he were studying it. "Back to O'Higgin—he plans to keep Clarry by his side all the way, then deliver her to Anna."

"And Virgil? What's to become of him? I guess he needs help. He's a human being—even if he *is* a subspecies. Oh, darling, we are sending them a pack of trouble. I thought we would be safe here, protected from trouble—but I guess," True said with a sigh, "the devil does his work well in all places."

"As does God! Maybe the Lord sent us these people to remind us just how needed we are everywhere. Their being here has served to convince me that the subject I want to pursue is essential. I will need your approval, your help—your understanding—"

A rare uncertainty stopped his flow of speech.

"Wil North," True bristled, "are you implying I wanted to return with this group without *you*? 'Until death do us part!' Not only will I cling, I will cling tighter each year. I am your helpmate, your Adam's rib, so," True was talking rapidly now, her breath coming in little short puffs of excitement, "I will study with you—learn—and do *my* internship in the classroom. Maybe I have taken too much for granted. Maybe there are cases like this," she shuddered, "in our own Valley."

"There are such cases everywhere, put under wraps, of course. I was reading the Old Testament last night and found so many references that it overwhelmed me."

"But ours is the age of enlightenment. We are under the New Law, the love of Jesus—and He makes it all so plain about responsibility to the family. How could people claim ignorance?"

"Because," he said slowly, "they can't read, particularly in Appalachia. Law and order, civil or Biblical, comes by word of mouth. They have survived simply by their own laws, which hinge on two, I guess: 'Thou shalt bear arms.' They simply shoot down the stranger—meaning preachers, teachers, revenue officers . . . and every now and then when somehow a would-be peacemaker manages to break down the barrier . . . well, there's either a hanging of the victim or a lynching of the 'furriners.' "

Oh, dear God, I didn't know, True's heart whispered. Audibly she whispered, "No lawyers to defend them? You said *two* rules?"

"How could a penniless mountaineer afford a lawyer? There's occasionally a kangaroo court. But bear in mind that the population has intermarried—and worse!—that everybody's related. And Rule Two is: 'Thou shalt protect thy family!' They enforce it, welcoming no outside interference. That includes the law—and the Almighty Himself—God forgive them."

But they receive forgiveness by asking, True argued. *Ask?* Her husband shook his head sadly. One did not seek forgiveness unless one saw a wrongdoing. True must try and understand that for generations—was she up to hearing this? Of course she was! Else how could one help?

"Darling, they don't want to be helped—not now. Killing is a—well, a game up there in the tanglewood of laurel, ivy—and primitive thinking. It provides excitement in their dreary world. This handful of mountaineers sneaked away from 'the family' after hearing a hellfire-and-damnation sermon by a man who had never attended a school, his only qualification of his words being 'Leastwise, that's the way I heered hit.' " He sighed in a way that made True hurt. "And look what they found out here!"

There was a long silence broken only by the hoot of an owl in search of food. And then the fiddling changed to off-key hymns, as the pathetic fugitives had "heered" it.

"We must go back, sweetheart," Young Wil said, trying to coax her into a lighter mood. "Unless you want them sending out a searching party to eavesdrop like we did—"

"Oh, Wil . . ." True pulled back, clinging to the safety of the shadows. "Is there hope—I mean that these people will learn? After all, isn't it a good sign that they're stopping over in Slippery Elm—"

She stopped, realizing the folly of her own words. How could they learn with no schools, no seminaries—not even a preacher?

Young Wil must have read her thoughts. "Who can know the mind of God? I wish they could have heard some sermons of salvation here, but at least they have not killed each other, dancing in the victim's blood and then attending the funeral the next day! Come on, darling, we must—"

"That's the way I 'heered' it." Wil attempted a second lightness, which failed miserably. "I'm sorry I upset you—yes, there *is* hope. After all, their belief has roots in the Scriptures. Who knows but what they can shake off the ironclad conviction that folklore takes care of the rest... If they can take away a mustard seed of truth, it can sprout like mushrooms in the devil-darkened hollows. So, come, sweetie—no tears of goodbye. We'll pray instead..."

13

The Twain Shall Meet

It was only a fortnight from the time the newcomers left Centerville until O'Higgin returned. Ordinarily it would have seemed much longer to the families awaiting his return. But there was such frenzied activity in the Valley that nobody chalked off the days after the first night. Jerry moped. Kearby, seeming to sense that something dreadful had happened to Clarry, steered away from all men—even those within her family—and kept up an endless wheedling in favor of having her parents send her to Wilbur's Academy for Girls. She won her case and, with the aid of her father, was admitted, carrying with her a near-perfect report card, a trunkful of attractive school clothes (only to find that uniforms were required), and an outward bravado.

"Are you sure you want to do this, honey?" Aunt Chrissy asked gently. Kearby's waspish reply canceled out her affirmation.

"Would my talking to her help reassure Aunt Chrissy?" True asked Young Wil.

His answer was a shake of his head. "She's in no mood. We have to allow youth to find its own level, like water. Now, darling, lighten up as we probe the human mind together. Kearby, Jerry, and Clarry are at an interesting stage in human development, weighing and reweighing their chances for success out there in the world which looks exciting and frightening at the same time. Their insecurities come out in mood swings—sometimes high, too high, like spirited starlings, and at other times deliberately stoking the fires of pessimism. Follow me?"

Indeed she did. Wasn't she guilty of the same thing? Deliberately she dismissed her misgivings about those on their way to Slippery Elm, about the twins, about the somewhat empty feeling she had about the rather meaningless church here—about *everything.*

Young Will had told her once that when one took away something undesirable it must be replaced by something better—a more desirable substitute.

So she filled her mind with readying for occupancy the cabin that Aunt Chrissy had once occupied with Uncle Joe. The formula worked. It would be such fun for her and Young Wil to be alone for the first time! Picking and slicing every event that came their way was no way to live. Neither was her tendency toward overprotection. God would look out for them all...

"But," she smiled to herself, "I suspect He will leave ironing of those ruffled curtains, washing windows, and beating carpets to me!"

And almost in a "jiffy" (Grandma Mollie's word) the cabin was sparkling and the happy couple were moved in. "Just look!" she said with pride as her husband picked her up and carried her over the threshold.

"I looked," he grinned, easing her onto the bed, then sitting teasingly at a discreet distance. "Double Wedding Ring quilt... feather mattress, downy as a cloud... and..."

Impulsively he eased toward her, inching slowly, as if courting her anew. Then, leaning forward, he kissed her boldly with a force that caused her to blush. She was the bride again, but—

"The gingerbread! It's burning!" True jerked free with a giggle.

"Methinks the lady protests too much—"

True grinned wickedly, waved, and backed toward the woodstove.

Early the next morning school commenced. True had to forgo breakfast. She was too on edge to eat, so great was her concern for the day. Swallowing her coffee with a force that almost scalded her throat, she tried to rationalize her queasiness. *I have taught before,* she told her reflection in the hourglass-shaped mirror above the armoire in the larger of the two bedrooms which the small cabin afforded. *Yes,* the True in the mirror affirmed, *but that was only to fill out the year when your aunt was confined before the birth of the twins.* Teachers were hard to find then, Mr. Goldsmith had reminded her with a hint of warning in his voice. He would be on hand a lot, of course, in case she needed his help. One needed *his* kind of help in the same manner one needed laryngitis on the night she was to solo in a concert!

"Why so pensive, darling? You'll do well and you know it!"

Young Wil, bless him, with all he had to do (judging by the entries in the old ledger which served as an appointment book) took time to bring True another cup of steaming coffee.

"I'm not pensive!" True denied with too much feeling. Then, whirling, her mouth filled with tortoise-shell hairpins to hold her heavy hair in what she considered an appropriate "teacher hairstyle" halo, she mumbled a garbled apology. "I'm sorry—of *course* I'm scared. I—I've had no time to get things ready—room's a dis-disaster—and my hair absolutely won't behave!"

The last words came out as she sneezed. Pins flew in all directions like ill-aimed arrows, causing both of them to laugh. True needed the release but realized that her laughter sprang more from nervousness than amusement.

"Go ahead, laugh it out," Young Wil encouraged in the same manner he had urged her to cry so many years before when Angel Mother was taken and her little heart lay about her like shattered glass.

"It's just—it's just that I must look like Mr. —Nate Goldsmith when he—he spits that cud of tobacco—and it runs down on his chin—"

"Parting his beard like the Red Sea—yes, he's still on that filthy weed. Come here!"

True obeyed. Young Wil snapped the three top grippers on her high-necked pink blouse (which made her pink cheeks all the pinker). He then kissed the back of her neck where three gold curls, held prisoners by the pins, had escaped, and turned her toward him—drawing her close. And suddenly she *was* crying—crying her heart out as she had when his awkward adolescent arms had held her on the night of her mother's death, bringing comfort as nobody else could have. Even then she had known it was young Wilson North to whom her heart belonged.

"It's all been too much, sweetheart," he was saying now. "You held up commendably—perhaps too well—"

"Wil North!" True said with spirit, "are you going to read *my* mind, too?"

"I always have," he replied almost humbly.

The two doctor-husbands had hitched the buggy to the most trusted roan. Obediently he clopped along, like a four-legged clock, ticking away the time, telling Chris Beth and True that confrontation was near at hand.

The morning was bleak and sunless, with a hint of rain in the air, unseasonably cool after the heat. And now a brisk breeze was rising.

"I feel dressed all wrong," True said against the teeth of the wind, "and I feel a sense of foreboding in spite of my husband's sweet efforts to erase it from my day. If only I had my room ready—"

Chris Beth urged the roan forward. Then she laughed lightly. "Don't let Nate bully you, True dear. You provide a necessary service which cannot be imitated, and he knows it. Anyway," she inhaled, hesitated, and then burst out, "you have nothing to worry about. It was supposed to be a surprise—that old faker made me promise—Nate, I mean. But, well, so I won't be guilty of talking too much, the charge he brings against *all* women, let me give you only a hint. You have nothing to worry about, absolutely nothing. Just prepare yourself for a nice surprise—and a wonderful day!"

And then they were there.

The surroundings were dearly familiar, yet excitingly unfamiliar. True somehow felt she was drinking in the beauty of the land for the first time: seeing the mountain ranges fold one behind the other as if they were in motion... marveling at the green-upon-green of the hills looking so deceptively close. Patches of emerald-green, like the design on a five-point star, appeared stitched between the wispy clouds that climbed the hills and then stopped to rest. Then, like a backdrop, the purplish-blues began, peak after peak of towering heights—their heads capped by bonnets of snow—probing today's gray of the vaulted sky. Who could fully understand this glory? To True, it was as if God's voice thundered through the surrounding canyons, only to drop to a loving whisper in the fir trees and the mountain stream that flowed around her...

"Oh, the school has a new coat of paint," she whispered in awe, "and a new roof—oh, Aunt Chrissy, another room!"

"*And* another teacher," a man's voice said very close to her ear. The voice, like the surroundings, was familiar, yet so unexpected that it came from a stranger—a stranger who was tethering the roan to a shady oak and emptying a generous portion of what Young Wil had laughingly called the horse's "sack lunch"—fat, golden oats from a gunny-sack.

"Good morning, Mr. Prescott," Aunt Chrissy said to the stranger's back. True stiffened and came out of her fog.

Prescott! What was the young minister doing here? Or were there two of them?

Not unless the Reverend William Prescott had an identical twin. No, she thought, the delicately carved features could hardly be duplicated, even in a twin! The finely drawn but firm lips curved into an engaging smile. But for some reason the deep-set eyes did not. They still reminded her of hardened quartz, and again she compared him with one of Robin Hood's men. Something about him—

"You are staring, Miss North," William Prescott said, eyebrows arched in amusement as he reached to help her from the buggy.

"*Mrs.*," True reminded him as she gingerly lifted the peg-top skirt an inch and accepted his hand simply because she was unable to alight without it. "And you are to please forgive my staring. It—it's just that I did not expect to see you here—and—"

She hated herself for fumbling for words. "Is this customary—I mean, for ministers to attend the opening of school? Is there to be chapel?"

"Whoa, one question at a time. Yes, it is customary for the new teacher to put in an appearance. And, yes, again, there is to be chapel. Unless you object?"

"Of course I do not object!"

"Mr. Prescott is to serve in several roles—teacher, preacher, and principal. We needed someone like him, as you will see," Aunt Chrissy told her.

True stood very still, listening to the drumming of the grouse and an occasional gobble-gobble of a wild turkey joining in protest of the invasion of their privacy. Nearby evergreen berries offered an abundance of fruit, and hazelnuts were in their prime. Probably that was what all the fuss was about.

Chris Beth, aptly described by President of the Board Goldsmith as being "high-stocked with brains 'n allus busier'n a couple of honeybees in a sweetbriar patch," tactfully moved on. She must have suspected that William Prescott and her niece had something to settle between them. It was true. But for the life of her, True had no idea what. The man was arrogant, a characteristic unbecoming a minister. True was not even sure she liked him. He was learned as far as a formal education went, but there was an aura of mystery that made her suspect him.... It should be of no importance to her, but it was.

"You'll need to know the facts about the people with whom you'll work—that is, if the mountaineers (only don't call them that) all show up as promised." The man's tone made her sound like a newcomer.

True's chin jutted out defensively. "You forget that I grew up here—" and there she stopped. "What do you mean *mountaineers?* We have no mountaineers here, Mr. Prescott."

"Not by that name—they prefer being called 'Highlanders.' They are really Scotch, but—well, it's a long story.

I suggest that you take a quick look up the mountains to your left. Or is that your blind side? Maybe you would prefer not to look."

True ignored what she considered to be insulting words. The man was impossible. But she did look upward and was surprised to see that a narrow path sliced out the side of the almost-vertical wall of the mountain. Up, up, up it went, sometimes losing itself as it jutted sharply to avoid an unexpected outcropping of jagged rocks. And along the shocking trail were shacks, hastily erected of the crudest logs, held intact by dried and cracked mud, and windowless. The cluster of lean-to's, huddled together as if seeking protection by numbers and separated only by gawking, squawking chickens, extended to the backbone of the mountain. A large, black pot swung from a tepee of poles centered the pitiful scene, its immensity suggesting that it was community property. There was no movement. Even the trees stood windless in spite of the stiff breeze. And then hounds, skin stretched tightly over their ribs as if there were no flesh between skin and bone, appeared from all directions. They bayed without enthusiasm and then sat down to scratch. There were no other signs of life.

True was speechless. Were there children here—children she was supposed to teach? Where had they come from, and when? "Who—?" was all she could manage.

"Appalachia—Great Smoky Mountains. Starving, frightened, trusting nobody. Chestnut crop failed, and they had to leave—some, that is. Others are fugitives from the law. Either way, they're hostile, ready to shoot their way out of any situation that's threatening."

"But—but why didn't somebody try to get them together with the group we helped?"

William's laugh was without mirth. "Them they hate worst of all—totally different breed. O'Higgin can explain matters better than I can. I think he can crack the barrier. I can't offer any other hope—"

"*Can't* or *won't*?" True spoke the words before knowing she planned to—and then wondered why.

"Both!" he said tartly. "They're dangerous—stubborn—feuding—"

True sighed. "I must get to my room—but these people—well, 'East is East and West is West—'"

His voice was so low she could scarcely hear: "But the twain shall meet . . . someday . . ."

14

The Light of the First Day

Stepping into her classroom, True experienced a peculiar, otherworldly feeling. She had crossed into another time, another century—walking backward. All progress seemed to dissipate, and she was back at the beginning of the American frontier. She did not exist. In her place were Angel Mother . . . Aunt Chrissy . . . all who came before her.

She was unable to settle the butterflies in her stomach even though she had handled classrooms before. She wished momentarily that she were as cocky and overconfident as William Prescott. It was then that she realized he was neither of those. Of course not—he was scared silly! Sure, he had been in the pulpit, where he could and did hold his congregation at arm's length. But he had had no experience in teaching, where small human beings swarmed about one's feet seeking love, understanding, and "learning" as a swarm of bees clusters in search of nectar for honey. Nate Goldsmith had appointed him to be principal simply because he was a *man*, and because women, through no fault of their own, were not very bright. So unabashedly (lest Mr. Goldsmith, Aunt Chrissy, or True herself would think of him as a beginner) William Prescott spoke and behaved in an arrogant way which the more experienced would avoid at all costs. She smiled to herself. Here was Study Number One for Wil's book. And she had expected it to be a child . . .

Eyes adjusted to the dim classroom, True looked around

her in amazement. Why, all was in readiness! There was a large brown crock filled with colored leaves on the worktable, where paper, pencils, and primers had been laid out with the same precision that one arranges the place settings for a formal meal. And right in the center of her desk lay a fat, rosy-cheeked apple for the teacher! Books, which had not been there before, lay in waiting on shelves which lined the walls. Where had they come from? And when?

Somehow she knew who had prepared the room even before William Prescott himself told her. He had entered the room quietly and his first words were, "Do you like it?"

"Like it? I love it—and what's more, I am deeply appreciative, Mr. Prescott."

"William, please, when the children aren't around."

True smiled. "I appreciate all you've done, William."

He colored, then managed a smile. "At least it earned me a smile, my first from you."

Was this what Wil's psychology book had described as a "compensatory act," one performed in order to gain favor or make amends for some imagined shortcoming? Perhaps she had made him feel it necessary. The thought made True feel a little ashamed.

"I have been unfair to you, Mr. —uh, William. Let's try again."

"My pleasure! Oh, the books—I've been boning up on Oregon history, and I find that people in this state are literary-minded. They pooled their books like their food and circulated them even before the first wagon trains—but I'm sure you're well-versed in history?"

"Quite well. Of course, Daddy Wil's a native and taught us that back in 1848 or so—anyway, when Oregon was a Territory—Congress set aside about 5000 dollars for a Territorial library. Unfortunately it burned, and we're still struggling to increase our books—"

"Struggle no more." William looked complacent. "Your friend, working with the government and the railroads, has arranged all this, with more to come—"

"My friend?" Surely he didn't mean—

But he did! "Michael St. John, the railroad tycoon—and look at this. Mr. St. John himself collected writings by some of the fur traders, scientists, missionaries, and explorers such as Cook, Vancouver, Lewis and Clark, Slacum, and Wilkes—all careful journals, sort of travelogues. But the first works of fiction, too—you know, Moss with his *Prairie Flower*, Joaquin Miller, Edwin Markham—"

William Prescott was rubbing gentle fingers along the spines of the books. But True, excited as she was, felt her mind pulling in two directions, one part of it wanting to listen and the other part marveling at Michael's generosity.

And then the principal had her attention again. "Oh, here it is, True—I mean Mrs. North—"

"True's all right," she smiled, wondering if he heard.

"The best-known of all books written on Oregon is Frederic Homer Balch's *Bridge of the Gods.* What an interesting man! Born in Lebanon, Balch didn't attend school until he was 15 or so, and then very little. But he learned to read at home, and—here's what may appeal to our charges—his ambition was to make Oregon as famous as Scott made Scotland!"

"Scotland—yes, that may appeal to their background if—"

"But wait! There's more! The author converted to Christianity and burned the manuscript he was working on—said what he was working on was sinful!"

A little like Michael St. John. "Then—what—" True began eagerly, then stopped. Michael, in his new life since his own decision to walk with the Lord, was seeking ways to serve. He was a brilliant businessman but neither preacher nor teacher, so was using his money to furnish needed supplies. And, oh, how money was needed—both there and here. *Bless him,* she thought as her eyes misted over.

"You're wondering what contribution Balch made?"

True came back to the confines of the classroom with a jolt. "Er—yes. Yes, I was. If he burned the manuscript—"

"That was the one he was working on then. But he kept remembering stories of the Columbia River Indians which he'd picked up as a boy. Characters kept haunting his thoughts, begging to be born—writers being a peculiar lot, I guess. At last he took up his pen and wrote *The Bridge of the Gods*, but never lived to know it would make him famous. Just as well, perhaps, although it's sad, as it could have made him feel guilty."

"Oh, but it shouldn't! He made a great contribution—"

William was watching her closely. "You think we can remove guilt—shame—and fear?"

"God can!" True's reply was instantaneous. And then she realized that the man beside her was fighting an inner battle. She could hardly wait until tonight to share her news with her husband. But ahead lay the day. How long had they been talking, anyway? Only a few minutes, actually, but to True it seemed an eternity.

Aunt Chrissy's head popped through the door. "Time to ring the bell, Sir—that is, if we plan chapel the first day."

"Absolutely—but—" William turned to True, "take one quick look out the window and get a view of those who are waiting to meet Teacher."

The schoolyard swarmed with children. True hardly knew what she was expecting—but not this. The children were beautiful, though fragile to the point of looking undernourished. Flaxen-haired and pale, they looked like little celestial creatures.

Almost all were barefoot, some with feet bleeding from the jagged rocks in the winding mountain trail they had descended. But their clothing was clean and surprisingly well-fitted. Except for their tendency to clump together, removed from the other children jumping over lumber piles reserved (she learned later) for a new library building for community use, their high-pitched squeals of laughter rang like bells in the clean air, and one would not have thought them different.

Chris Beth peeked around the door frame again. "Ready?" she smiled.

True nodded absently, her mind on the contrast between these children and the others of Appalachia. Why the difference between the "Highlanders," who chose (she supposed) to climb higher, and the "Valley Folk," who occupied the rich river-bottom lands in their former home?

"The children—they're so tidy. I just never expected the difference—fact is, I never expected *them*."

"It never pays to generalize, does it now?" Aunt Chrissy chided gently, her eyes glancing at the tiny watch pinned to the bosom of her simple white blouse. "There was never time to prepare you for the onslaught, not that I know the whole story. O'Higgin will have more news. You and I had our hands full, and then some. There goes the bell!" Its clang announced "books time" to the eager newcomers.

But at the hall entrance where the children were lining up, Chris Beth paused, turning long enough to say, "About the clothes—Bertie, Nate's wife, Olga, the Chu's, and all the Basque people, led by Rachel Beltran, collected outgrown clothing. Miss Mollie took a nip and a tuck and the proud parents 'biled 'em' in the black pot. The Solomons furnished notions. Oh, dear, here comes Nate! Shape up—make him feel important—"

Nate Goldsmith was wearing—to True's surprise—a white shirt with a stiffly starched bosom and collar, which being about two sizes too small, caused his Adam's apple to be thrust almost to meet his chin. Even his voice was strained when he strutted in to introduce the man at his side. Rolling his eyes without an attempt to turn his head, the Honorable President of the Board said importantly, "This here's Mr. Courtland," then turned his body to the immense shadow which loomed to shut all light from the door.

"Howdy," said the man wearing patched but clean overalls, his deep-set blue eyes probing True's. He removed the old felt hat which had been pinned up in front with a thorn and bowed in a surprisingly gallant manner.

"How do you do, Mr. Courtland?" True greeted him with a smile.

"'Bout as common. Glad t'have ye here—shore 'n we are. Now, Wife 'n we want that our little Josie, Nellie Sue, Charming, Eliza, 'n th' boys be larnin' a heap—case we find we wanta go back thar as missionaries. Welcome a'gin, sweet Ma'am—'n iffen we kin he'p—?"

"I will let you know," True smiled, warming up to this proud, courtly gentleman. Mr. Courtland seemed to know.

"Here ye be now—bein' all Wife 'n me had t'offer. Want t'wear this t'adorn yore purdy hair?" His offering startled her to silence.

Nate Goldsmith winked at her—his signal that she must not refuse. Not that she would have. But why rob him of his joy in authority?

True accepted the long owl's feather and tucked it in her hair, realizing that with the feather standing at attention at the back of her braid she was sure to be a subject of ridicule among local children. She must look exactly like the ghost of a young Indian maiden.

Pleased with his simple, artless gesture, the man turned to go.

It was then that True froze. In his back pocket was the imprint of a gun, the handle barely visible above the frazzled top.

She did not hesitate. "Mr. Courtland, Sir, I'm afraid I must ask that you leave your gun at the door."

The man turned in surprise. "Leave me gun? Why I wouln' be drest without it—no he-man goes about half-drest." He patted his pocket. "Hit's my best friend—protects me 'n my family, provides food—why, I've promised me wife I be bringin' home th' meat. Planned on squirrel stew—"

"Which you probably will have," True smiled. "But I cannot have guns brought inside the classrooms. That is against our rules. Just lay the gun by the door, please. Then you can recover it as you leave. We are so happy you came," she said winningly.

The man grinned. Maybe he was getting soft—maybe a little henpecked—but, then he'd never met so brave a lady. Fine job she'd do. Yep, fine job!

The children's bright eyes all focused on Teacher as pupils of all ages shuffled to find seats without a word. Above the tom-tom rhythm of her heart (either from excitement or a delayed reaction to her impetuous order to Mr. Courtland), True was dimly aware of two circumstances. These children, all with bisque-doll skins, were all ages even though she was to have beginners and chart-class. And here were the larger ones struggling to fit themselves into small desks (replacements for the battered secondhand benches). And there was the overwhelming, almost intoxicating, smell of varnish, new paint, and a strange food-smell similar to the odor of the strung-together pine cones, red peppers, garlic, and something else that True was unable to identify—a "good luck charm," said one of the children, that was as "important as a man's gun."

A man's gun. True tried to push the idea to the back of her mind as she assessed the group, wondering what to do about the assortment of ages and sizes.

The children's bright eyes remained glued on her. "Fine fix," True said to herself. She had never felt so helpless in her entire life. Preoccupied with the problems at hand, she took no notice of the amusement in the eyes of the local children whose parents she knew, so was unaware that they were about to explode into laughter. Actually, she might have welcomed it except that other matters were more pressing. In fact, they were closing around her—the children looking like giants.

One tiny girl, looking too young to be there, caught True's eye in an amazingly mature manner. What a lovely child! Fat-cheeked, with a high, rounded forehead and wide-open blue, blue eyes.

"Are yuh stuck, Teacher?" The voice rang out like a tiny silver bell. "Pray—thet's whut our maw does when her's got too much t'housekeep, 'n th' floor's all covered in slut's wool—"

"Shet yore mouth, Little Josie!" ordered the awkward boy of about 13 who was wedged into one of the desk seats so tightly that his breath came in difficult gasps. He was obviously the tiny girl's brother. Looking sheepishly at True, he volunteered, "We ain't 'posed t'be talkin—'n anyways, our paw ain't so pious, jest shoots up the chim'ley lettin' sparks fly—skeers our pet pig 'way from th' table—"

The suppressed laughter exploded somewhat like one would expect from a shotgun. This she could handle. Raising a hand for silence, True said softly, "You must be members of the Courtland family. You are Little Josie—and you?" She turned to Little Josie's brother.

"Nathan—Nat—'n we's all Prim'tive Babtis'—don' talk uh heap—"

"Praying's better anyway," True smiled. "We'll be gathering for chapel and then—"

There was no time to discuss seating. William Prescott was pushing back the curtain which made the large auditorium into three rooms.

Nate was suddenly back. "He's a-gonna read 'bout Creation—th' light of th' first day—larnin', I guess he means—'n he's hopin' *you* larn somethin' too. Dangerous thang—disarmin' a man—sez you'll be payin'..."

15

And Then the Dark

It was indeed an enlightening day—a day of discovery. It had thrown True only briefly when the children of the Appalachian families showed up. After all, "Come one, come all" was the motto of this Valley. Here was a new way of life with which she must become acquainted. Already she was planning home calls so that she could familiarize herself with their expectations. In fact, there was a certain challenge, a renewal of the spirit of adventure that she had come by naturally. It "ran in the family," according to Grandma Mollie. And to think, True had thought everything was under control here, that the Valley, beautiful and peaceful as it was, was finished. It had hurt when they left Slippery Elm, because of saying goodbye to Marty, Midgie, the baby, and all the new friends. But even more, she had known how much remained to be done. She still missed it, but now—well, thank goodness, God was in charge of the future. He had given her a new assignment, and He would help her fulfill it.

But she had to admit that it was a tough one. And just how much help she could expect from human sources remained to be seen.

True had hoped that Jerry would be around to help. After all, if all ages were to be scattered like the tribes of Israel, his presence would afford her a hand. But she should have known that Aunt Chrissy would want him with her. To their surprise he ended up with one Mr. William Prescott, who dangled a carrot before the boy's nose—one that was obvious to the point of being ludicrous. Except to Jerry! It was not every young man who was appointed to the position of Junior Vice Principal!

Well, if ever a principal needed a helper, it was this one. True's own apprehension melted away in sympathy when she saw the violent trembling of William's legs as he read the planned passage. And he had an inattentive audience. The new children, although quiet, fumbled with their new supplies as if they were from the king's counting house. Even a sheet of lined paper was a treasure. They were lost in a world of magic, staring in fascination as if they expected the lines to disappear. But that accounted for only part of their preoccupation. They did not understand a word that this strange man was reading.

The Valley children behaved even worse. They were squirming and giggling. The squirming came from boredom, and the giggling, True finally realized, sprang from amusement at the feather perched in her hair. Well, Mr. Courtland was still there, taking it all in, so she would just have to put up with it. Afterward there would be a lesson on manners—she would see to that. Meantime, she shook her head at the gigglers, who went right on giggling while the Appalachian children saw and took her disapproving glance seriously. Their faces blanched and they laid the supplies down as if they were burning their hands.

When William Prescott stopped to catch his breath, the children's faces went even whiter, if such a thing were possible. Thinking they were in "big trouble," one small boy called out, "We declare, Teacher Sir, we don' know them words—never heered 'em—'n they skeer us—'cause our Paw'll bust our britches—"

The principal's face went as white as theirs. He looked hopelessly at Chris Beth, then directed his question to True. "Uh, should I dispense with the reading—or have prayer—?"

A forest of small hands waved back and forth. True bit her lip. He had prepared the rooms but not his words or his heart. Obviously he was fearful of offering a prayer before this group of restless children, perhaps fearing their laughter, even though he was accustomed to praying from the pulpit.

"Pray," True said crisply, adding to herself, "you need all the prayers you can offer!"

"Don'chu know how?" The artless question came from the Courtland lad who was still squeezed into the tiny desk. "We do—but we don' wanna be throwin' off on you—less'n we git our hides tanned." He glanced uneasily over his shoulder at his father, glad perhaps that the gun lay outside the door!

The fairylike creature called Little Susie stood up. "I kin—"

All the Appalachian children clapped as their hands went down. True cast an anxious glance at Mr. Courtland. To her surprise, he was smiling broadly.

"Go ahead, Little Susie," True said quietly, seeing that William seemed to have lost not only his poise but his voice. Was he in shock?

"Shet yore eyes 'n bow yore heads," the little girl said sweetly. And then she began an odd sing-song of words which obviously made sense to her peers.

> Good Lawd, we thank ye-hey-tank-toodle all day—
> Come 'bide with us, hey-tank-toddle, 'n take our sins away...

Feet tapped. Fingers drummed. And, with eyes still closed, the children swayed in a sort of trance, all singing the words unself-consciously together with a certain charm that expressed deep emotion.

The day rocked on, frustration after frustration looming to destroy all hope that it would get better. First came the commotion of trying to place children where they belonged, which never materialized. For some reason William Prescott held fast to the idea that it was unwise. About the only thing he held onto, True sniffed inwardly, except a desk or chair to hold him on his feet!

"But why?" she asked quickly as he was drawing the curtains to separate the rooms again.

Glancing over his shoulder furtively as if he actually believed "Walls have ears," he whispered nervously, "You'll see."

What on earth bothered the man? But he was right. She did *see.*

There was no need to fill names in the register until the matter was decided. "Some of you are uncomfortable. Just bear with us and I'll try to get you older boys and girls into other rooms—or make some arrangement about desks—" True stopped, realizing that she had no authority to promise anything against the principal's wishes.

Wails of protest filled the classroom.

"I fit in here like a bird in a nest," one Huck-Finn-looking boy objected . . . ragged overalls torn off just below the knees . . . barefoot . . . a cowlick . . . with a sprinkling of freckles crossing his stub nose . . . gray eyes lighted with innocent objection. "Paw put me in charge of th' little 'uns—an' we gotta stick t'gether, us Prim'tive Baptists!"

It was the second mention of Primitive Baptists, so it must be an important matter. But there was no time to dwell on the thought; the overgrown Courtland boy needed attention. His father had left the room, so he was in charge. "Please, Ma'am, hit ain't good t'go separatin' us. Me, I kin fit in this here seat better'n I kin fit in with furriners—now, don' go thankin' I'm a scalawag—we love one 'nother—"

"Aw, Miz North, let 'em stay," the youngest Beltran boy put in on behalf of the newcomers. "Cain't you see . . ." His voice trailed off.

Oh, she saw all right! The Appalachian children were soft-spoken, well-mannered, and eager to learn. But they were not going to be pushed around. And they had no intention of making an effort to fit into a new group. That she saw—and something more. She saw, as Mark Twain must have seen, a moment in history, and she longed to preserve it because it represented a valuable record of a rapidly disappearing social order. She could learn much from these people . . .

The next lesson came with an "Eeeek!" as bedlam struck. The Valley children leaped to safety on top of their desks. The Appalachians remained seated, eyes puzzled.

"Dunno why they's sech skeeredy cats—hit bein' jest a skunk wantin' t'larn like us. Granny makes skunk oil fer us when we got the grippe—keeps 'em cooped like chickens, tho' I'd not be ahankerin' fer dumplin's," the Huck Finn character volunteered.

The fluffy little creature, blinking in the light, waddled down the aisle, nose twitching slightly as if others than himself contaminated the air, little front feet turned inward toward the white spot on his black chest, and tail up suspiciously straight—right toward True. It was all she could do to keep from leaping on her own desk. Then she saw the culprit—Huck himself. It was not what he did but something he did *not* do. His face was straight, too straight. It looked like a mask.

"Do you know anything about this—this creature?" True's stride, her route bypassing the trespasser, took her quickly to his desk.

"Me—yessum, some. I know they kin stink purdy bad."

He wouldn't lie. That would be "sinful." He would just withhold the truth, bypassing the facts no matter how long the dialogue continued. There could be no doubt that he had masterminded the skunk's appearance. But why give him the satisfaction of a scolding?

"You seem to know a lot about skunks—what's your name, anyway?"

"Ebenezer—named after my paw 'n his paw—'n yessum, I know—"

"Then toll him out of here, Ebenezer!"

The boy stared at her blankly, his freckles standing out on stems. What had gone wrong? Why hadn't his plan worked? his eyes questioned. Aloud, he said, "What's *toll?*"

"Coax, beg, drive—do anything to get him out—"

"Oh, thet. Ain't no problem." Huckleberry Finn II stood with pride, took the striped creature by the tail, and marched out with all the dignity of a soldier goose-stepping off to war.

"Now," True pitched her voice low, exuding a calm she did not feel, "you boys and girls be seated, please, and let's get the register ready for tomorrow's roll call."

They complied, ready to right the wrong as well as regain the dignity they had lost temporarily in the eyes of the new children. One volunteered to write down names. Another would follow and write in addresses, while others would check with the preacher—no, the teacher—that is, uh, the principal, and ask for some other desks.

There was a general commotion as the desk-swapping took place, but at last it was finished. The helpers did a good job with the names, but when it came to addresses, they'd had no cooperation. The mailman wouldn't come "up thar," the children said. No need anyhow, since not many folks could read. They all knowed where t'other lived, which trees had notches carved, where there wuz a hole 'twixt th' rocks, or a rail loose in th' fence, so who needed this—what was it, address? Well, that part would have to wait until her house calls. For now she must show a few books that might hold appeal for the older children. Most were unable to read, but they would be embarrassed by *The Three Bears*. *Treasure Island* was entirely too difficult, although the plot would fascinate them. Thank goodness, most of the books had synopses. She could garner interest by reading these aloud. She must write to Michael, thank him, and congratulate him on his wise selections.

She wrote herself a reminder and added several others. Ask for a fan, since the room was stifling. And more firewood (the potbellied stove would gobble the rick outside the window). And surely the Board would understand a need for something other than the communal cup that True suspected one of the mountain children had brought—a long-handled, hollowed-out gourd to dip into a tin bucket which was already rusting where water had run down the sides. Somehow her mind wandered to the other Appalachian folk who had gone to Slippery Elm. Those children had no school at all—no church—and—

Her thinking was split in half by a loud *clang-clang-clang* of a bell, the three clangs signaling lunch. Jerry must have told Mr. Prescott or rung the bell himself. She was about to explain to the new children when there was a nerve-curling clanging of the clapper which seemed to go on forever. Didn't Mr. Prescott know—

"Fire! Fire!" screamed the Valley children for the benefit of the new pupils, then stood at attention, awaiting Teacher's orders.

The Appalachian children panicked, some scampering like mice into the other rooms, others jumping from the windows. Someday perhaps True would laugh about this, but for now it was almost more than she could bear. And ahead lay the lecture she must make on how to conduct themselves in emergencies—maybe a few terse words for the principal himself. Imagine a fire drill on the first day!

Order restored, lunch ("dinner" to her new pupils) gave True reason to write herself another note. The contents of the "dinner pails" were so pitifully inadequate that she felt she was about to be sick. Thick, half-cooked "sow bosom" hung limply from between heavy, yellow biscuits. The rinds (bristles still intact) had not been removed from the pork. Surely something could be done to supplement the children's diet. Of course, there was pride to reckon with...

At last the day ended—almost. As True saw the children off, William Prescott shouldered his way through the group to stand by her side. The hand he pointed up the mountain trembled. Following the direction his finger pointed, she saw a shoulder-to-shoulder troop of mountaineer men, descending the mountain on sure feet, their hands on holsters strapped openly to the side-front of their bibbed overalls. She felt a bit queasy herself...but why had William fled?

True managed a smile and a wave of her hand. The men lifted their assorted hats and returned them to their heads. But they did not return her smile. Maybe it was fatigue which caused a sudden dread of the future. Momentarily, the hand of darkness clutched at her heart...

The darkness became real as she, Aunt Chrissy, and Jerry rode home in the gathering twilight. There was so much to talk about; but Jerry monopolized the conversation. Mr. Prescott said...Mr. Prescott made me responsible for this...Mr. Prescott made me responsible for that...and then, "This will be my best year, being in charge, then next year—well, I've got plans already. Mr. Prescott and me."

Chris Beth frowned a bit, then smiled. "I'm glad to see you so happy, darling. You never liked school so much before. And I know you'll do a fine job!"

Aunt Chrissy's words translated into: "This is the beginning of a change in our Jerry." And she would have been right. But for now True was unable to care. She was tired, tired . . . tired . . .

At home she fell across the bed, too exhausted to undress. Her husband was gone when she awoke the next morning.

16

The Return of O'Higgin

Two weeks passed quickly as True worked her way through a wilderness of problems. "Do you think we'll ever get this year on its feet?" she asked Aunt Chrissy over and over. And always the answer was the same: "Of course we will—although I'm not just sure what the Lord has in mind. These children are so interesting—so unique—so *precious* in their own way. Sometimes," she said with a wistful look in her dark eyes, "I almost wish we didn't have to 'civilize' them—impose our standards on their simple ways."

"But we're doing it for their own good," True invariably protested. "And I doubt if we're going to *impose* much on them. Some of mine are as stubborn as mules—gentle and sweet, but not about to be persuaded to change their ideas."

They agreed that they must move slowly with the new curriculum. Chris Beth was in a quandary as to the children's insistence that they learn Latin. Each day one of the fathers came down the mountain to observe what took place where his child was supposed to be "larnin'." They themselves, almost without exception, were unable to read. Why then was it important that their offspring master Latin? "'Cause th' Good Book once was in thet speech till them whut s'posed they be a-knowin' more'n God hisself begun messin' up His words 'n tamperin' with our child'run's brains—got 'em all churned up—'n in danger of hell's furnaces. Latin, hit's gotta be like once 'twas—'n you teachers, bein' smart 'nuf t'read, know 'bout th' Lord God's wrath fer him whut changes one teeny word—er goes takin' hit out."

The most immovable of them all was a man by the name of *Goodman.* He was "hidebound on a-livin' up t'th' name like unto how th' Old Country ancestors tooken pride in hit." Like their bloodline, they had to keep away from "messin' 'round with silly games 'n fancy stuff which hafta be forged out in th' devil's workshop—hit's Latin er nuthin'."

True shook her head helplessly, feeling drained of her sanity. She knew the Latin words to "Twinkle, twinkle little star..." and that was the extent of her knowledge of the language. "What will we do?"

Aunt Chrissy laughed. "We will ask our husbands to help, that's what! For some reason I never understood, Jerry took an interest in your Daddy Wil's work and pestered him until he dragged out his old textbooks and helped him a bit. It's a dead language, but—"

"Better it be dead than all the teachers!" True said with a shudder, remembering that it was her frightful duty to disarm each mountaineer. It had become so routine that, amusingly they had begun to drop their weapons of their own accord. Which was not to say that William had not created a wall of fear, no matter how careful she was to conceal it, around her heart. One of the men would balk one day...

For the most part, the men were polite and appreciative, each making it abundantly clear that "facts" were what they had brought their families here for. Facts. Truth. "Light"—only to be found in Latin. But one man by the name of Hank-John Brown was different. He was surly, even angry—and seemingly very frightened. He made her uneasy with leading questions concerning the group from Appalachia which had come before his "flock." "Skeered, they wuz—'n well they ought-a be. They's settlin' up t'do one day. Don' let 'em come near—don' want them nasty-minded filth tryin' t'mate up with our virgin daughters—no incestin' 'mongst us. An' we don' go co-minglin' 'mongst them what fornicates 'n desecrates—me, I be ready t'shoot any boy what goes courtin' me daughters afore he's got a chance t'draw! Don' go 'lowin any boy settin' near my girls—ye hear? I never shot me no woman—still—" he rolled bloodshot eyes to peer out the window where he had reluctantly dropped his weapon, and without so much as a "Good afternoon" he sprang from his chair, recovered his gun, and disappeared.

True felt almost out of touch with Young Wil. She was buried in a sea of work but had to postpone questions and relating incidents from the classroom because of his demanding schedule. He kept long hours (he was often still out on house calls at bedtime and did not awaken her on returning), and then he spent hours working by lamplight on his book. When there was a moment it was like doing battle with a shadow to get her husband's attention.

"I wish you wouldn't work so hard, Wil," she said wistfully on one of those rare moments. "There's a moon—a full one—just waiting to be shared—"

True paused, wondering if he had heard. In the quiet, the music of their private stream stole into the livingroom-dark. A bird twittered and the mountains, wrapped in twilight's purple shawls, beckoned.

Hard work had burned away the daylight hours for them both, stolen away a margin of togetherness she needed. Now, teasingly, she paraded before him—flexing her muscles in luxurious pleasure. "What a relief to move—we could walk—talk—oh, Wil—*can't* we?"

Wil's eyes had a faraway look in them. And the sheaf of papers waiting on his desk told her the answer. Women could *make* time for their husbands, she thought a little bitterly. But men—well, whoever said, "'Love to man is a thing apart; 'tis woman's sole-existence' had it right." She could tell him that Chicken Little was right, that the sky was falling, and he wouldn't hear!

And, then without warning, True had a chance to test her theory. There was a distinct crackle of brush right beneath the front window, a muffled voice, and then the warning cry of a bird of prey closing in on its kill.

"What was *that*?" Young Wil was at her side immediately, a steadying hand on her arm. "Oh—I see." And his hand pointed at a great bird, motionless in the darkening sky as if poised to reconnoiter before sailing in on silent wings to dive.

"Birds don't talk—you know that!" True said a little sharply because of her fear. Mindlessly, she pulled away and eased to the window, peering out in spite of her fear. There she saw a menace behind every stump, a lurking danger behind each tree. Then her courage floundered. But, hypnotized by the lazy blue sweep of the mountains (where she was sure the object of her fear had originated), she felt unable to move. Until some movement, some motion turned her around.

Young Wil was not there!

True came to her senses then. She had sent the man she loved into a danger he knew nothing about. Perhaps even now, he was surrounded by mountaineer men with six-shooters dangling at their sides. Even now a shadow was crossing the yard—

"Wil!" she screamed in warning, and wondered later if her feet touched the braided rug even once as she rushed out the door.

A hand closed about her own. But it was not herself for whom she feared. It was her husband. "Let go of me—you—you—"

"Watch your language, Teacher!" an intimate voice whispered in her ear. "Some detective you'd make." But the mellow laugh gave away the identity of the shadow.

"Wil—Wil North—you scared me out of my wits—and if you dare tell me it's my mind working overtime—"

He was guiding her footsteps toward the door of the cabin. "My, my! What length some women will go to in order to get attention—"

"Only when they're neglected by their mates!"

It felt good to release all her pent-up emotion—no matter what the cost. And they'd have to talk now. Already she had postponed telling him about the odd manner of the mountain men dangerously long.

"Thank God I haven't made you hate me," Young Wil said fervently as he gripped her cold fingers in a warm, comforting grasp with such strength she wanted to cry out. But, oh, it felt good to hurt!

She was putty in his hands. But she had *not* imagined the sound!

As if reading her mind, as always, Wil closed the door behind them, the cozy room jealously guarding their privacy. "There was someone out there," he said flatly, "and I can't tell you not to be afraid because I have no idea who or why—but I *can* beg you to be careful, darling."

He slid down into his favorite easy chair, drawing her into his lap. True made no protest, winding her arms about his neck instead.

"Of course there was! And what do you mean—you haven't made me hate you? How do you know what evil lurks in my heart, you overconfident, impossible man? Talk about male ego—"

"Who wants to talk about it?" He buried his face in her hair. "But I'll answer your question before devouring you completely."

True snuggled closer with a giggle as in mock seriousness Young Wil said smugly: "Women *pretend* to hate us—hate being close to love, you know. But to despise me, find me loathsome, now that's different."

She nodded. "Something you're picking up for your research? Studying *me*, then generalizing about women? Oh, well," she faked a sigh, "I don't mind being your subject—and darling, although we've been apart far, far more than I'd like, I've been working right along with you—studying influences of—the newcomers—"

True poured out the whole story then, every detail. And when she finished, Young Wil said quietly, "I've known, sweetheart—and I've done my share of watching from a distance and praying. Now I'm even more afraid for you—and if anything happened to you—"

His voice broke in several places, and he held her closer as the darkness folded its arms around them.

Sunday brought three surprises. True glanced around, hoping to see some of the new settlers at church. Seeing none brought keen disappointment. But not to William Prescott, whose eyes surveyed the congregation anxiously. Relief spread over his delicately formed features, a reaction which still puzzled her. What was he afraid of?

Afraid? His sermon certainly reflected fear. It was as if he were two persons—except that she did wonder at his text. "Come now, and let us reason together..." he read from Isaiah. Somehow she felt that the passage had to do with his problem. Yet his poise surprised her.

The second surprise came at announcement time. Nate Goldsmith stood and with his usual pomp presented a report that one would expect to hear at a school board meeting. All was well, he said of school. Lots of new books... extension of the curriculum to include Latin...two new cedar watering buckets, a dipper, and individual paper drinking cups "fer hy-*hy*-gene, y'know, 'n a coupla privies fer th' same purpose." But, best of all, Nate said with a lift of voice, was the newcomers who visited school daily—and it was the "bounden duty" of others to do likewise. *O, no!* True's heart cried out. But the report was interrupted by a merry whistle. O'Higgin was home!

17

Understanding— and Lack of It

A burst of applause greeted Irish O'Higgin. But it did not seem to bother William Prescott, who wanted to hear a report as much as the congregation. News of the "folks over there" was of even greater importance to him, True was sure. Somehow he fitted into a strange puzzle here involving both the group in Slippery Elm and those choosing the higher elevations here in the Valley.

"Greetings from th' goodly folks ye befriended, in th' name o'th' Lord Jesus Christ!" O'Higgin boomed, his merry blue eyes dancing with pleasure at the stomping of feet almost drowning out his words. "Now, be still, dear ones, lest me voice not be heard in God's hoose—*house*!"

Why, that rogue! He actually winked at his "Mollie-gal"! His boldness brought even more applause. True looked at Grandma Mollie, who sat there poker-faced. Not that she fooled anybody. Theirs was a good marriage, an inspiration to all who took marriage seriously, binding them with sacred vows—in contrast to the growing number who seemed to have misunderstood the terms. Did they really suppose the final promise was "until *divorce* do us part"?

O'Higgin doffed his plaid-and-tasseled tam-o'-shanter to expose a near-bald head (with the few strands of red hair that were combed forward to cover the loss failing in their mission). He compensated by allowing his always-abundant red facial hair to grow into an enormous beard.

"I be knowin' 'tis hard waitin' on a full report," the big Scotch-Irishman grinned winningly, waving a ruddy hand for silence. "'N ye kin depend on receivin' it—but first," and there was a rare near-pleading tone to his voice, "'tis patience I be askin'—patience whilst I be informin' me family. But this day jest 'low me t'tell ye them mountaineers Jeremiah 'n me be takin' t'be pasturin' in a new land be more ignorant than vicious—victims more I'd be thinkin' o'Blue-Ridge environs mix't with whut Young Wil here'd be referrin' to as heredity 'n ye old demon rum . . . their region was invaded-like by outsiders with dif'ernt idees. And—well, th' pore ignoramuses—they gotta be changin' er they're goners. Tempers flared when some Prim'tive Baptis' hiked up them hills t'tell 'em guns be a tool o'th' devil—'n a man caught aimin' one o'them tools at a brother, kinfolks er not, was predestined t'be takin' th' fire-stoker's hand 'n go Down There. No power on earth be able t'undo that—not even God."

There was an outcry of protest. But O'Higgin's powerful voice rose above it. "Now, ye gotta be rememberin' them mountaineers see their reflection 'n be believin' it—seein' theirselves as good folks who jest be misbehavin' onct in a blue moon . . ."

Not to worry, he declared. The believers separated themselves from "th' infidels" and, deciding they were "God's elect, chosen ones, baptized into heaven" before the Creator finished earth's foundation, up and got themselves out.

"But," and here O'Higgin's chest swelled with such pride that True feared the buttons would pop off his vest, "they're a-changin—shur'n they be! Ye gotta be rememberin' our Marty's where I be placin' him—right there in their midst—bein' no preachers thereabouts, 'n him 'n Midgie, praise be! jest up'n prayed 'n prayed 'til th' prayers be answered—they got it straight from above they gotta be fillin' in where them saddlebaggers leave off—you be knowin' 'bout them kind what used t'come through onct a summer—passin' th' hat—fervor dependin' on how much be put inside. Well, begory, t'God be th' glory! Onct our Marty be tongue-tied, 'n now th' words come a-flowin' like Moses struck th' rock!"

There was such a roar of shouts that True wondered which would go out the top of the building first—her sanity, or the roof itself, or, judging by his face, the Reverend William Prescott!

"Lots more t'be said—but ye, bein' devout like ye be, understan'—I kin tell by th' gleam in yore eyes thet a man bes' be sharin' with 'is family afore he goes spoutin' off too much. Some o'this is family talk—"

They understood, but with reluctance.

And now here they were, the family—the O'Higgins and the Norths. The setting, of course, was Turn-Around Inn. The weather had cooled mercifully, "'nuf t'thin th' blood," Grandma Mollie said. To which Aunt Chrissy had answered (with a secretive smile at True), "Yes, until we can get it thickened with fall's molasses."

A fire chuckled in the big fireplace. The kettle sang merrily of coffee-to-come. A gingerbread-scented woodstove made promises of its own. The newest litter of kittens tumbled in Miss Mollie's yarn, batting balls in unnoticed glee. O'Higgin opened his worn Bible, read selected passages concerning love, and called on Daddy Wil to pray. It all made a beautiful picture, one that would live forever in True's heart...

The rest of the evening was spent in one long soliloquy by O'Higgin.

"Brother, them Scotch-Irish be like unto yeself—'n thet be th' reason ye got so all-fired worked up, begosh 'n begory!"

The men were rugged six-footers—like unto the giants of Canaan who made the children of Israel look like grasshoppers, O'Higgin's monologue with himself began. Come to think of it, the story ran a heap like the Bible's account of spying out the Promised Land. Only it was King James who sent *these* giants out, well as the rawboned but "fertile as th' soil" women to America's shores. Supposed to intermarry and replenish the land with Protestants! Sad to say, they did more "fightin' than courtin'." They took up their muskets instead of their Bibles and did more washing down meals with stilled liquor than serving communion...

But the first immigrants were pure of heart—smart, too, sharper than a tack. They knew it was God's will that they build churches and schools. They knew rich land when they saw it, so settled in the valleys as pure and virgin as their women. All stuck together, helping offspring build cabins instead "o'pitchin' lots elsewheres." First crops were good; but eventually the bottomlands could hold no more " 'count o'them prolific girls a-marrying' at 12 or so turned out many as 30-some-odd wee lads 'n lassies."

So families pushed higher and higher up the mountains, where farmland grew more and more shallow, not near as productive as the womenfolk. By and by the folks up there got to be as uppity as the shallow soil and began a war of words, claiming 'twas God's will they eke out a living by the sweat of the brow. And that was easier to accomplish by using hoes " 'mongst th' rocks 'n fern-feathered dells" than down in the bottoms where the oxen did all the sweatin'. The mellow soil produced enough corn for johnny ashcakes. Awful good with wild turkeys and acorn-fed coon meats. And already the trees were big enough to hide their whiskey stills—natural to have them, elsewise they'd be wastin' a lot of that corn as well as the wild fruits.

Each generation took them higher into the hills, where hunger prevailed. But they were too proud to admit it. They were deprived in other ways, too. No learning. No law. "No women fer th' lusty men with big appetites—so's they be gittin' theirselves all cantankerous t'live 'round." That spelled out the history of the intermarriages " 'n worse."

By now the war of words had ended. Arguing was "ole woman's meat." Men wasted no time at it. "Shot other men dead 'stead." That was Giant Number One, a man's gun! The other was "th' Prim'tive Babtis' church—kinda germinated from th' Good Book, then went 'Calvin'—still makin' claim on Baptis', cuz o'th' duckin' required when they got religion." The shooting continued, as did the whiskey-making and the intermarrying " 'n th' like, includin' concubines." Religion never changed a man's *ways*—just his heart. So the rest of their self-styled religion took its "proof" from superstition, dreams, and "visions" that they shared in white-faced fear. Now a body could shoot a blood-'n-gut mortal. But a ghost—well, now that was different.

The hate burning in their hearts shot its flames higher and higher among the mountaineers. Nobody dared invade their privacy. For sure, no trespasser would be coming back—except as a white-faced corpse. And that's where O'Higgin stopped, his face drained of all color. "'N that's what I be fearin's a-gonna happen t'my Martin-boy!"

The group tensed. Then, white-lipped, all tried to speak at once. After all, intriguing as this account was, it served only to give them insight into the tension between the two groups with whom they had dealt. It told them nothing concerning their own!

"Then you truly feel that Jeremiah's group is a threat to Marty?" Young Wil's question rose above the others.

"Could be—jest *could* be now." O'Higgin's near-bald head bobbed up and down, gleaming in the firelight like a polished marble. But True saw tears in his usually roguish eyes. He leaned forward, bracing his elbows on the still-open Bible, and cupped his bearded chin in the ham-sized hands. "Meself, I be takin' no pleasure in bearin' bad news—but best I tell ye I ain't feelin' tip-top 'bout me lad—er—"

"Midgie and the baby?" Aunt Chrissy cried out with seldom-heard alarm in her voice. "They're in danger too—was that what you were about to say?"

"O'Higgin! Don' you know better'n shatterin' all our nerves? You got no proof now—'n I'm not one bit sure the Lord takes a likin' t'such talk—less'n you *know*?"

O'Higgin looked remorseful but made no effort to amend matters, even though a scolding from his Mollie-Gal was more threatening than facing a grizzly bear.

True's thoughts deserted her body. She imagined herself in a tub of comfortably warm water, sinking into its depths, letting its warmth untie the muscles of her taut body. For a moment it worked. Then Daddy Wil's voice brought her back to the problem at hand.

"But if they're Christians, like they claim—"

"Nay, nay!" O'Higgin lifted a hand of protest. "I ne'er be sayin' thet—not onct did me ears hear mention o'Christian—jest Prim'tive."

"Well, they're that all right," Daddy Wil said crisply, "but they seem to know little about laying aside arms and repenting!"

"No exposure, shure 'nuf. Me lad be tryin', but he be no preacher—'n then there be th' rascal namin' hisself Clarry's stepfather—reminds me—got a letter from th' bonnie lass fer Jerry—'n 'nother fer True—"

Jerry and True snatched for them hungrily.

18

Midgie's Letter

Although the hour was late, Mollie Malone O'Higgin busied herself in the kitchen of Turn-Around Inn. Hospitality kept late hours. A body just naturally felt better about matters when the tummy was satisfied.

"Skim the morning's milk, O'Higgin. This gingerbread behaved itself, all tender to th' touch 'n is deservin' th' richest cream."

The two of them argued, scolded, and laughed in their unique way which created the signs of a happy marriage. Jerry had taken himself upstairs, two at a time, in order to be alone with Clarry's letter. By now he would have read it three or four times. The two Wils were deep in conversation, eyebrows knitted in thought, voices pitched too low to be heard above the sleepy whisper of the dying fire. Outwardly it was a cozy scene, but the air was charged. A log shifted to break in half. The snap brought everybody to their feet nervously.

As the men sat down to resume their talk, True motioned toward a corner in invitation for Aunt Chrissy to join her. The up-ended logs sent a shower of sparks up the chimney, then burned like twin candles, making it unnecessary to light a lamp.

"Let's share Midgie's letter," True said quietly as she pulled two ladder-back chairs close together. Chris Beth waited in anticipation as True unfolded the three sheets of paper and smoothed them in her lap.

It was hard to read the squeezed-together words crowded

so childishly together. True noted with a smile that Midgie had written on both sides, making the thin paper even more difficult to read. But she noted also that the language and the punctuation continued to improve.

The letter was so refreshingly "Midgie" that it was easy to forget the frightening news that was sure to follow. But at least the words started with the usual bundle of household news—another room added, a sunny corner papered with rocking-horses and reserved for the March Hare ("we call him 'Christian' when we can remember"), next spring's bulbs planted ("you know how welcome they are in the confusing month of March, everything covered with dirty leftover snow, winds bitter and bound on taking out their fury on the world, all that mud... then up pop a million crocuses as numerous as stars, daffodils so gold and shining they almost sound their trumpets like Joshua's troops marching around Jericho seven times").

True paused to look at Chris Beth. Both were smiling, each knowing that tears of understanding were close to the surface.

Midgie, almost as if postponing the burdens of her letter, talked about the season at hand.

> I will never forget the beauty of autumn there. Marty and I will cherish the memories forever. But they are fading, no longer outdoing the special show of God's handiwork here. Remember, True, how fall days always look like a sunrise—the earth, the rocks, and the mountains declaring His glory? The whole world's a brilliant red such as described in Revelations...

Revelations. Midgie was working up to her own gradually. But first, didn't they want to hear about the family of friends there?

> Things were better for Tillie, the adorable March Hare's "Grandy." Midgie was uncertain which was a greater factor in the restoration of her sanity—love for her precious great-great grandson ("and, oh, lineage counts with Tillie Caswell!") or the come-to-stay arrival of Reverend Randy after Mr. Caswell's terrible fate. They were doing a lot to the store—

True wished that Midgie had gone on to tell more about their ministering to the newcomers. But instead she switched to other matters without indenting for paragraphs.

> Mariah and Billy Joe, the "Beetle" (True, noting Chris Beth's questioning eyes, took time to explain that he was once a bowlegged squatter who made claims of being Uncle Artie's foreman and did such a good job that Marty kept him on), had replaced their tent with a house. "A *real* house—well, a kind of lean-to, but cozy with a little-mouthed fireplace and lots of wall hangings, all cobalt blue and turkey-red—colors that only Mariah could make like they belonged amongst the dresser with a cracked mirror, rag rugs, and strings of colored gourds mixed with red peppers and garlic! Mariah's so happy and keeps those knowing fingers busy sewing—her and Tillie—for the new folks—"

Once more, the letter stopped where it should have begun. There was news about each of the farmhands. And, oh, the best part:

> Mariah was having them come for Thanksgiving—Augie, Tex (his new kind of wheat *had* done well and a government man was coming to take a look, might even buy some to recommend to a big seed company), Pig Iron, and Slim. All were modern-day disciples—how on earth could Marty do as much as he did trying to spread the Word without them? Not that Marty could do what needed to be done, but . . . well, back to Slim—his withered arm was on the mend and he was as good at breeding fine cattle as he claimed . . . oh, such longhorns, shorthorns, Holsteins, Jerseys, and Ayrshires . . . right proud of them she was until the silly critters took to running like they were calves, trampling down her garden and the morning glories . . . good that roses had thorns. Of course, Slim was "getting on." That's why her heart was gladdened that he was seeing the Widow Grant even though the poor creature had her problems. Real plain woman, salt-and-pepper hair pulled back so tight that her scalp

> shows through. Tied up in knots, too, hands always moving, but it was plain to see that she was gone on Slim. Betrays herself by sucking her lower lip in every time she looks his way. Well, anyway, I'm going to ask her over for the holiday, too—a good start to get to know these strange new folks—hoping we can avoid trouble..." *more* trouble than they'd had. But who knew? Look how much trouble Abraham had finding ten good men. Did True suppose God might look with the same disfavor upon Slippery Elm in view of all this wickedness and destroy it like Sodom and Gomorrah? "Sin's great and grievous—like I'm about to tell you—"

True inhaled deeply and prepared herself for what lay ahead. Miss Mollie's interruption at that critical moment, although she was generally welcome in any circumstance, was a disappointment.

"I come in 'bout middle-way through, quiet as a mouse—was agonna tell our menfolks I'd added sourdough griddle cakes 'n maple syrup, it bein' so late 'n all . . . but," the older woman fanned herself with Midgie's envelope, "I got t' thinkin' thet's a good idee she's got, ain't it though? How's about we include them peculiar folks up th' mountainside? Yep," Grandma Mollie answered her own question, "we do it!"

"Begory! We do, me bonnie one!" O'Higgin, restored to his jolly self, boomed as he dumped a fresh armful of wood to rekindle the fire.

It was useless trying to read further. Midgie reluctantly laid the letter aside until they completed refreshments. Young Wil called Jerry, but there was no answer. When Daddy Wil suggested that boys this age needed a lot of privacy, his nephew nodded thoughtfully.

"Now," Daddy Wil surprised True by saying "I think I speak for us all when I ask that you share the rest of Midgie's letter with the entire family. I have a feeling we all need to know."

"I agree," True said woodenly. He was right. It was only that she, like Jerry, felt a sudden urge to be alone. Reluctantly she began:

> We don't know which way to turn. Things were bad before the new people came—and now it's so

confusing we don't know who the enemy is. The militia is still here, our only protection. But they're more on the lookout for deserters and bootleggers—I do believe some of these men would make whiskey from other men's blood if they could afford the sugar! Mr. St. John—and saint he is, too, creating a library, only to have it torched—

A gasp went up from the listeners. "Burnt *books*! Thet be a downright sin in me mind. Think ye th' same? Best myself be there—"

"Best yuh be settin' yourself down, O'Higgin!" Miss Mollie declared, followed by a low-pitched, "But I'm beholdin' to yuh!"

The big Irishman poked the fire, then obeyed. "Go 'head, lass."

"Where was I?" True murmured, her mind more on Michael's new image than the loss. Books could be replaced—"Oh, here—" she said, a little embarrassed that she had allowed her mind to wander, "still talking about Michael St. John—"

—thinks the railroad feud has died down. He's doing what he can to restore law and order, watches his men. But he can't be everywhere at once. Nobody can but the Almighty, and sometimes I think He's turned His back—what with all this cursing His Holy Name by some of these Appalachians. Why, True, they'll kill *anybody*—enemies, friends, kinfolks. The militia tried disarming them, but they crush skulls with sharp rocks. Oh, how they misquote the Bible (can't read it, of course) . . . and us with no teachers to educate them. No preachers to teach them about God's forgiveness and how to get it—and no doctors to patch up the wounds. So they bleed inside and out. Even the nonviolent Shakers have had to learn to shoot straight. That's where that sweet Clarry is—with AnnaLee—or *was* till Virgil Adamson found her. The child ran here pale as a cauliflower . . . then disappeared. *Oh, how we need you . . .*

19

"Mica, Mica, Parva Stella..."

Exhausted though she was, True was unable to sleep when, as dawn was nearing, she lay down with senses spinning. Young Wil had insisted that she rest even though he and Daddy Wil had to respond to a call by a man who, faceless in the dark, waited at the gate of the Big House when they returned. "Hit's serious, Doc—Docs—needin' of you'ns—"

With a shock True realized later that she had heard nothing regarding the nature of the emergency. The words blurred together. Didn't these people realize that doctors' families had problems too?

"What should we do, Lord... *what*? Help us... we are stumbling... falling..."

A knock on the cabin door startled her. "Who is it?" she managed to mumble, feeling for her slippers.

"Jerry—" his voice came out uncertainly.

"*Jerry*!" True was wide awake as, barefoot, she hurried to lift the heavy board which barred the door.

"I—I heard part of Midgie's letter," the boy confessed.

"That's perfectly all right, darling—you're a part of the family," True assured him, managing to find a match to light the oil lamp.

"I know where she is," he said flatly.

"*Clarry*?" True whirled to face him.

He nodded without accepting her motion of invitation to sit down. "But I'm not supposed to tell—"

"You *must*—it could mean her life." True was having trouble breathing. Should she promise to keep her whereabouts secret? Bargain to get the truth? "*Tell* me, Jerry—*please.* I'll do my best to keep it between us—"

"With Kearby."

True caught her breath. "But how—I don't understand, Jerry."

He shook his head, face white with pain. "I don't either—that's why I have to go—Kearby can't keep her."

It was a delicate situation, one which should be faced with a clear head—certainly not by a person who was herself exhausted. *Think!* True commanded herself. *Move carefully...think before speaking. Let the Lord lead...if Jerry were convinced he knows best, would he have told me, when the girl's whereabouts were to be kept secret?*

At length True spoke. Did her words come out as thick as they sounded to her own ears? It was as if her tongue were too large for her mouth. "Sweetheart," she said slowly, "I know exactly how you feel, because I feel the same way—torn different directions—knowing that Young Wil and I need to be with Marty and Midgie, but needed here, too. I—I haven't had an opportunity to talk with anybody—so it's good that we can talk, just the two of us—think, plan, and *pray*—that's the first step, Jerry. We both know that."

He nodded while making a circle on the braided rug with the toe of his shoe. "You feel that way too—then you understand. But, True, I *have* to go to Clarry—don't I? I mean—oh, True—I *have* asked God—*why doesn't He answer*?"

True walked toward him. "Are you too big to be hugged, sweetie?" He made no objection, so with her arms about him in a comradely fashion, she was able to get the words out. "I'm guilty on that count, too, Jerry. We don't give Him time, really wait for an answer. We just make up His mind for Him. Remember the saying, 'Doubt is out'?"

Again he nodded.

Without warning the answer came—and in such a strange way that neither of them recognized it at the time.

The handful of pebbles tossed against the window could have been the gray-fingered dawn scratching to be let in by the two tense persons inside the cabin. The faces pressed flat-nosed against the panes were leering skeletons in the half-light.

Fright changed to indignation. Who were the intruders and why—

Jerry recovered first. "What are you doing here, Loren—Josiah—Billy Jack?"

The frightened faces withdrew, and their owners would have fled had Jerry not opened the door and commanded them to stop. "What's the trouble—why are you here at this hour?"

All talked at once. It was that new boy and his followers, Master Jerry (*Master Jerry*? True was intrigued by both the title and her young cousin's mature behavior). Bigger'n a growed-up man, they babbled, big knuckles he liked to use on littler kids. They said, "We—" more, but Jerry said, "Come on!" and, before True could collect herself enough to try to stop him, he was gone—the children at his heels. Taking a dark shortcut through the trees, the group was swallowed up in the now-pinking dawn. What was she going to tell Aunt Chrissy?

Why, the truth, of course.

Forewarned, True braced herself for the worst. And found it! The walls of the schoolroom were covered with brown spittle and the chalkboards were smeared with crude but explicit drawings. She would have to notify Mr. Prescott the moment he arrived.

Only he did not arrive. Instead there was a note on her desk stating that "business" had kept him away—and could they manage?

Anger boiled up inside her. Somehow he had known; nothing could convince her otherwise. This had gone far enough. Nate Goldsmith needed to know the truth—whatever it was—about William Prescott. Meanwhile, God would have to see them through this day. *Where was Buster*?

She found him quickly enough. The gawky giant-boy was sprawled at her desk, muddy bare feet crossed on top of her register. Sullen, insolent, vacant-eyed, the youth's swarthy skin covered with red pimples, he leered at her in a way that resembled pictures she'd seen of the devil himself.

"What are you doing at my desk?" True asked angrily. "Get your feet down *immediately*!"

Buster made no move to obey. "Nothin' else fits—wanna see iff'n ye're able t'make me move?"

"That won't be necessary," Jerry said from the door. "Move—*now*!"

Buster showed no signs of moving. True was dimly aware that this was a showdown of sorts, and that there was a large audience of spectators gathering—more than the sum of the three rooms added together. *More* students . . . from where . . . *Appalachia*? Buster was staring at her, daring her. But she ignored him, knowing that she must retain her composure. Knowing, too, that Jerry stood at the crossroads of his young life.

The overgrown bully looked mildly stunned. A woman not knuckling under was reason enough to raise the eyebrows, and an upstart kid ordering a he-man around was downright shocking. His bravado showed signs of weakening.

"Go chew yer cud, half-pint," Buster tried again, turning his attention back to Jerry. But "thet stupid kid glared at him!"

The onlookers laughed, causing indignation to flood his pudding face. Losing control, he began sputtering. Then, when the snickers continued, Buster's snake eyes narrowed as he stared at True. Why, he wasn't right, True realized. His eyes, slitted like those of a reptile, showed a sickness of the brain. He needed help . . . but Jerry needed protection . . . what was she doing here among the spectators?

But there was no time to move forward. Jerry had grabbed the muddy feet, flung them from True's desk, and—with a quick, fluid motion—grabbed the insolent intruder by the ragged collar of his dirty shirt. "Apologize for your bad manners. The lady's name is Mrs. North—or some of the pupils call her Miss True—"

"Thet ain't a-gonner be whut I call 'er—"

"Say 'I'm sorry,' " Jerry ordered, his grip tightening on the collar. "Say it *now*—if you want to draw another breath!"

And then came the surprise of True North's life. Buster

cowered, his thin lips whitening as they shrank to a line. A snake. A *scared* snake.

"I—I—*let go*, yuh stumblebum—sorry I sed thet—*let go*—I uh—uh—cain't ketch a br-breath—chokin'—"

"*Say it!*"

"I—I—did'n' mean nuthin'—Missus—jes' had—a—hanker'—t'swap out—'Howdys'—"

The mouth opened to reveal rotting teeth. The slitted eyes bulged. And his face turned a frightening blue.

"Let go, Master Jerry!" Chris Beth stood at the door, her composure reminding True from whom she herself had fallen heir to courage. Even in a crisis, Aunt Chrissy used a low voice in giving commands—also remembered to call her young son by a title of respect.

Jerry's grasp relaxed, but his eyes remained fixed on Buster, whose bluff had been called. What's more, he was in trouble—bad trouble. True felt her heart go out in pity for the bully whose image had tumbled. And now—

"I'm a gonner," he whined. "Thet man a-bustin' in's me paw, 'n he's pizen—he's a-gonna whup me—'n beat Maw 'cuz I ain't got me no brains—" Buster's entire body shook with fear.

"Whut's goin', shoolmarm? I brung yuh 13 a-needin' larnin'— 'n don' see no hopes—better I line 'em up 'n thrash 'em one by one—"

The man's walrus mustache divided as he wiped tobacco from his chin. "Ain't got no sense—never learnt Latin 'n I heered ye cain't larn 'em—so's I best jest beat hit in—"

Jerry smiled, his composure regained. What he said was:

Mica, mica, parva stella,
Mirror quantum sis tam bella,
Splendens eminus in illo,
Alba velut gemma calelo.

"Well, I'll be a suck-egg mule—yuh young'uns behave!" The stranger removed his hat and flattened it against his belly, then stumbled out.

The rest of the day was unnaturally quiet. "I was proud of you," True whispered to Jerry at one point. "Twinkle, twinkle little star . . ." "My star's here—for now," was his reply.

20

Quiet—
and Then the Storm

The lines were drawn. The children knew where they stood, and seemed comfortable with that. Discipline was something they understood. What's more, True felt an overwhelming relief that parents had learned to respect her, Aunt Chrissy, and Master Jerry. Mr. Prescott was another matter. He was still a question mark in their minds, as he was in True's. Why wouldn't a teacher—particularly a minister of the gospel—be seeking out these people, becoming acquainted? Why no home calls? Yes, she must talk with Nate...

But, True wisely decided, she would make no issue of the matter. An opportunity would present itself. And in the meantime she must fight the battles within herself. To be sure, the children were entitled to an education, a part of which was a better command of the English language. But how could she go about unsnarling their grammar while preserving their heritage, a part of which were their quaint, mystical idioms that was so much a part of themselves? "Paw, he's discomfortin' real bad 'n our meanness is a'tendin' t'worsen 'im"... "Come Sat'day last Maw went a'washin' body-cover clothes"... "Us'n cain't eat 'til th' noon-high sun sez 'tis th' dinner spell"... "Frawgs make music down by th' slough when they go courtin'." And, often as not, mixed in with what she had come to regard as their "hill talk" were such courtly words as "sires, dukes, and duchesses" occupying the "thrones" at their "gloaming supper."

Now that they had overcome much of their shyness, there was genuine desire shining in their bright (and often intelligent) eyes to mingle with the Valley children. But they shied away, sticking—in obedience to their parents' orders, True suspected—with their own clan, engaging in folksong games.

Gradually they attracted an audience. Well, could she help it if integration worked from the opposite direction? If only she could guide them into Sunday school through the local children. But for now a step at a time, True reminded herself.

Meantime, she made behavioral notes faithfully just as she made lesson plans which would include them all. She talked more with Jerry than with William Prescott, who had developed a peculiar twitching of the nose which would have been comical had she not suspected something serious as the cause, or Aunt Chrissy, who seemed preoccupied. None of them saw as much of the North men as they would have liked. But that was soon to change!

And meantime a letter came from Kearby. It bubbled with school news. Her grades were top-notch. She had made the girls' choir. There was to be a school party which boys would attend. And the head mistress was letting them wear bows in their braids . . .

True wished details were less sketchy about the co-ed party. She hoped it meant that Kearby was overcoming her fear, which had become a near-obsession since Clarry's ordeal (yet to be spelled out). But no word about Clarry herself. This, too, was destined to change. But for now there was relative calm. And the children were learning at a pace which surprised the two teachers, the teacher-principal, and his "vice-principal," Master Jerry. There was no change in those with learning disabilities, but they too had learned to socialize—consequently, were less disruptive. Even Buster. What a pitiful piece of humanity! The clumsy boy often came to school with purple rings around his eyes, obviously resulting from his self-described "long head" of a father.

"What should we do? I've met Buster's father, and he seems different—" True began, hoping for William Prescott's counsel.

"He *is* different," was the immediate reply. "A stubborn Scot. And, of course, we have a sprinkling of flinty Irish and closemouthed Germans mixed in with the English gentry—"

"Yes?" True encouraged. But his mouth had clamped shut.

"I—we can ask O'Higgin to help. He'd love it. Then there's Nate's wife, who speaks German fluently—if you approve?"

He turned palms up. Why? Well, she would find out!

"You seem to know a lot about these people's background—"

"Yes," Prescott said bluntly and stalked out of the room.

All right. If he refused to cooperate, she would take the lead. Thanksgiving would be a good time. Which reminded her that Grandma Mollie wanted parents notified to come for dinner. She was already preparing, with help of the neighbors. Baking, mending...

It was a struggle getting invitations to parents. The children were overjoyed and labored over the notes with a dedication that was heartwarming. But to no avail. The parents, of course, were unable to read. But, even with the children proudly showing off their writing and then translating the words, the adults refused hands-down.

Bitterly disappointed, True made preparations for the holiday with her family and friends. Yes, of course, they would help, O'Higgin assured her, and agreed to show up Monday. "As fer their not bein' on hand fer th' Lord's celebration—well, now—iffen th' mountain ain't a-comin' t'Mohammed, Mohammed'll be a-goin' t'th' mountain, begory!"

"Yep, yep, thet we will!" Nate Goldsmith was jumping up and down like an undersized grasshopper. "Whar's thet principal?"

True motioned him aside. Nate trotted along behind her like a terrier about to receive a bone. Suddenly he spun on the heel of his boot, went back to pick up his loaded plate (although dinner was yet to be announced), and then joined her. They had the talk that True had planned. "Sumpin's mighty wrong—I sensed hit—" Nate said between nibbles. "Well," proudly, "I'll fix thangs—good!"

There were prayers and hymns. Disappointments dwindled. And outwardly the crackling fire and enormous bouquets of chrysanthemums, rivaling the color of the flames in reds and golds, spelled tranquility. But True sensed that it masked an undercurrent of premonition—one which she felt perhaps most of all.

"What did O'Higgin mean?" she asked Miss Mollie suddenly.

"We kin plan a feast fer school—maybe they'll come to thet—"

True was about to express doubt when the rumble of hoofbeats sounded and the air was split by a frenzied yell. A mountaineer man.

"Th' wound's opened up, Doc—one from th' gunshot—you gotta' be acomin'—you wuz right—bullet's gotta be tooken. Family's all riled—sayin' you gonna die afore Jim Haley. But I'm a-takin' you in—you 'n th' teachers here. They'll safen hit fer you. Comin' peacable-like er do I hafta use force?"

A stillness fell over the great livingroom. Faces went rigid with fear. They were accustomed to hardship, but this was different. The people they loved most of all were in danger. And they were helpless. Even now, the stranger was fingering his coatpocket for a gun.

Already the doctors had their black bags in hand. Why the hesitation? True had recognized the man as the one who came for help at dawn the morning after Midgie's letter came. "Comin'?" The man's voice carried a threat.

"Of course—we're doctors," Young Wil spoke for them both. "But not the ladies!"

"It's all right," True said calmly. "They know us. Put away your gun, Sir!"

21

Death March

"Cain't no ani-mule make hit up thet hill," the man's eyes, deep-set in their sockets, seemed to penetrate True's very soul. "An' ain't fair fer you city-gal women t'try."

Was he weakening in his decision? Her husband's life was on the line. She would beg if she had to. "We are pioneer women, Mr.— sorry, I didn't catch your name?" Bloodlines were important, making the question flattering—particularly when it was accompanied by a warm smile which turned on all the feminine charm of True North.

"Kimbell, Ma'am—Ryan Kimbell—'n (hat in hand) most call me Ry—'pendin' 'pon if they's friend er foe—'n you got yourse'ves a rep'tation of friend, but now I got hit 'pon my shoulders t'warn you, hit's damned iff'en you go 'n damned iff'en you don't. Clear?"

"To us both." Aunt Chrissy's voice was steady, her eyes unafraid.

"Don't do this." Daddy Wil walked between them, taking each's arm.

"True is not going!" Young Wil's voice was a command rather than a statement. Their dark eyes locked.

"Wil North! Let go of me, there's no time to waste."

A grin of admiration creased Ry Kimbell's slim, weather-creased face. "Gotcha some gal-woman, man! 'N you better be grateful—whilst you try on savin' my brother's life, Miz North here's gonna be tryin' on savin' your'n. Fo'ks up thar trust 'er 'n I cain't say th' same fer you doctors . . . shudda done whut we tole you, bored a hole in th' skull 'n dug out thet lead—even iff'en hit meant 'is brains'd leak out. No need fer a man's dyin' from a bullet, jest needed blood drained."

Chris Beth smoothed her husband's face and whispered something in his ear. Then, freeing herself from his protective grasp, she sidled back up to True. "We'd better waste no more time talking."

Already Young Wil was bringing the buggy that Jerry had hitched. "We'll follow your lead to the gap—then walk." True thanked him with her eyes.

"I'm a-bettin' my last sixpence all of you's not a-comin' back—but—" attempting a grin must have cost the man more than that, "I got me woodchoppin' shoulders iff'en they're needed fer survivors."

Sounds of their hasty departure drowned out the tearful farewells of those left at Turn-Around Inn and their promises for a prayerful vigil. There was not one among them who would not have changed places with their beloved North family, but reason told them that nobody hereabouts was qualified. God had given them special gifts.

"We shudda stopped 'em, blowed th' crazy man's head off," Nate Goldsmith was screaming, his words falling on deaf ears. His intended audience was already kneeling in fervent prayer. So fervent that nobody except Miss Mollie saw O'Higgin, Jerry, and Olga Goldsmith slip away to take a shortcut, unarmed but unafraid. They "spoke the language" of the Appalachians. Both meanings implied...

"I'd be cautious—hit's nippity-tuck your bein' able t'keep up—but I'm th' only hope you got," Ry Kimbell warned at the bottom of the climb. "A'ready we're on th' aidge o'dark—an' bear in mind hit's a death march we're on!"

Death march. The near-whispered words rose and fell in True's ears, filling the Valley with a dirge. But she squared her shoulders and, taking hold of her aunt's hand, motioned their guide ahead.

"Yea, though I walk through the valley and the shadow of death, I will fear no evil—for thou art with me..." *Lord, lead us*!

"Now," Ry said as he positioned himself in front of the procession, the ladies sandwiched between him and the two doctors who brought up the rear, "this trip don't pleasure me none."

It pleasures none of us, True thought, but saved her breath. The trail wound sharply upward, then became so steep that conversation was impossible. Several times Young Wil attempted to communicate in a low voice, breathing heavily. But True was unable to hear with her heart drumming like the muffled drum of the grouse. Her legs ached. She felt light-headed. And certainly her skirt was too long and too wide for the steep, narrow trail. It was all a bad dream.

If so, she, Aunt Chrissy, Daddy Wil, and Young Wil were to awaken suddenly and simultaneously. Back a way, True had been convinced that traveling conditions could be no worse. She was wrong.

There was the sound of churning water, tumultuous in its rush to the sea. So this must be where one of the rivers headed. There had to be a bridge—only there wasn't. Just an enormous log tossed across the depths without an anchor at either end. How on earth—?

Ry Kimbell's hobnailed boots saw him across and, surprisingly, the man offered a hand to Chris Beth, who reached to grasp True's, thus forming a human chain.

"Don' go lookin' down!" the mountaineer shouted above the roar of the water. "Th' logs is slippery-like, bein' barked in parts—keerful, iff'en you fall, there'll be a drownin' afore a shootin'!"

True gripped Aunt Chrissy's hand and felt her uncle's gentle hand supporting her back. He was trusting Young Wil to make it on his own. But, knowing her husband, True was sure that Wil's eyes were glued to his loved ones, readying himself to do whatever he must. She must try and make it. *Don't look down. Careful...catwalk...*

And then the log began to sway. A sudden dizziness overwhelmed her, the roar of the water below reminding her of the great height to which they had climbed. And then a piece of bark on which she had positioned her foot sideways gave way and the river rushed up to meet her.

"On your knees, darling, quick! Straddle the log—oh, would to God I'd had sense enough to leave you—"

Dimly, his voice penetrated. "Wil North—" True panted. And then she went down with a jolt that surely must have split her in half—one leg dangling helplessly on either side of the slippery log.

How her husband managed to bypass Daddy Wil, put his strong hands beneath her armpits, and all but drag her to safety would remain a mystery the rest of her life. As would the remainder of the death march...up...up...up toward the razor-sharp backbone of the mountain, with bottomless ledges dropping steeply from both sides.

And then the welcome sound of a rooster's crow! Something resembling civilization. *People*—never mind how dangerous!

A cabin loomed out of nothingness, unbarked logs, cracks chinked with mud...a pack of half-wolf dogs, and any minister would envy as large a congregation as was assembled, men wearing slouch felt hats, bibbed overalls, hands jammed in their pockets threateningly. Not a word of greeting. Something warned True to retain her silence.

The only light inside the crude cabin came from a sputtering candle which sent shapeless shadows in ghostly dance from the rough-hewn rafters to the bare floor. A man, white as a corpse except for a circle of blue on his left temple where the bullet must have entered, lay motionless across a straw-stuffed mattress.

"Is he—?" True swallowed the word, *dead*.

"In a coma—right, Doctor?" Young Wil addressed his uncle.

"Whet's that? Speak up so's we kin hear," one of the men ordered.

"Coma means unconscious, Mr. Kimbell—unaware of what's going on around him," True heard herself saying as the two doctor's examined the patient thoroughly. Aunt Chrissy, she noted in the unnatural silence, had opened the medical kits and spread the instruments on a sterilized cloth.

"The doctors will need a brighter light. Have you a lamp—uh—" Aunt Chrissy hesitated, then went on, "Which of you is Mrs. Kimbell?"

"I'll be answerin' fer th' widder," Ry interrupted.

True's chin shot up. "You'll do no such thing!" she said with spirit. "What's more, your brother's wife is *not* a widow. Chances are good she isn't going to be, if—" True swallowed and went on, "you call off your watchdogs and cooperate! Now—we need a lamp if you expect my husband and uncle to do the job you brought them here for."

Several of the men stepped forward threateningly, one reaching for a double-barreled shotgun lying across a moose-head rack. "Rest up, fellers, th' gal-woman's a real lady—a *teacher* lady, braver'n a wildcat. *Clara Belle!*" Ry Kimbell spoke with proud authority.

As the men looked on in awe, Clara Belle Kimbell answered, her body pressed against the wall. "Yessum, I have a lamp." The sweet-faced woman in a faded calico dress and no shoes on her feet stepped from the shadows. She slipped from the room with surprising grace that whispered of a better environment than this once upon a time.

There were no further interruptions from the bystanders. Teachers were smart, a whole "covey" smarter than doctors. They, not "medical quacks," were the ones what were to "larn th' young'uns." And wasn't that the whole purpose of being here? So they could learn and take back their learning to Appalachia? Most teachers could "tote a tune."

Clara Belle was back, the rubbed-brass lamp she handed Chris Beth chasing the monstrous shadows away. "What more?" she asked through tightset lips which spelled fear and grief-in-restraint.

"Some boiling water, Clara Belle—I'm True, by the way—and some extra sheets just in case—"

"What else were you going to ask for?"

Without hesitation, True answered: "Prayer."

The next few minutes were critical. They determined whether her husband would live or die. Clara Belle knew it. And True knew that not only a man's life but their entire future lay in the hands of the two doctors. But they must be inspired by the greater Hand...

Clara Belle turned her back to stand in the corner in silent prayer. Young Wil took note, spoke a few low words of consultation with his uncle, and—motioning all others from the room—called the wife of the dying man to his side.

Outside a strange jumble of conversation was in progress, something akin to the Tower of Babel's confusion of tongues. Latin . . . German . . . English filled with idioms . . . and English in classic form.

True and Chris Beth glanced at each other in wonderment, while their ears were attuned to their husbands' simple explanation of the task that lay before them—praising the Lord for Jerry, O'Higgin, and Olga Goldsmith, who could communicate with the enemies-turned-friends.

Did Clara Belle understand that the bullet was pressing against *this* part of the brain? Dr. Wilson North, the senior doctor, showed the quiet woman a hastily drawn sketch. That removal could cause massive hemorrhaging? *But wasn't the young doctor here a specialist, writing a book on the matter?* Not exactly . . . he was doing a different type of research . . . but, yes, it would help, Young Wil tried to explain. *But they thought it was safe?* The eyes of the stanch lady were filled with confidence. They were gentle men. And she had prayed. So, "What are we waiting for? I trust you both."

"Your approval," Uncle Wil said quietly, a somber note in his usually jovial voice. "We are uncertain as to whether your husband can withstand the operation—and yet, if we don't remove the bullet—"

"He won't pull through? And if you *don't* operate?"

"He—what's his name, Clara Belle—did I hear you say Grady?" At her nod, Young Wil went on: "I have to tell you the truth, my dear, and I know the decision is hard. But you are a strong woman—you will bear up—" he paused to nod at True, his signal to embrace the brave woman facing the starkest alternative of her life, "so let me tell you that even if Grady lives, there may be brain damage—blindness—"

So sure was Uncle Wil of the wife's decision that he and Aunt Chrissy were pulling the lamp closer, adjusting the tasseled shade, and placing the instruments in order of their use. True's arms were folded about the woman, one of her hands wiping away the beads of perspiration from the cold forehead. Clara Belle turned pleading eyes to meet hers.

"You're a woman—what would *you* do, Mrs. North?"

"I would go ahead—*now*. Your husband is dying, my darling."

Clara Belle clung to her momentarily. Then, letting go, "Proceed!" she said loud and clear. "Mrs. North—True—help them. I'll pray—"

The rest was a horror story. People tried to crowd in, morbidly curious. "Stay out—all of you! You're using all his oxygen," True ordered. Outside, she heard Jerry, O'Higgin, and Olga's voices promising to explain every step providing they would stay put. They obliged.

"Razor—have to shave off the sideburns...antiseptic...ether..." True and Chris Beth handed the supplies from the table, each trying to breathe naturally as the sickly-sweet odor of the anesthesia closed around them. A first incision...an order for a sponge...forceps...and then the blessed words: "Close up! We're finished—and he's breathing!"

True came out of her reverie as she heard the men's voices outside burst into a hill-splitting shout. The crowd closed in—and her husband's arms closed about her. "You did it, my darling—you saw me through!"

22

Turning Point

In the days that followed, the seriousness of the circumstances under which Young Wil and his uncle had performed the life-threatening operation struck True with full force. How impetuous she had been, leading, as it were, the men to do the job at what amounted to gunpoint! Why, they could have been killed—all to save the life of a man they didn't even know. And for what reason? At times, an inner fire grabbed at her insides, squeezing, burning, rendering her almost helpless in a delayed reaction.

And then, just before her mind and body melted, it all made sense. Like a sudden parting of the clouds after a storm, the world righted itself. Her hope for peace gained sturdiness. Could it be true—the way God sometimes performed His miracles? Did He sometimes send out stern reminders that peace is a fragile thing, hanging from threads and pinned in a fear-conquering manner by small acts of love-in-action? The premise, then, was that peace was never rock-solid. But the underlying concept, God's love, had proven sound. It could be demonstrated only by human hands—hands that did His will. And hearts that endured?

Surely, yes!

The week after the ordeal brought a swarm of incidents to reveal that circumstances were dramatically altered among the mountaineers, and consequently between them and those in the Valley below.

"How is Mr. Kimbell?" True inquired of the children.

"Mendin'." It was Buster who loved to report. "Safe fer th' docs up thar now. Fo'ks aint' never 'lowed sech a'fore."

So Young Wil and Daddy Wil—probably taking turns—were making house calls. Why hadn't either made mention of this? But she knew why, of course: They did not wish to worry her and Aunt Chrissy. And, with a wry smile, neither did they wish to become "hen husbands" tied to their wives' apron strings. It was important that they nourish the new image of themselves.

"One day I will visit your homes," she promised instead, and was surprised at the look of amazement in the eyes of her charges, which now numbered 65! Well, thank goodness, most of them came from large families. "Maw'll be right proud," came from all directions.

"The children tell me that you plan home calls." William Prescott said one day as the children sat in circles (now mingling groups), having lunch. His tone registered disapproval.

"It is time—actually overdue," True said a bit defiantly.

"I wouldn't encourage it—you are often foolish."

Foolish? True felt a dart of anger shoot through her heart. "Why are you avoiding these people like the plague, Mr. Prescott?"

"William."

Her anger enlarged. "All right, *William*—what are you afraid of?"

His eyes took another arrow from his quiver. Then, spinning on his heel, the principal, now drained of anger, replied simply: "I am one of them."

Shock kept True from responding. And after that there was no time.

Christmas was nearing, and Grandma Mollie, unbeknownst to True, had assembled the Valley women together for quilting covers for the mountain folk. The ladies seemed better informed than True herself of their troubled history... starving for food back in the Blue Ridge country, both for body and soul... feuding between clans (some saying that one or the other groups had been responsible for the attack on the wagon train, its refugees now in and around Slippery Elm). Little solace they'd found here... just new entries in the catalog of catastrophes. Just more blood and sweat. Working on shanties with bare hands seven days a week... too proud to accept help... breaking around boulders that an earthquake couldn't budge... soil so "pore up thar" that it wouldn't produce enough for one square meal, planted as it was by hand around those immovable objects. Took a year readying the land and, discounting the bugs and varmints, there was the weather. A body could just about count on a frog-strangling rain to wash away what little soil they had.

"Well," Mollie O'Higgin said proudly, biting off the string dangling from the final knot of another finished quilt, "things are improvin', thanks t'them wonderful Norths, well as my Irish—not to mention Olga here! But we can't be settin' down on th' job now—come on—hep me hoist this quilting frame so's we can git another underway."

"They'll be comin'?" asked Bertie Solomon. "I'd have supposed their kind would be stone-deaf to invitations—"

"They're coming!" It was Chris Beth who made the announcement quietly from the doorway, where True stood beside her. The two of them had made the trip to share the good news as well as check on progress.

The applause was deafening—as was the jabber of what O'Higgin would have called a "roomful o'women all a'talkin' at onct, bless em!"

By gathering bits and pieces of the talk, True and Chris Beth were able to piece them together like one of the complicated quilts.

Plans were made. There would be food such as those pretty-eyed children had never before seen—and enough to take home. Since the school was neutral ground, there could be a brief program (maybe some Bible, although Brother Prescott had been behaving mighty strange lately, and rumor had it that those folks didn't take kindly to "educated preachers" anyway). But mostly there would be games with prizes! Clothes all wrapped up in disguise. Shoes which the Solomons said were just a wee bit dated. And more—bundles and bundles underneath the biggest tree in the forest. Couldn't be called "charity" this way. "Now, here's whut we're a-gonna do..."

"Can wars end like that—I mean—maybe we're expecting too much," True, ears still ringing, said on the way home.

"There could be a temporary truce—a start—" Aunt Chrissy's voice trailed off.

"Is something bothering you, Aunt Chrissy?" True had been concerned for some time now over the distracted look that her aunt wore.

There was silence as the buggy creaked on. "Aunt Chrissy—"

"What?" Chris Beth said with a start. "Oh, yes—it sounds fine."

True reined the horse to a stop in a shaded strip of woods. "We'd better talk. What's bothering you—other than our common concerns?"

Her aunt fidgeted, then answered slowly. "I—we almost never have time to talk. I—I was glad you asked no questions—but wondered why not."

"About William Prescott—I was wondering the same about you."

Chris Beth disregarded the question. "About Kearby—Thanksgiving."

"Her not coming home? I *did* wonder—but thought with only a day—"

"It was more." Aunt Chrissy's voice sounded almost sad. "Her excuse sounded flimsy—just a note saying she had a friend who came first."

True had never felt more guilty. Kearby meant Clarry—and she was bound by her promise to Jerry. She would talk to Young Wil . . . but, no, the promise included him!

"I'm sure Kearby meant just what she said," True murmured. Then, gathering strength: "She'll be here for Christmas. You'll see!"

Just how she was going to arrange that was beyond her at the moment, but arrange it she would. She would begin by talking with Jerry, then writing a letter to Midgie. Midgie! Guiltily, True realized that she had been in such a turmoil that she had not answered Midgie's letter—although the problems in Slippery Elm occupied equal time with the problems here. How did life get so complicated?

Now she broke the silence. "Aunt Chrissy—surely you aren't entertaining any idea that Kearby is—well, involved with some boy?"

Her aunt's head jerked erect. "Is there a possibility?"

"No!" True said flatly. "Don't ask me how I know. I just *do.* It's only that we are all so overwrought. It is easy for doubts and fears to creep in. Tell you what," she said brightly; "let's pray."

And, there in the sky-cathedral of the eternal evergreens, with the sun shining through the stained-glass windows of the autumn-painted maples, the two women clung to each other and prayed for the hope that endures... although, surely the Lord in heaven knew that it was theirs already...

True followed through with all her promises, writing a hasty note to Midgie, asking an update and promising a lengthy letter later, then concluding with a Midgie-like postscript: "Can't you arrange to visit us?" The opportunity to talk with Jerry came about naturally. He would show her the shortcut to the mountain settlement, he volunteered when she made mention of home calls. On the way, she asked him to release her from the irresponsible promise regarding Clarry's whereabouts. He was remorseful that his mother was worried. He would see what he could do. But, meantime, he was adamant about keeping the promise. A promise was a sacred thing. "Remember your wedding vows?" The question startled True to silence.

23

Revelations, Uncertainties—and a Promise!

Climbing the mountain was easier the second time. The shortcut route was shorter, of course. But there was something more, something True would have been unable to define: a new source of strength, a stabilizing energy that quieted her heart and gave her the peace and strength to see her through the crises to come.

They stopped by the Kimbell cabin first. Clara Belle met them at the door, her features softened by the miracle which had taken place here. "Can you come in?" she asked a bit uneasily. "Grady ate his breakfast—and heartily—but I—I am doubting if you would care for cornmeal mush."

"Oh, we ate hours ago—and it's best we not disturb your husband," True said quickly, saving this gracious woman further embarrassment. "Actually, Master Jerry and I stopped in order to check on Mr. Kimbell's condition—"

"And," Jerry interrupted, "to invite you both to be our guests at the big school program—dinner, games, a program planned by your children. It would please us all so much!"

The woman cringed. Her lovely eyes turned toward a fleecy, lamb-shaped cloud that appeared to be grazing on a distant high meadow of sky. But she was not seeing the view. She was seeing some specter beyond True's cone of vision. "I went to such a celebration once—and the ladies wore lovely gowns—" Clara Belle looked down at her bare feet, trying to cover one with the other.

"You will wear such a gown yourself," True declared rashly. "The Solomons are too busy to make calls but want to do something special for you—"

Sheer joy flooded Clara Belle's face. "You mean—*clothes*?"

And then she seemed to fade back into an earlier century, a world of omens and witchcraft—a world that doctors and teachers could not comprehend. Bringing together the two worlds could only feed the jaws of evil. True had never before witnessed such a mixture of faith and joy, wiped out as one erases a blackboard.

And then an amazing thing happened. From inside, Grady Kimbell called out in an unbelievably strong voice, "We'll go—we owe 'em thet. An' count on th' young'uns—"

Some women would have wept, but Clara Belle said simply, "I'm obliged to you, Mrs. North. We will bring wild holly and mistletoe."

"Well," Jerry grinned as they turned away, "there goes my Christmas money."

True's heart swelled with pride, but she dared not risk a reply. Tears would embarrass Master Jerry, who was emerging into manhood at the speed of a bullet sure of its target.

"This is the Craytons' place," Jerry whispered when another cabin—shanty, really—loomed out of the trees. His announcement was verified by Sammy Joe's sudden appearance at the crazily slanted door.

"Teacher," he gulped, trying to swallow the chunk of cold cornbread he had stuffed in his mouth. "So'ghum!" He all but choked as he pointed to his mouth in an announcement he need not have made. Rivers of the thick, brown substance flowed down from each corner to drip on the bosom of his shirt. "Maw!" he managed to yell before going into a spasm of coughing.

True decided against entering when she surveyed the yard. Pigs wallowed in ankle-high waste—both animal and human. The stench was unbelievable as the morning sun sucked steam from the soggy filth.

Maizie Crayton, wearing an ill-fitting apron-dress, answered her son's call. "Ye be our brood's teachers, I'm a-s'posin'—stop tryin' t'show off, boy!" The woman pushed at her hair, which may have been combed a month ago, although True wondered about that. "Yep, we be a-comin' t'th' blowout et th' school. Glad we be thet they's larnin' stump'n more'n me 'n me ole man got knowin'. Las' church doin' we go'ed to didn'n make no mention of th' Almighty—jest ranted 'bout some feller named Calvin. I reckon ye be knowin' 'im?"

True mumbled some kind of feeble response, an overwhelming nausea threatening to take over. How could they contend with such living conditions? And she was expected to teach their children?

She would have picked up her skirts and fled down the mountain except that Jerry was steering her limber legs toward a tall, slender woman who stood in the yard of another shack, waving a hand in welcome, her beautifully cut features carving into an uncertain smile.

"I am Mrs. Courtland," said the lady, who in her ragged garments maintained dignity with a touch of regality. "You and my husband have met. Please come inside."

Courtland. Oh, yes, of course. The man who had come to school the first day armed. How in the world did he win this fair lady?

The children, so like their mother, ventured out—as tidy as they were at school, one part of True's mind thought as the other part wondered in surprise at the warmth and color around her. Everything was clean, spotlessly clean. A million questions flooded her mind. What had held them together—this strange group? There was squalor here, and filth—and yet there was also a certain grandeur that harked back to their pure-strain past.

One of the children brought True a chair. The child was, she realized, less at ease than her hostess. And Mrs. Courtland had noticed.

"You are wondering," she said gently, "what has bound us together?"

"I—I'm sorry that I stared. It—it's just such a contrast—"

A ray of sun came through the spotless glass of the east window, picking up gold lights in Amy's (she learned Mrs. Courtland's name later) crown of hair and bouncing back from a pewter pot filled with colored leaves. "Our proud heritage, I guess—born and bred in us—a sort of snobbishness, really." She laughed softly. "Imagine my choice of words—snobbish—when," her soft voice took on a distaste as if she had bitten into bitter fruit, "we would be begging were it not for our stiff-necked pride. Oh, Mrs. North, help our children see what our ancestors saw." Amy leaned forward in her intensity. "You are our last hope—you, your family—and I should like to include the teacher or preacher—which is Mr. Prescott?"

"Both—and I regret that he has been unable to call—"

"So do I, not that he would have been welcome by some."

True drew a deep breath. "He seemed to sense that. May I ask if you know why, Mrs. Courtland?"

"Amy—and I should like to address you as True. It gets so lonely for me. Seeing you is like—well, going home—being with my own kind. I know that makes no sense—"

"It makes all the sense in the world—Appalachia being home to you, then coming into another—well, culture. You see, my mother and my aunt came from Boston after attending school in Atlanta." True told her then about her mother's diary, how two young girls had come to the American Frontier with romantic notions, only to feel lonely and homesick. She stopped short of mentioning more, and ended instead by telling of her own search for her roots in their homeland.

Amy's eyes were shining. "Yes," she said dreamily, "I confess that I miss the Blue Ridge, but it goes back farther back to the courtyards where lords and ladies strolled through formal gardens... drifting away in the misty past of the moors. I hear ballads that I have never heard but somehow passed down to me in these few heirlooms, ancient letters, and stories told and retold through the generations when there was no question who God was. You see, True, we are not all repulsive. We have blue blood flowing in our veins."

"Oh, my dear," True protested, "I never thought of you as such! The God you knew then is the same now. It is ourselves who in one form or another draw a curtain between. Maybe we can rediscover that lost past together. Originally, the purpose of education was to teach children to read His

Word—and, in your way, you have tried to preserve that. Even your men want that back. I am so glad that we had this illuminating visit—it's like—well, walking backward into the past—"

Amy Courtland rose slowly from her chair and glanced through the back door. For her husband? Perhaps it was time to go, True suggested. But Amy detained her with a timid hand placed on the cuff of a simple blue dress that True wore. "Lovely—" she said, and then: "Not backward, but forward, like seeing more clearly through the glass that Paul wrote about—catching a glimpse of what was, yes, but what is to be—if we can bring them together. I want to move forward—"

True nodded. "Yes, take a stand as you have taken in accepting our invitation to the Christmas festival."

Amy smiled radiantly in anticipation. "We can hardly wait—even my husband, who, as you know, is a master at 'taking a stand.' But wasn't it Oliver Wendell Holmes who said, 'It's not enough to take a stand; we have to know what direction we're going'?"

True nodded. How wonderful to meet someone here who spoke her own language! And, strangely enough—as is always true when people open their hearts to one another—she was learning much from this woman. "I believe," she said slowly, "that it's possible to go forward without letting go of the past. It is the Bible which has shaped our lives—and, even though most of its foundation is built on the past, its truths endure. After all," she tasted the words and found them sweet, "it is our common heritage. Isn't our culture somewhat the same—coming back in little glimpses that bless our lives?"

"Precisely. And I hope, dear True, that you will remember and preserve the good in us—bits of our language in poetry and song—forgetting the crudeness—when we are gone . . ."

"*Gone*?" True's mouth felt dry with disappointment that she would have felt impossible just an hour ago.

"You surely must have known that was our plan—to learn from you and have you teach our children so we can take it back to our people?"

Had she known? True found it hard to remember. But suddenly she wore a new yoke, that of preparing the children as *missionaries*. It was a tremendous responsibility—almost terrifying. But hadn't Jesus promised that His yoke was light? Joy replaced the terror.

How little did she know that the next stop was surely arranged by Satan himself in an effort to wipe clean the slate of her buoyant spirit, to rob her heart of its joy...

"One more stop," Jerry said. And, in her state of euphoria, True did not protest.

An older woman—tall, gaunt, and angular, with once-lovely golden hair now snarled and twisted like a rope around her head—met True and Jerry at the door in answer to their knock.

"Yeah? Whatcha be wantin'?" she asked suspiciously.

Jerry explained their mission, to which the half-hidden face lighted up. "So ye be comin' to'call? An' git th' lowdown on folks up'n th' mountains, I betcha. Well, now, I be th' one ye best see," she said, her gossip-loving tongue licking the thin, pale lips. "Bes' ye set a spell. Ned, he be gone, so git askin'!"

The children slipped inside, sticking their heads in curiously, only to be ordered out by their mother. "Yer paw's a-gonna be late. So set y'se'ves down without a peep 'n git eatin'."

The children sat down at the rough-board table without ceremony—taking no time to wash up, although there was a basin by the back door. Memories of the pigs came back, and True longed to leave but felt herself being pushed into a rickety chair without invitation.

"Jest as well yuh know th' truth. Me—I be knowin' a heap 'bout both bunches, meanin' them whut lef'. Bad—really bad, thet mess—a whorin' bunch, even 'mongst theirse'ves! I be scarred by th' mem'ries they lef—men usin' li'l-girl folks lack they wuz women—'n all th' while a-claimin' to'be full'a religion. Course some of 'em wuz trespassin'—comin' in whur they had no bizness t'git loose of th' lawmen. Take thet 'un whut raped a chile—crippled 'un—'n married th' mother cuz she wuz a-gonna be birthin' a bastard-chile. Musta knowed it'd be a girl he cud be usin'.

Got 'erse'f shot—th' woman—'n kilt in th' gun battle a-comin' hereabouts, I heered—hate 'em all, we do, but," she rolled her colorless eyes, refusing to meet True's penetrating gaze, "we live by our own code so didn' have nothin' t'do with th' attack—"

True found herself wondering about the truth of her statement. No longer in a hurry, she leaned forward, every muscle tensed. "The man—the trespasser—what was his name—Mrs.—?"

"Trevor—my name, thet bein'. As fer 'is name—let's see, I be forgettin'—but I'm recallin' a name. Coulda been 'is wife-woman's er her bastard-chile—'twas C-C—I be' forgettin'," she sighed, "too much biz'ness needin' me here."

The Trevor woman was hedging, but she had given True what she wanted to know. Her concern now was for Jerry, but his mind seemed to be elsewhere. The girl's identity would hurt—in case it was Clarice—

"Is there something we need to know here, Ma'am?" he asked politely, causing True to exhale audibly. All clues pointed to the awful truth.

"Oh, lots. One of yore chid'run down there—ain't saying' who, mind yuh—saw with 'er own eyes th' hangin' of 'er maw. Th' Paw bein' a real devil cuz of strong drink—even a-threatenin' t'do th' same thang t'li'l ole Lucy iff'en she so much as breathed a word, sayin' he'd toss 'er body on top of th' grave fer raven food—"

It was Jerry's turn to become sick. True saw it in his eyes. And his nostrils were actually turning green. But Jerry shook his head. "Why," he asked, spreading his fingers apart and looking at True desperately, "would God let that happen?"

"It's hard to understand, darling. I get confused myself—but we have to remember that God doesn't *want* it to happen. But there's so much wickedness in the world and we are here to help Him combat it—"

Mrs. Trevor snorted. "He's forgot us—ain't no way t' com'cate with 'im, cuz we forgot 'is language—thet's why we gotta be larnin' Latin. Yep, thet's our deadliest sin—we up'n forgot 'is way of talkin' so th' Almighty paid us back good 'n planty. Jest plain forgot us fer punishment—we're all doomed fer th' fiery furnace."

Deep emotion swept True's mind and body, shaking her very soul. But how could she respond? *Put the words in my mouth, Lord.*

"God understands all languages, Mrs. Trevor," she said slowly. "All He wants to hear is that we are sorry for our sins—and that we love Him and will serve Him—then some of these things will not happen—"

The woman's mouth gaped open. "Now, how kin thet be?"

Jerry's color was back. "Because," he said with a bold lift of his young chin, "we will all love one another as He loves us. *But*—" Jerry hesitated, seeming to sense that it would take more to convince these people, "as for the Latin, we *are* teaching it, and maybe one day we can send a minister back to the Blue Ridge country—"

A look of horror crossed the angular face. " 'N git 'im kilt? A ed-ja-cated preacher—back thar? I cain't begin t'tell yuh how many's buried in th' chestnut groves—with no tombstones. Which reminds me," her eyes brightened like a vulture having found a bountiful supply of carrion, "rumor's got hit thet a few slipped outta them hills 'n is plannin' on goin' back totin' them big words. Know anybody fittin' thet mold? Could be a—teacher—er—well, speak up."

True's heart missed a beat. And surely her body was sheeted over with ice. One wrong word and William Prescott would become a missing person right here in their own Valley...

It was past midnight when Young Wil found True propped in bed trying to concentrate on lesson plans. "Darling!" he exclaimed in surprise, "those violet eyes should be shut, proving you're in slumberland." He came to lie on his stomach beside her. "What's the problem? Don't deny it—I see it on your face—" and then his arms were around her, "Oh, little sweetheart, I've made you cry!"

In that tender moment he let her sob out her account of the day. "Oh, maybe the man who monitored our tests was right in questioning us about being sure we belong here," she said at last. "*Wil North, you knew*!"

"About it all," he said smugly, then with a kiss, "We'll have the best Christmas ever!"

24

A Most Amazing Christmas

The best Christmas ever? True and Young Wil were to remember his words forever. In a way his prophecy was right—one brimming with wondrous amazement, as if the Star of Bethlehem's beams had led the mountain people into the Valley and stopped immediately over the school. Steeped as they were in superstition, half-truths, and folklore, it was an omen once the events of the evening came to a close. And to them the "larnin' place" would become forever "Th' Church of th' Nativ'ty."

That was the miracle—the miracle which made the world shine briefly with "best ever" glory.

But it was an evening filled with perplexity as well. "Fear not..." the angels had sung. But it was raw fear which clutched at True's heart—no, she mustn't feel like this, else the Baby Jesus would have been born in vain. Somehow she must achieve a certain peace. "Lord—oh, Lord, my God," she whispered over and over as the evening unfolded, "stay with me—see me through..."

The crowd began congregating early. Before dusk the auditorium was overflowing, the guests spilling outside and not seeming to mind as the black-velvet of the Christmas sky was lighted by a million brilliant stars, twinkling as if to upstage the Star which had led them here.

True had a blurred-together impression of candles glowing among sweet-scented evergreens...children's eager faces scrubbed until they were as rosy as apples...and a general milling of friends and strangers offering to help the Valley people set out the makings of a feast. There was a feeling of breathless waiting—anticipation—which seemed to hark back to the hills of Judea.

But where was William Prescott?

"It's imperative that he be here," True whispered to Aunt Chrissy. How glad she was that she had shared the mixed emotions of the home calls. Somehow her aunt had a way of coaxing her gloom to fade, even wiping away her fears of inadequacy by repeating her own misgivings as a beginning teacher. And, as for her fears—well, yes they were well-founded. But one did not run from them. God had an oversupply of ivory-tower dwellers already. And now, Aunt Chrissy was speaking as calmly as then.

"Yes—if our program is to go the way we planned," she smiled, "but (and she consulted the small, enameled locket-shape watch pinned to her shirtwaist blouse) there's plenty of time. He could have been delayed—"

"*Way*laid, you mean!" Jerry said in a small voice. "Mr. Prescott promised to be here early—and he always keeps his promises."

Jerry had behaved so calmly when they visited among the mountain people. Why was he so nervous now?

"Teacher, I cain't git these angel wings on straight—do angels hafta have wings?" True's fingers trembled as she helped adjust the wings. And then she, Chris Beth, and Jerry were surrounded by excited children who eyed with longing the giant fir decorated with Miss Mollie's gingerbread men. "When'll we eat 'em?" "When do we have supper—before or after the program?" "Why are we so late?" "Teacher—I—I—forgitted—*forgotten*—my lines 'n my paw he'll be hoppin' mad—oh, I 'member. Let's git startin'!"

Outside, the flaming fire had dwindled to brilliant red coals. Just right for setting the coffee to boiling. But the program was to precede the meal, and there was still no sign of the principal.

"Get your father, Jerry," Chris Beth said quietly. But there was a note of urgency in her voice.

Both doctors responded to the summons. Yes, it was odd. And people were getting restless. The O'Higgins were keeping up a lively conversation. But for how long? Yes, it was best to switch plans, have the meal first.

Jerry made the announcement and the shout of glee was reassuring. Maybe things weren't that bad after all, the teachers told each other in an effort to shake off the feelings of apprehension.

"Did ever y'see people so hungry? Fine thang, th' board's decidin' t'feed th' multitudes." Nate Goldsmith had managed to shoulder his way through the people who stormed the table, most of them refusing to stay in an orderly line. "Yep—good thang—"

He waited just long enough for a compliment. When none came, he blurted out the matter which had brought him to True's side. "Now, whar's thet principal of our'n ? He's done a heap a peculiar-like thangs," Nate paused to wipe gravy from his chin with the back of his hand, "but this 'un takes th' prize!"

True was able to move away when one of the small boys, too young for school, tugged at her skirt. He just had to "go"—and would it be all right to "git 'hind a bush cuz hit's dawk 'n people's cain't see. Nate grabbed a small, uplifted hand and hurried him away.

That gave True a chance to rush to her room. Why hadn't she thought of it before? Maybe—just maybe—William Prescott had left a note again. That was most often his way of dealing with situations.

She was right. Propped against her desk copy of *Elementary Latin for Teachers* was a bulky envelope bearing her name.

Quickly she turned up the wick of the kerosene wall lamp, tore open the flap, and read the first line, stared at it with disgust, and thrust the pages under a stack of spelling papers to be graded. Her face was flushed with anger when she hurried back to the group, where the women were hastily picking up the remains of the meal and packing them into containers for the guests to take back with them. The games were already in progress.

There was a general state of confusion as children played the musical-chairs game, the winner of each stop of Mr. Beltran's harmonica being allowed to open a package of clothing. True welcomed the opportunity of organizing the squealing children and their excited parents into something resembling order. It helped her work off the fury churning inside her. And by the time the game (in which everybody won a parcel) ended, the fury had turned to fear, triggered by a fragment of conversation reaching her ears above the pandemonium. Two men, whose faces she was unable to see, were whispering.

"Yep, thet's th' way I heered hit—sad-like, 'ceptin' he 'ad hit comin'. He's been astin' fer hit fer a long time—"

"Agreed—but, whut a hor'ble way t'be leavin' this ole vale of tears—swingin' by th' neck like he wuz. Pore man, rest 'is sinful soul, wuz 'lowed t'hang thar still breathin' fer hours, 'cordin' t'reports—yuh know, dyin' by inches. 'Course he 'ad it comin'—"

The voices drifted away, leaving True frightened, remorseful, and sick... *sick*... had she ever been so nauseated? That's when she prayed as she had never prayed before. "Oh, give me strength to get through this, Lord. Surely something good can come of this... let us somehow get Your blessed message of love across to these lost souls...."

Dead, William Prescott is dead.

The words pounded at True's temples as Jerry maneuvered the children through the Nativity Scene while parents, caught up in a spell, leaned forward in pride and wonder. If the young actors stumbled over their lines, nobody noticed. It was the first time their parents had seen their own children perform—and, for most, the first time they had heard the message of Christmas.

God is at work here, True's heart whispered one moment. The next, it harked back to the dark world into which He had sent His Son. *Dead, William Prescott is dead*...

Olga Goldsmith rose to play the secondhand piano which the church had found at the Saturday afternoon auction in Centerville. The Jericho Singers, the all-male chorus formed by the church, followed. Moments later their voices filled the church with carols with what Grandma Mollie often described as "awful majesty," bringing tears to the eyes of the listeners. And then—one by one—the listeners joined in the singing, bodies moving slowly back and forth in a strange rhythm, known only unto themselves, their eyes closed as if seeing another Christmas, one so different that it could have happened in Appalachia—or beneath the silent stars of Bethlehem.

So caught up was True that again she forgot the terrible present. An inner voice seemed to be proclaiming that things would never be the same. The people, including the scoffers, had begun the long journey home—ready to savor the splendid misery of the climb.

And so their hearts were prepared for O'Higgin's reading—not the account of the Holy Birth, for they had *witnessed* that, but Isaiah's prophecy of God's Gift which offered freedom from captivity and salvation to a world "as filled up with sin as this very night—'nuf t'make a body shake, lest he be of a mind t'hear!":

> For unto us a child is born, unto us a son is given; and the government shall be upon his shoulder; and his name shall be called Wonderful, Counselor, The Mighty God, The everlasting Father, The Prince of Peace . . .

"And t'think He be born lovin' th' likes o'me—'n all of ye, good brothers—th' whole wicked world." O'Higgin closed his worn Bible, tears of joy streaming unashamedly from his merry blue eyes. *Oh, praise the Lord for O'Higgin—and for the person who had presence of mind to invite him to fill in tonight,* True whispered in her heart.

Young Wil. It had to have been Young Wil. He always knew how to right the world when it spun off its axis. And hadn't he said this would be the best Christmas ever? The stream of people pushing their way forward to pump the Irishman's hand proved him right. What could they do to help? How could they find out more? Was it true that the Bible he read from "tole hit same as in Latin"? That being so, maybe they had ought to learn reading, too, not waiting for the offspring to be spreading the gospel. And was it true—"Swear on yer maw's grave"—this gift was for everybody, even women and children who could be mighty ornery?

Overcome, True slipped out the side door and into her room. The wick had burned out, extinguishing the light. True shivered as she fumbled for a candle and then a match. How could it be so dark when there burned in her heart such remorse that it threatened to ignite? How the words seared, scorched, and pained. *Dear True: I deeply regret that I will be unable to attend the program. It is better this way...*

Better? When hours later he was swinging from a tree?

Laughter, unrelated to mirth, clutched True's throat. "I laugh because I must not cry," Abraham Lincoln had said.

And then a hand reached out to touch hers in the darkness...

25

Aftershocks

The touch on True's hand must have been startling, but she had no clear memory. No memory either of her husband's concern when he caught sight of her face after he had lighted the lamp. But the words in William Prescott's letter would linger forever . . . at first to shock her, then to haunt her, and later to take a place in the orchestra pit of her mind as an overture to introduce an unfolding drama—a drama with climax after climax, seemingly without the usual falling action which led to an ending.

"What is it, True? What has happened, my darling?"

Without awaiting an answer, he gently removed the letter from her trembling fingers. "Sit down," he pleaded, "and try to relax. Everything's under control—people are filing back up the mountain. There, hear the singing, the caroling—darling, *please* sit—"

Young Wil pushed her gently into the chair at her desk. "I'll read it aloud if you wish. I've a hunch it's from Prescott. Right?"

Yes, and he's gone—forever. You'll be reading the words of a dead man. That was what she wanted to say but could find no voice.

Maybe it would be better if she never knew the contents. No—what was it Aunt Chrissy said about God's having enough ivory-tower people already? If she had a part in his demise, she would never forgive herself. Yet if she never knew, she would feel equally guilty.

"Read it," she said at last through stiff lips. "I have to know—"

"'Dear True: I deeply regret that I will be unable to attend the program. It is better this way,'" Young Wil began, pausing where True had left off, his brow puckering. "We could wait if you aren't up to this."

"I'm up to it," she said, feeling stronger. He read on then, his voice never faltering but his head shaking in disbelief at points.

> You are more capable of facing the audience than I. In fact, I would fear for my very life, as I have no way of determining who among them are friends, if any, and who are the enemies. For, yes, I have enemies among the mountain dwellers, people sent here from the Blue Ridge country to spy me out and bring me home for punishment. Don't ask me why an education is a sin—it just is, like trying to escape and "mate-up with a furriner—jest lack th' Good Book warns 'gainst." Can you imagine my suffering, True? I am asking no sympathy, mind you, just begging you to understand.
>
> My father was what is commonly called a "liquor-head"—hardworking when he was sober, but that was seldom. And a real devil when he was drunk, cursing and beating my mother. She forgave him, saying it was Bible-like to forgive. And we little ones believed her, saint that she was. The child of a minister who harked back to more enlightened times, she was less superstitious, more steeped in the true meaning of the Bible and better educated than those around her. "William," she used to whisper as she heard my prayers at night, "you have a fine mind. If something happens to me, take the cash I have put away from the egg money and use it for an education. You are different. You can change this place, put it back together for the Lord. I have dedicated you to Him, promised. So your destiny is pre-ordained. I will watch from heaven—"
>
> I used to cry myself to sleep about that. Lose my

mother? It was unthinkable. What would I do? She was the only one I could talk to, the only one who loved me, the only one who cared. Imagine growing up with eight brothers (most brandy-drinkers like my father) and five sisters who were afraid to speak aloud. But I could dream. Wasn't I pre-ordained to melt down the golden calf of their drunkenness and absolute love of bloodshed? Oh, the blindness of it all. You see, the mountain folk gloried in their "religion," calling the senseless killing "pleasin' t'th' Lord—regular human sacrifice." That was just the way the world was, one tired-looking lady told me when she caught me crying after an emotional funeral—God's plan, and nobody could change it.

Oddly, my father made no objection when Mother started me to Sunday school. Hetty Amerson didn't know any more than I did, he said after two drams of brandy and just before he'd reached the beating stage. So he guessed the teacher'd not be "contaminatin' my mind with notions of changing things. Only the ignorant could praise the Almighty." Learning was sinful. It was trying to steal God's wisdom, so man could take control.

I guess I didn't learn a lot from Miss Hetty, except about David. He was my hero. I made myself a sling, gathered up a secret pile of stones, and waited for a giant (the devil himself, I guess) to hack his way through the bushes past the whiskey stills so I could destroy all evil. As the years passed, with no giant appearing, I grew weary of waiting and gave more thought to my well-meaning mother's plans for me. But the call I was supposed to hear never came—or maybe I wasn't hearing it above the gunfire, cursing, and screams of heartbroken widows on weekdays and the drunken shouting of the Primitive Baptists in response to a "Revival Preacher" (unordained) who confided to me that he had to "get gloriously drunk" to keep up his courage. But he did know how to read, and he taught me secretly. I wondered why he never read the Bible, but he explained that he had it memorized—only would be "shot down" if he quoted from it "proper." True or untrue, I will be forever grateful for his "You can do it, Sonny, you being a lot quicker than the others. And, as you know, there's only two kinds of folks—the quick and the dead."

And then my mother died. It still hurts remembering but I've managed to put it all behind me except her last words, "Remember, William—remember." I promised. That night my father went crazy, drank brandy like it was lemonade, while I shrank in a dark corner and wondered if he would beat her after the spirit had left her body. But he worked off his frustration by hammering together a pine coffin for the burial, then joined his cronies in the tobacco dryer in a game of strip poker. When he'd gambled away our last cent but refused to strip off his long johns, one of the men shot off his mouth and then his gun. That meant a double funeral—biggest one ever. Thousands came to the celebration, some on foot. Some of the bereaved (kin counting down to thirtieth cousins) had to camp outside, and I could hear their moanings and groanings all the night before. The women kept it up as they dished up food following the "divine experience" of the two of them going together. The men, of course, had finished their wailing, having uncorked a jug for getting brandy-eyed. That was the day that set me wondering what life was all about. How could God love us and yet will these things to happen, while some said it was pre-ordained before Adam was formed and others just laughed at their bloody hands, saying they'd helped the plan along? I slipped out and sat under the sweetgum tree and prayed the best I knew how. And the answer was that this was wrong. But I heard no voice thundering from heaven. It was left up to me what to do about the money in the sugar bowl. I realized finally that I had no choice. Everything was pre-ordained . . .

"Poor William—if only I had known," True whispered at

that point. Visions of a hanging body, gasping, and then going limp tore at her heart. As if the rope were about her own neck, she could say no more, need as she did to share her suffering.

"There would have been nothing you could do, True."

Her voice came then in rasping gasps. "You—can't—can't mean it was—*pre-ordained?*"

"Of course I don't mean that! I mean that the man had to find his way, make his own choices. Forgive me if I sound abrupt, darling. It's just—well, I believe that we should stop here—"

True shook her head vigorously. Young Wil bit his lip and read on:

> And so I ate of the forbidden fruit from the sugarberry bush growing in the graveyard just to prove to myself that I wouldn't die of dysentery. But I felt sick and ran, stepping on graves in my haste—then running faster when I remembered that this would bring their ghosts back to get me. You see, I didn't believe these things because God was in charge; but I could not escape the superstitions of my childhood. I am still afflicted at points. I guess your husband will understand that, being as informed as he is in the workings of the human mind. But I am not paranoid. I *know* my life is in danger and that it has been since I slipped away wearing a hand-me-down suit with red suspenders which caused the other students to laugh when I entered school.
>
> You know the rest, the important parts, at any rate. You've heard it from the pulpit. And, as you know, I was never an inspired minister—never able to bring the gospel message. Maybe, I decided, the Quaker girl I loved was right, the Voice I thought I heard being that of my conscience at having failed my mother. Why not try teaching for awhile? But it wasn't right either. And then when I saw my people again, it came! I knew what I had to do—do *now* before I was killed. I must go back and try to get the message of God's love across.

Yes, I know the danger, but I am willing to lay down my life . . . I can no longer be a Jonah . . . God has found me . . .

"Why, thet dumbell—crazier'n horseflesh! I allus knowed he wuz queer in th' head. Expectin' us'll be organizin' a searchin' party—thet's whut—'bout as apt t'happen as bein' bit by a snake with four legs!"

It was Nate Goldsmith. True, eyes closed and face covered by her hands, had been in another world, totally oblivious to the one which briefly she and Young Wil had escaped. Neither of them had been conscious of the silence outside nor the quiet footsteps which brought an audience now lost in the shadows beyond the pale halo cast by the flickering lamp.

Without looking around, she answered now, tonelessly and without emotion: "William Prescott is dead."

The blue haze, as William had described the mountains of his childhood, closed in around her. The room was alive with the sound of voices, voices filled with questions. But to True the world lay hushed, the spirit world more real than the cosmic one over which man had dominion. *Or did he?*

"True, True darling—look who's here!" Young Wil was gently shaking her shoulders. *"Look!"*

But she was unable to turn. "They hanged him—others found him—swinging from a tree—"

"Who be ye talkin' of, lassie? Be ye meanin'—"

O'Higgin was unable to continue. "Leave th' lassie be," he said at last. "She'll be a-sharin'—oh, could ye be meanin' *he*—he be Brother William?"

There were more questions which True was never sure she answered correctly. But she communicated with the one person who knew the truth.

"The man they found was—it has to be—my stepfather!"

The voice was low and musical, almost childlike. Only one person sounded like that. And it was that voice which brought True to her senses.

"Clarry!" she gasped. "Oh Clarry, *are you sure*?"

"She's sure. 'Twas I who brought the message." Jeremiah

stepped from the shadows. The fog was lifting to reveal faces. Only True North could not trust her eyes. It couldn't be. *It just couldn't!*

26

What Christmas Is All About

True slept late the next morning—if one could call it sleep. The small remnant remaining of the night (when at last all were in bed) she had spent dreaming of roaming the Great Smokies, not bodily but as the "voice in the wilderness" trying to prepare the way for William Prescott's arrival, pleading his cause—only to realize that she was neither seen nor heard. She was transparent and voiceless—struck dumb, rendered helpless. The dream was so real that right now she touched her body, tested her muscles, just to make sure she was of the flesh.

The events of last night had an illusory quality as she tried to piece them together. Bit by bit it came back... the program... the principal's letter... his demise... no, he was alive. It was Clarry's father who was hanged. *Clarry!* Thought of the girl brought True from her reverie. Clarry was here—Clarry, Kearby, Jeremiah—*Midgie!* Fully awake now, joy flooded her being, sending blood flooding the body that was very much flesh indeed! Midgie, Marty, and the *March Hare.* It was the warmth and sweetness of the drooling baby, pink-cheeked and heavy-lidded from need of sleep, snuggled against her bosom which restored her sanity. A baby... a squirming real-life baby who sucked his thumb and dimpled at her even as he fell asleep. The baby Chris... the Baby Jesus... that was what Christmas was all about...

A faint sound came from the livingroom. Young Wil would probably have had breakfast and be working on his book. He was incorporating the notes that True had made in the classroom and on home visits. Jerry, she smiled to herself, would have gone back to the Big House before the birds knew it was morning. He had volunteered to sleep on a cot here at the cabin so Kearby and Clarry could have his bedroom. Now she must join them all before O'Higgin and Grandma Mollie (who had taken the overflow of guests) returned. Time was short, and—

The noise again, a sort of scraping, as if a reluctant door were being forced open. Something cautioned her not to call out her cheerful "Good morning, darling!" as she usually did on the seldom days that Wil was home. Instead, she slipped into the daffodil robe he loved and gently turned the knob, hoping to find him at his desk. She would put her hands over his eyes, give him three guesses, knowing very well she would be drawn into his lap instead.

Clarry! But what was she doing here? Dusting to surprise her? The girl was propping a note against a cologne bottle. *A goodbye?* True was about to call out when she noticed how cautiously Clarry was moving, something clutched in her hand—something bright and sparkling as only a circle of pearls centered by a beautifully cut sapphire jewel could be. *Her mother's brooch!*

True stood transfixed, unable to believe her eyes, as she watched Clarry hesitate and then white-faced, thrust it into the pocket of her sweater. "Clarry!" True found her voice as the girl reached for the latch to let herself out quietly. The jewel box was gaping open, so there could be no mistake.

"Put it back, Clarry," True said calmly. Her voice was sorrowful but grave.

Clarry turned with a little half-sob, her young face twisted with fear.

"I—never—oh, Mrs. North—I beg you to believe me—I *never* took anything before—"

"The word is *stole*, Clarry. And, yes, I believe you—so replace the brooch. It belonged to my mother and is far more precious to me than it could be to you."

Clarry's face looked blank, as if she were unable to

comprehend the words. "Precious? I—I—didn't think of the pin's importance—I mean—*that* way. I—oh, Mrs. North—"

"True."

The girl looked even more stricken. "You—you would be kind—after what I've done—I thought—thought maybe I could sell it—" Clarry gulped, "and run away—"

"Put it back, Clarry. Nobody can solve a problem by trying to outrun it. And no amount of money would be worth the price you would pay—"

"You—you mean—you'll report me to the militia? Oh, Mrs. North—*don't*, I beg. Some of the soldiers came with us—to make it safe when they brought us out of Slippery Elm—while it's under martial law." Fear turned to defeat. "Yes, that's what you'll have to do—but (remorsefully) I deserve it—"

Head down and shoulders slumped forward, Clarry walked—*crept*, really—to the highboy, placed the piece of jewelry back onto its blue-velvet bed, and closed the lid. The sound reminded True of the finality of the carefully controlled metallic click of a coffin lid. The child was burying all hope—her very life—in this heartbreaking interment. But she must guard against being too soft if she wanted to help Clarry. She was *not* a bad girl, but what she had done was wrong. Understanding must wait.

"You have returned my property, Clarry. But I am unable to help until I know the truth. So, forget punishment, and explain what it is that you are running away from. Your father—stepfather, whatever he was—no longer has a hold on you—don't be afraid."

Silence stretched between the two of them as long as True could endure it. "Sit down, Clarry. Take the slipper chair. I'll sit here in Dr. North's desk-chair. He doesn't seem to be around."

"No," Clarry said in a small voice as she eased her thin frame into the slipper chair with a puzzled look "I—uh—heard his uncle say there was a call—somebody's appendix—then I—oh, Mrs. North—uh, True—I'm so ashamed—I slipped in—and the devil told me to—steal it—"

True inhaled deeply. Already some of the Appalachian thinking, or rationalizing, had rubbed off on the orphan girl, although she was not "one of them."

"What," True said, choosing her words carefully, "do you suppose the *Lord* would have told you?"

"To leave it alone—but I couldn't take time to ask Him a favor—"

"God always has time, Clarry. But He deserves an explanation—and so do I. Why did you do it, darling?"

When the word of endearment slipped out, Clarry opened her eyes to look at True in admiration. And her whole lurid story came out.

True knew that "that terrible man" was not her father, not even her stepfather, didn't she? Virgil never married her mother, just bullied her into living a lie. Because (the girl hung her head) "I am a bastard—dirty, unlovable—disgraced."

"You are none of those things," True said softly. "We will talk about that later. But, for now, please stay with your story."

"I loved my mother—but she neglected me—I guess," the lovely girl said bewilderedly, as if she were making a new discovery, "she did the best she could, giving me to Grandma, only I was stolen time and time again. I loved her," Clarry's voice was defensive now, "oh, I loved my mother so much—but she was afraid of *him*, afraid of disgrace—afraid of everything—even afraid of loving me. I guess that's just the way life is—people can't change what they are—"

Clarry looked up at True. There was no change in her facial expression. And, although the tragic eyes did not blink, a tear trickled down one cheek. "I guess you hate me."

"I do not hate you and you are wrong about people being unable to change, Clarry, but go on with your story."

"I need to know what's going to happen to me—now that you've found out what I'm like. And," her voice strengthened a bit, "what does my family, such as it was, have to do with the pin I—I stole?"

"I want to be fair. I respect the law, but I want to hear your side of the story. We've never really talked. Try to trust me."

Incoherently the story came out then—the ugly truth told in words that tumbled over each other as if they had been bottled up far, far too long. Virgil Adamson was downright brutal. He beat her when she tried to protect herself, and, being a coward like her mother, she guessed, she—well (a shudder shook her body) allowed herself to be abused "the other way." Then he got involved in robberies, killed some people, too. He forced her at the age of nine to sell stolen jewelry because, he said, her mother was in need of a doctor and would die without the money. He was sent to prison, telling Clarry that she was his accomplice and would be put in the cell with him if she told. A group of grim-faced women from some church placed her in an orphanage. All she could remember was a high iron fence with a locked gate and that there were no other girls her age—mostly boys who snickered when they saw her and spoke in loud whispers behind the angry-looking matron's back about taking her out in the woods. That's why she ran away to find an aunt. The woman meant well, Clarry guessed, but she scarcely had enough for herself, and she called her niece a burden. And then *he* escaped . . . and the whole sordid affair commenced again. Grew worse, in fact.

"And now he's dead—and I find myself *glad*—do you understand? Glad, *glad*, *glad*! Only they're going to find me—"

"Who, Clarry?"

"The outlaws with him—they'll think I helped before so I'm helping now. So I should know where the stolen money's buried—"

"Do you?"

"No! I've been living with Miss Anna-Lee, and she's good and kind, but she can't protect me. And besides, I don't want to embarrass her—and—if those church people find me, they'll send me back to that horrible place. Oh, can't you see why I *had* to run away? Kearby has been so kind—but I'm a burden to her, too—and hiding me out the way she's been doing is bound to get her in trouble—that's all I've ever caused is trouble—can't you see why I did it?"

Poor child. Poor innocent victim who had seen nothing but the power of evil. How could one expect her to recognize the power of good? Compassion overwhelmed True, and she was about to reach out to the child who saw her as judge and jury when Clarry crumpled to the floor and crawled like a legless reptile to coil at her feet. True was so taken by surprise that she was unable to move momentarily—just looked with horror at the stricken face, so pale in dismay and distress at her confession that surely the blood had been driven from her young heart.

True regained her composure, slid down beside Clarry, and cradled her in her arms. "Nobody will harm you, darling—we love you."

"You—you *forgive* me? If only I could have known you—*forgive me?*"

"Yes, darling," True said gently, "that's what Christmas is all about."

27

Life Must Go On

A week was not enough, but it was all they had. And True was grateful for the seven days. It seemed symbolic somehow: The Lord had created the entire world in that length of time. The North family must somehow rebuild *two* worlds from chaos and somehow bring them together, even hang a sun in the sky, for there must be a shedding and spreading of light. Just why the burden rested on their shoulders nobody seemed to know. Except Aunt Chrissy, that is.

"Because," she reassured Marty, Midgie, and the O'Higgins as they shelled walnuts for the holiday puddings that she was late in making, "we are His 'Chosen People'."

She cast a misty-eyed smile at Daddy Wil, who smiled back tenderly, the message saying they would never forget the details in Angel Mother's diary. "We can be proud of God's choosing us as His elect. The holy election puts us in the governmental position of the Supreme Court Justice—it is for a lifetime."

The three younger ones did not understand. Jerry laid down the two walnuts he had been pressing together to break the shells, and rubbed his reddened palms. "I've a feeling this goes far back. Tell us about it, Mother. There seems to be some mystery."

"The works of th' Lord are always mysterious," Grandma Mollie volunteered. "O'Higgin, cain't yuh keep th' fire goin'? Add a log!"

Chris Beth continued, "You're right, Jerry; but it is True's story, recorded by her mother in a diary. We are all mentioned, except you and Kearby, the end being before you were born—before your father and I were married, in fact. He was Vangie's—Vangie was True's mother, my sister—before Vangie—left us." Her voice broke.

All seemed caught up in emotion. The room lay in solemn stillness except for the occasional crack of a shell and the muted hiss of the backlog that O'Higgin had heaved into the widemouthed fireplace as it cast alternate fading and flaring lights—shadows dancing against the homey wall hangings. Homey. And it was Christmas. Yet the atmosphere seemed subtly portentous. So much was at stake.

It was True who broke the silence. "I think," she said with just a hint of unsteadiness in her voice, "that the time has come for sharing the diary with you, Jerry—you, Kearby—and Clarry. I want her to read it too."

Clarry's lips whitened. "What! *Me?*" Her voice was strained, humiliated. And her eyes, just before she lowered them, reflected a look of betrayal, their message clear: "I trusted you—and you let me down, just when I thought you understood. You promised we would never speak of the unpardonable thing I did—and now I am at your mercy, without defense. You will see that I'm punished—and you are wrong about God's love. I am *not* an innocent victim—I'm bad, *bad*, BAD. Nothing can change it—I was born that way—"

The look broke True's heart. She had a difficult role to play. "Of course you are included, Clarry dear. The diary will bring all the family skeletons out of the closet—let you see that none of us is perfect, although sometimes we adults try pretending we are. We are all sinners until we confess our sins and ask forgiveness—and then we become perfect through His love. All of you are old enough to see us as we are—"

O'Higgin slipped a stubborn walnut beneath the rocker of his chair and came down on it hard. The crash might well have heralded the end of the world.

"O'Higgin!" Miss Mollie's voice filled the room. "Talkin' of sinners—what's under thet thatch of red hair—anything? Causin' us t'jump outta our hides 'n need a doctor!"

"Now, now, me Mollie! There be two in this room—'n be 'avin' ye a peek et th' fruits of me labor. A perfect nut!"

"You got thet one right!" she muttered.

Laughter filled the room and the tension was broken. True cast a quick look at Clarry, whose eyes were shining, lighting her lovely face with relief that came close to spelling happiness. *Oh, praise the Lord!*

"We were going to make fudge, remember?" Kearby reminded her brother. "Come along, Clarry."

The girl cast True a heartbreakingly touching look of gratitude as she followed the twins into the great kitchen, where she would take part for the first time ever in Christmas preparations. And something told True that Clarry Hancock's mind was making preparations for Jesus' coming into her heart. One need not travel, for within each heart lay a Bethlehem... an inn where ultimately each mortal must decide whether there is room... and, one by one, those True North loved were deciding.

True wanted—*needed*—to talk with everybody individually, but time forbade. The only real group togetherness was at mealtime. And then there was such a joyous babble that she wondered if anybody heard a word anybody else said—except when it was quiet and Jeremiah prayed his beautiful prayers. Otherwise it was a natural pairing-off dictated more by priority than choice.

Chris Beth, obviously wanting to spend more time getting to know the "New Marty," recognized that her son must talk business with Irish O'Higgin. She longed to hold her first grandchild, too, become acquainted with his adorable baby-ways. True could see the desire in her eyes. But Aunt Chrissy, rendered him to Grandma Mollie, who—for the first time ever—allowed others to do the work while she rocked, sang, and (according to Midgie's hurried whisper) "spoiled him rotten." However, Chris Beth was able to spend some needed time with her daughter; and for some unaccountable reason she seemed worried about Kearby.

Clarry monopolized Jerry's time, who looked "mooneyed," Nate Goldsmith observed. He had come, of all the improbable times, to deliver a wagonload of books and brightly illustrated maps with real roller-cases which could be fastened to the wall! True sucked in her breath with admiration and surprise. Oh, what a boon—but who on earth was the benefactor?

Nate, chest out with pride, took time to spit (and keep her guessing) before his announcement. "Thet railroad feller—what's th' name? Oh, Saint Something—right fittin', ain't it now?"

"St. John—Michael St. John." For some reason True wanted to cry. Biting her lip instead, she turned a few pages joyfully and managed to thank the President of the Board. "They—Marty 'n th' others—knowed 'twas comin'—jest no time fer grabbin' hit in their hasty exodus. Bad, thangs is bad thar, I'm a-tellin' yuh—did'ja know 'bout th' hangin'—I'm a-meanin' t'other one, th' straw-stuffed dummy, strung up lack thet Virgil outlaw, hung on a rope in—uh—uh *ef*—some big word—"

"Effigy," True supplied, then in horror, "did Clarry see?"

Nate spat again. "Nope! Thet's why th' militia scampered 'em all out—'n I'd be guessin' with a pinch of relief, too, whut with th' meanin' of th' hoax. 'Twas a warnin' to 'em, yuh know, but now with th' new marshal—"

"There's a marshal?" True interrupted, hope rising inside her.

"Hasta be—with marshal law—ain't thet how they said 'twas?"

Disappointed, True tactfully explained the difference between the needed marshal and the "martial law" temporary takeover by troops. But she doubted that Nate listened. He was too busy stroking the treasure he'd delivered and asking Jerry's whereabouts. The boy could help unload, he said, since 'twas his bounden duty (importantly) long as he'd have to fill in for that sneak of a Prescott. After all was said and done, 'twouldn't change things much. The young man had been packing the load anyway.

"Jest whut he—Jerry, that is—seen in thet cowardly calf beats me. But would'ja be believin' he claims Prescott he'ped him make up 'is mind t'be a teacher—decided faster'n greased lightnin'—when he shudda tooken a run-ago at 'im—"

"A *what*?" Thrilled though she was to hear of Jerry's ambition and eager as she was to get the precious cargo unloaded, there was a point to make here. "I've never heard you use that word."

Nate removed his slouch hat and scratched where his hair used to be. "Ain't jes' fer certain—reckon I borried th' word—"

"From the mountain people," she smiled. "We all rub off on each other, don't we? Oh, here's Jerry—"

Young Wil, finished with house calls, joined them. Boldly he kissed a curl at the nape of her neck, then just before she could hiss "Wil North—mind your manners!" her husband took a look at the wagonload of supplies and whistled. "What a blessing! If you can manage, Jerry—you and Nate—I'd like some time alone with Clarry, please."

Daddy Wil and Jeremiah were strolling toward the ever-gurgling stream, buried deep in conversation. About the need for a church in Slippery Elm? Probably. It occurred to True then that the school was in need of a pastor too. In True's mind it had been for some time. Surely there was a minister who could win the respect of the Appalachian folk through gentle persuasion—kindness, patience, peacefulness, and understanding—then emphasize salvation, spelling it out, making it clear, pounding the pulpit if he must!

And then her thoughts changed. Oh, here came Midgie! They needed to talk and talk. But first, just to hold one another. *Close!* Men would never understand, they admitted laughingly, that crying together sometimes spoke louder to women than words. Chris Beth, looking out of the upstairs window, where she and Kearby were having their mother-daughter talk, looked down on the scene below. And history repeated itself. True and Midgie were herself and Vangie. The diary would tell—also reveal the fears in her own heart. And that was, at this point, how it should be...

The warm embrace had covered a lot of ground. It spoke of undying affection. It spoke of happiness found with men they loved. It brought back tender memories, shared dreams, and the need of togetherness for the four of them, just as Mary Evangeline North, heart breaking with the ache of temporary parting, and wasted body wrenched in pain, had written her final entry in her diary: . . . *so long as you're all together.* That would have been Uncle Joe, Aunt Chrissy, and Daddy Wil, the bereaved husband. Angel Mother, in human form, would be gone, but her spirit would linger forever. It was here now—with her and Midgie.

But there were other things to talk about, a world that the two of them shared—had helped to build, in fact. And now it was crumbling. Unless, of course, True and Young Wil would come back . . .

"Oh, darling, we can't consider a move—can hardly plot our future—until life levels here. It makes me ache to talk about it—"

"Then I will tell you the news." Midgie's dimpled smile brightened her round, girlish face with a lightness that True was sure her sister-in-law did not feel.

And talk they did, words tumbling out nonstop as if they must be spoken on deadline—which in a sense they must. The ranch hands had taken over, refused to leave, saying they'd help restore law and order . . . still trying to "teach Bible" . . . but Midgie wondered if 'twas smart, seeing that they needed schooling . . . needed a preacher too—but, oh, True, there was a teeny-weeny chance . . . the Reverend Randy having just taken over handling of the Caswells' business . . . and, yes, Tillie *had*, by the grace of God, become her old self since losing her husband . . . not that it would last without some doctor like Young Wil who knew the workings of the mind. Same for Mariah. Back to help Spanish tongues speak English while Tillie did it the other way 'round. But as for morality, what little the handful of decent folk had been able to instill had shriveled up and died, forcing decent God-fearing people to bear arms—allowed by the Constitution, but was it Christian? Midgie wished True could see how beautiful their house was now, spring bulbs sprouting already, bumper crops harvested, and ground "turned under" and allowed to fallow just before casting Tex's new strain of wheat. The cattle were multiplying and trying to replenish the earth as if they'd just stepped from the ark . . . same for the horses, real thoroughbreds . . .

True savored every word, but waited for Midgie to run down before bringing to the forefront questions which she knew were of critical importance to them both: the newcomers, the Appalachians.

At last Midgie inhaled deeply, almost painfully. "Your turn—you knew, of course, that Virgil Adamson was hanged?" She shuddered.

"Yes, I heard indirectly." True gave as complete an account as possible, except for Clarry's attempt to take the brooch. And the two of them pieced the story together, including the girl's flight from Slippery Elm. The stories coincided, including her reasons.

"Fear?" True said. "Didn't Anna-Lee befriend Clarry when she found she was a relative of her husband's? Couldn't Clarry look to her for protection?"

"Maybe I can understand better than you, True. I can identify with her, remember. Our backgrounds are different from yours—and, yet, we don't want to bring humiliation to those we love. But there's more—lots more. Clarry has real reason for being fearful. That awful gang Virgil Adamson was involved with will get to her if they can. So we might as well turn her over to them and get it over with if she returns. In fact, she would endanger us all—I'm so confused—but, darling, I don't dare take her back until the gang's rounded up, which will be the case when we get home to the Double N."

True could see the logic—could even see the wisdom of keeping her here—but, she evaded, it would be risky, too. Clarry and Jerry shouldn't see so much of each other day and night. And that's what it would amount to with Jerry's taking over—well, it would rest with the family. And with Clarry. That was another consideration. Young Wil would know how to talk with her. And the diary would help—at least, in letting Clarry know that she was not alone in being illegitimate. "But you were not abused," Midgie pointed out. "Oh, True, that leaves scars that even love can never wipe out. If you were there, we could form a little group—open up, talk things out—Clarry, Tillie, Mariah—me. You could lead—"

"But I am not there," True pointed out tiredly. "Let's see what develops, involve the Lord in this. And, meantime, I guess it will fall on our shoulders to deliver food to some of the needy. Feel brave enough to help? When you see more of how the Appalachians try to exist here, it will help you understand those in your area who, in their blindness, are at war with each other."

Midgie fidgeted. "I saw enough at the program to scare me—but," with a lift of her chin, "I will come. I—I can't help wishing one of the men—no, this is my Christmas gift. I had no time to prepare gifts, and I'm sorry."

True put her arms about Midgie and felt her trembling. "Don't be afraid, Midgie dear—" she paused, a bit shaken herself at the parallel between Aunt Chrissy's reassuring Angel Mother, remembered from the diary—"just keep the peace of Christmas in your heart. And, as for gifts, we had no time either—our Christmas is giving to the poor. Remember that the Baby Jesus grew up . . . walked among the poor . . . and, like the Star, said 'Follow me.' I—I'd rather sit safely by the fire and make popcorn balls—don't I owe that to my family? But—Midgie—think about what I owe *Him*. A pilgrimage—to a land of hunger . . . misery . . . and hate-filled faces. Yes, following is risky . . ."

They delivered the food but said little of the journey. On Christmas Day six bewhiskered men of the mountains brought down a roasted pig, its eyes still intact and the skin rubbed in alcohol "t'tighten th' hide fer cracklin's, savin' need t'scrounge round fer soothin' sir'p fer th' stummick afterwards of a square meal."

The family dinner was festive. But True and Midgie, recalling the pig sty, refused pork. Nobody noticed, as all were talking at once, Clarry and Kearby most excited of all. *Clarry was going to the academy with Kearby.* Just like that? How—? True, her eyes locking with Midgie's said Christmas was a sacrifice. Life must go on . . . and everybody would help. . . . They had handed the needy a Star.

28

End of a Silver Silence

Everyone was gone and the world lay in a silver silence. Nature had tiptoed in and dusted the Valley with the first snow, a grim reminder that winter was a reality of life. But it locked in the peace of Christmas in a mystical sort of way, just as the harsher freeze to the east would lock in the winter wheat at the Double N. Too, the quiet allowed time for reflecting as well as getting the school in order.

There had been a frenzied rush readying Clarry for the unexpected departure with Kearby. Fingers, the few sewing machines, and Mrs. Solomon's "Alteration Department" worked far into the night adjusting "dresses that didn't sell" to fit Clarry's slender figure. It was Jerry's admiring glances which brought to light a deeper relationship than his mother or older sister had allowed themselves to accept.

"It keeps happening over and over—history repeating itself," Chris Beth marveled. "How did your mother have so much foresight?" There was both admiration for her beloved sister and a concern for Jerry (which she tried to conceal) in her weary face. "I'm glad you let them share the diary—the girls, that is, since Jerry was bogged down with the school supplies—do—do you think things are serious between him and—?" Somehow she seemed unable to say the name.

True smiled. "As serious as they can be at this tender age." She was about to suggest that they waste no time fretting over it when she caught sight of the paleness brought on by her aunt's own words.

It all came to her then, the high-tide of revelation nearly sweeping her off her feet. "You are remembering Young Wil, aren't you?" she whispered, "Young Wil—and me—conceived out of wedlock like Clarry?"

"Oh, darling, *no*!" Chris Beth dropped the flatiron back on the bed of coals she had raked onto the hearth and rushed to take True in her arms. "If I ever, *ever* gave you reason to believe—oh, my darling, you come close to being my favorite child, if I would allow that."

True hardly heard. Her own mind was seeing too many parallels. Somehow she managed to mumble out her feelings.

Aunt Chrissy pulled True's head to her breast, stroking the golden curls back from her damp forehead the way she used to do when a bad dream had awakened True from troubled sleep. "There *are* similarities—I mean in our relationships—even with the changes. You have grown up knowing that we believe God brought us here for special work, and that it is to continue down through the generations."

Yes, that was true, True admitted to herself. And now she wondered if it had been her aunt or herself whom she doubted. Young Wil had told her as they studied together that the mind was tricky, not always reliable. That it tended to shift certain characteristics from self to another. But—

"I'm sorry, Aunt Chrissy—I shouldn't have said that. But," sitting upright, "what has any of this to do with Jerry's attraction to—perhaps love for—Clarry?"

Aunt Chrissy considered the question with puckered brow. "Her background," she said at length, "is so different. She has been through so much. I guess, to be truthful, I am afraid that her values—no matter how much she hates her past and what that man has done—make her more aware of her power as a woman. I don't want that for Jerry! But I'm wrong in assuming the worst, darling—I know that I am. You see, I am remembering what loose tongues did to your mother—and I don't want that happening to Jerry and Clarry, poor child—"

"I know," True said in a small voice; "it's all in the diary. I know, too, that scars will remain, as with Midgie. But Clarry is working her way through this. Young Wil is keeping me informed and says she will forgive herself of wrongdoing, real or imagined, once she realizes that God has forgiven *her*."

"Oh, darling, yes, *yes*. Sometimes I wonder if we mothers aren't bad for our children." Her attempted laugh faltered. "Is there something more you want to ask me? You still look troubled."

As True watched her aunt dampen her forefinger and test the heat of the iron, she remembered that she too must iron some white shirts for her husband. But she could not bring the conversation to a close until she had an answer to a question which had nibbled at her mind for far too long already. Sprinkling the starched shirts could wait.

Aunt Chrissy had begun the tedious job of ironing the pleated bosom, waiting—but not pushing—for an answer. When it came, she looked startled. "Jerry and Clarry I can understand, I guess. But why are you so concerned about Kearby?"

There was a quick intake of breath before Chris Beth said in a low voice, "I didn't know it showed. But her unnatural fear of men after Clarry's experience, followed by an about-face worries me. You see, Kearby told me, when we talked, that there's a boy she wants to bring home—brother of one of her friends there. Oh, just tell me I'm a goose!"

Relieved, True threw back her head and laughed, feeling the tension inside her melt into nothingness. "Is *that* all! All right, my precious aunt, you are a goose—a wonderful, normal, much-loved 'Mother Goose'!"

As True ironed and Young Wil worked on his book that night, the wind outside took on force, pushing against the invisible in a way that made her uneasy. Such a strange wind, advancing and retreating, like a mighty army. It played up and down the scale, discordant at one point, harmonizing at another. The room filled with smoke, making it necessary to open the door against a wall of wind.

"Did—you—get the—information you wanted—from Clarry?" True panted as they pushed against the door together.

"Here—stick this underneath while I hold it open." Young Wil managed to reach the fire shovel with his foot and kick it to her. Done!

In the freezing cold, True ventured to interrupt him again. "Did you?"

Young Wil looked up vaguely. "Clarry? Oh—ah—yes. I'm transcribing my notes—nothing confidential, I guess—" he paused to gather up papers the wind had scattered, "as she said she'd revealed the temptation to take the brooch."

He resumed his writing. *Confidential.* Young Wil respected that. But of course he would. Why should she have felt guilty for respecting it too? Relief swept over her. *Forgive my humanness, Lord.*

As they locked up for the night, Young Wil looked up at the somber January sky. "Snow tomorrow. Better get your boots out—my hands are frozen. Let's turn in and snuggle."

Warm in her long flannel nightie and secure in her husband's arms, True no longer felt uneasy. She listened until the wind grew hoarse and hushed its voice and Young Wil's even breathing told her he was asleep, then gave a contented sigh with no premonition of the greater storm which was building around them.

The next morning the world was white, with time, space, and substance tucked beneath the blanket of snow. School was to resume today. And the silver silence would be broken—ending in a number of ways...

29

Calm Before the Storm

January, True thought later, was the silver lining of an invisible black cloud. The North family (which included O'Higgin and his Mollie-gal), the Valley folk, and the mountain dwellers settled into a routine which Young Wil referred to in his doctoral dissertation (to be published in book form) as "a successful period of adjustment." Grandma Mollie sniffed and said 'twas more like the wolf and the lamb dwelling together. But Isaiah never made mention of what happened when the wolf sniffed fresh blood, did he?

To True it was much like the prophet's account of the restoration of Israel. *Peaceful.* So she encouraged her class to memorize the verse, "Sing unto the Lord, for he hath done excellent things..." After all, her prayers were being answered, her every wish granted. Didn't Michael's contribution to the library, followed so soon with textbooks and school supplies, stand out as a shining example?

The children stood in awe at the new materials, their eyes saying that Christmas was here to stay. They violated her rule by leaving their desks without permission and clustering around her. "Le's see, le's see... move, yuh upscuddle, lemme see... Teacher, Charmin' cain't see, her brother's a mean'un greedy 'n tetchious, allus packin' a gredge... *move*!"

True, as excited as the children, regretted that she must restore order. "Here, let's find Oregon on the map." Wordlessly their clumsy fingers located the Appalachian country, having no idea whether to trace their fingers east or west. It was as if they knew of no world outside their place of birth, even though they were now relocated.

Making note of their lack of knowledge, True asked that they wash their hands before opening the new books which two of the older boys would distribute. Again, the look of enchantment as they touched, smelled, and clutched the beautiful books to their hearts. True turned away to hide the tears. This was their first exposure to books with all the pages intact and unspotted by sorghum or lard.

Learning took on a new meaning for them. All embarrassment, bewilderment, and reluctance to learn faded. These books were *theirs,* not at all like the missionary barrels "of stuff," they said. True encouraged them to talk about the contents of the barrels. "Funny hats, right-smart purdy onct, but et up by moths . . . store-boughten lard buckets, right nice fer dinner packin'—'cept bottom's rusted outta th' critters, 'n thar warn't no bails . . . funny corset-thangs (*giggle,giggle*) fer fat womans . . . shoes thet hurt cuz of long nar' toes, not no buttons neither . . . some books whut was too colored-up fer readin' 'n pages tored outta 'em."

Then Buster's voice rose above all others. "Paw wuz hoppin' mad, built a far hottern hades 'n us'n all burnt 'em 'n roasted sow belly. Sed us foks don' be needin' no char'ty."

Sickened, True turned away to hide the horror she felt. *Think of something else,* she willed. She remembered then that Buster's teeth looked much better. Oh, yes, of course. Her wonderful husband had taken a retired dentist with him on some of the house calls. Which reminded her to tell the children that the doctors were coming in February to weigh and measure them. "Then," she smiled, "each of you will have a health record all your own. We'll learn how to take care of ourselves and (rashly) be fit enough to do battle with a lion like Daniel!" That she regretted, because one tiny tot said she'd be searching "fer th' jawbone of th' ass."

True seemed the only one flustered by the Bible quote. It was then that a strange notion crossed her mind. They were ignorant because they had no learning opportunities. But they were open and open-minded. What came out of their mouths was innocence itself. They appreciated what the

Lord provided, no matter through whom He doled it out, and they instinctively recognized His "good gifts" above the pitiful crumbs from do-gooders' tables. *Are they more civilized than we are?* A new sense of responsibility swept over her.

For the remainder of the week, True allowed the children to draw maps, label them, and try to pinpoint the ocean, mountains, and valleys. By Friday parents were coming en masse to see what all the commotion was about. That was when they decided to tackle reading for themselves...

All this True wrote in a letter of appreciation to Michael. He answered promptly, telling her that he had arranged through Meier and Frank's to have shoes of all sizes delivered, suggesting that Solomon's Store put on a "sale."

Meantime, Midgie responded to True's more detailed letter to tell of a similar experience with the missionary projects. "It was all disgraceful and degrading," she commented, then went on to relate how the contents were put to use in Slippery Elm, "only it would have been far better if they'd been sent up in flames like your people there. Poor darlings—they break my heart in half! Marty found bloody footprints—human ones—in the snow and hoped there would be some decent shoes. What did he find? Junk, *awful* junk! But the Appalachian people were so cold, feet all frostbitten, you know, that they grabbed at anything. It would be a riot if it weren't so downright pitiful—like having your heart carved right out of you. Why, True, it's not one bit uncommon seeing one of the men at Tillie's store wearing a frock-tailed coat over his ragged coveralls. One woman bought green satin shoes with heels sky-high to go with her shapeless calico that's worn so thin it's like gauze. She stumbled off the gallery of the store—nearly drowned in the rain barrel, and what did she say? First question was, "Oh, what 'bout my bee-u-y-fullest shoes in th' world?"

Midgie went on then with family news and views. True loved her sister-in-law's every word—the information and the amusing way in which she expressed herself. Midgie had managed to "study up" on her grammar and learned to communicate well without sacrificing her own unique personality. *If only I can accomplish that here,* True thought.

Quickly she scanned the remainder of the letter. There were papers stacked eye-deep on her desk and notes to prepare for Young Wil, some checking on Jerry (oh, dear, she had neglected him!), and so she read the next paragraph without really absorbing it.

"Things are still bad, even with help of the militia. They plan to get more help . . . but a bigger problem . . . well, let's not worry, but they've discovered she's gone . . . may go gunning for her . . ."

In fact, serious as the situation was in Slippery Elm, True had to smile at Midgie's constant reference to their need of Young Wil and herself. Not that she doubted it. But Midgie was so obvious . . .

Aunt Chrissy was as happy as True with all the supplies. They planned together for hours, listening always to Jerry, whose ideas were sometimes better than their own. Nate had managed to have the state issue a "Temporary Substitute Certificate" for Jerry ("nobody possessed 'nuf brains t'be askin' his age—'n me, I don't volunteer"). Aunt Chrissy was happy, too, about how faithful the girls were in writing home from the Academy. Her mind seemed to be at rest now.

"Sometimes," she smiled happily, "I think it's all too good to be true." That was before the wolf smelled blood, True supposed later . . .

30

The Smell of Blood

In spite of the Appalachians' progress in other ways, one thing was the immovable object: They refused to lay down arms—unless their weapons were within reach. Old habits dic hard. "Back home" men slept with their rifles cocked. Sure, things were changing here. Folks voted other folks in and voted them out. But in the long haul, did it matter much? Violence hid behind every bush no matter where a man was. The bulging hump of a mountain in these parts was as good a hangout as the brooding monsters of the Great Smokies. And what did the government care? Best a man be prepared. Even the Good Book said so.

The Norths prayed together often about the feuding mountaineer spirit that seemed to hold the people together. Actually, it was their source of pride. What help was a newfangled gas buggy if a man had no money? they reasoned. And who cared about that smart man called Edison—somebody who almost got himself killed trying to put lightning in a lamp? Both changes were more dangerous than bullets—and did nothing to protect a man's family. Better have a neck like a hoot owl that twisted round and round so he could keep watch behind him, that's what. And keep his powder dry.

"If only we could get a good minister in here—somebody like Joe," Wilson North said one evening. To which Aunt Chrissy replied that there would never be another like her former husband. "But," she reminded them all softly, "he left the torch in our hands. We must carry on."

That was when the two doctors began to approach the men with proposals that they put away their guns. To no avail. Everywhere the answer was the same: "We'd be kilt 'fore a week took leave!"

"I suppose," Young Wil said, his voice carrying a hint of defeat, "they're right, carrying grudges as they do. And somehow they're unable to bring together their new thinking—even after turning their lives over to the Lord—and the lifestyles which have been instilled in them. It's like—well, they continue living on an island unaffected by change."

"Don't give up, darling. I refuse to allow those weapons in my classroom," True began, and then stopped. After all, the guns were left within reach. "You're right, darling—we'll just have to keep working on it. Eventually something will show them the need for law and order—or will it? Change has to come from within. It's something that only God can do."

Young Wil's head jerked erect. "Are you aware that they claim to be studying so they can take the gospel back?"

"And how do they propose to present it—with a gun?"

"Actually, I think they're homesick for the most part—the men, anyway. Most of the wives seem more content, safer. But," he shook his head, "I keep hearing how good it would be to get back where the land is free of bullies calling themselves 'the law.' Better, they say, to be free like the Constitution promises—free to make their 'home brew,' kill if need be, and just watch the buzzard sail without flapping wings over cows that might be a little lean, but that was true only because they were allowed to be free—it's confusing."

"But," True said determinedly, "it's not futile. Somehow we have to shake them awake. And we will!"

"*We*? It well may be circumstances."

"Wil North, stop trying to scare me!"

For the first time her husband did not laugh or tease. His concern was too deep in the very core of his heart, she realized.

In February the weather grew milder, snow turning to rain. Snow thinned in the Valley, leaving the ground to look like threadbare carpet under which lay a bog of mud. It was a nuisance, but better than a shift of the winds to bring the warm Chinooks, triggering sudden thaws, mountain slides, and the threat of floods. The mountain children, still surrounded by snow in the higher elevations, were too excited to notice. They were getting health charts!

True watched with admiration as the two doctors examined them (often having to soothe the girls' fears and dry their tears), especially noting the reassuring way both her husband and her uncle weighed, measured, and made records while gently talking of proper foods to eat and the value of cleanliness. He knew that the eager children would take the message home. How true! Before the end of the month, parents were coming. First out of curiosity, then to ask shyly if maybe this would be a "purdy good idee" for them all. Young Wil cautiously caught True's eyes and winked.

"If you wish, yes," he said with just the right amount of hesitation. "Ladies first—and then, you men. Without your guns, of course."

True was relieved to hear one man actually joke, "I dunno, Doc. M'gun she packs a lotta weight!"

Maybe they *were* getting the message across in small doses.

And then a miracle happened! True received a surprise letter from William Prescott. He had arrived safely at his home country and was amazed at the reception he had received. A retired minister and his musically inclined wife had broken the ground for him—worked their way into these people's hearts somehow, and introduced William as if he were a stranger. Old-timers had clustered around him, some with suspicion, others just curious that an outsider would dare invade their territory—and, True could almost feel his shudder, some drawing knives and brandishing guns. And then—would she believe that a big square-ox of a man (noted for his "killing ways," William learned later) stepped bravely forward to say, "Don' I know yuh, boy? Ain't yer mammy th' one whut usta bake th' ashcake fer eatin' with th' wine in mem'ry of th' dead et fun'rals?" He'd thought there would be another funeral, he said, when he nodded. But instead, the people were afraid of "Ox," and when the giant of a man asked him to his cabin for ham-meat that night, there was an opportunity to explain his mission here. "Lordymercy, man," his host had observed privately, "don' yuh know whatta chance yer a-takin'? Still 'n all, iffen yer wantin' t'preach, tain't none of nobody's bizness, 'n I'll take keer of yuh bes' as I kin—bein' a shot lack I yam." Mr. Leady was a powerful man (both ways)...so there was hope...now, would it be possible that the Norths would be willing to allow Jerry to come and help...?

True threw the letter aside, horror rising to the surface. Send Jerry? *There*? Why, the man was mad. Stark, raving mad...

It was days before she could bring herself to finish the letter.

"Dr. Miller, the minister who helped me here, is tired and his wife is not too well. He would like to move to a milder climate for her benefit, but has no desire to retire. I have described Oregon and they would like your permission to come there. They are sweet, gentle people, but he is a fundamentalist—meaning that he sticks with the message of salvation, gently. Mrs. Miller is a teacher and will help in the classroom..."

True's heart soared then. And before it seemed possible, the family had relayed the message to Nate, who called a meeting of the deacons. And the Millers were invited to visit. Jerry's going was out of the question, of course. And, to True's surprise, Jerry agreed. "Besides," he grinned, "you couldn't get along without me—and neither could Clarry, maybe Kearby either."

The Millers were all he proclaimed them to be, and more. The day that Dr. Miller preached his first sermon in the Valley, the church was packed. Not an empty pew, with heads poked in at the windows. Those heads belonged to mountaineer men who claimed they'd not be caught dead in a church. "Well, now, ain't thet jest th' bes' news ever? That'd mean 'nother fun'ral," one of the insiders growled.

The man outside whipped out a knife. "Two of 'em—" he growled.

That was when the preacher, ears attuned to signs of trouble, said in a gentle but authoritative voice, "If all will lay down your weapons—guns, knives, rocks, anything which would harm your brother—we will get started."

Mumbling that the preacher wouldn't last a week hereabouts, the newcomers obeyed his request. After all, preachers had bewitching powers—last time they saw one shot right betwixt the eyes, the cows gave bloody milk the night of the ice-cream social. Real scary. Preachers were a threat—particularly this one—not like a saddlebag one who filled his stomach and flew like a bat out of torment. But this one, well, he was a puzzlement. Didn't shout. Didn't do much to make a man mad. Hard to hate a man whose words came as sweet as spring rain. There were questions needing to be asked, of course. Was he "Prim'tive?" Did he baptize or just "dry clean"? Why, even their kids knew better than dabbing down like Tuesday's ironing. Every gosling they owned had been baptized in the waterbucket. Better listen to this one, yep, lest he be casting a spell—

Well, by gum, the man made sense and he had a sense of humor. Never saw preachers laugh before—and make them laugh at themselves. Like saying "Hardshells are hard to crack—so I don't look for one immediately—"

But he got one anyway. He made the glory of God's love sound so appealing that one woman shouted right in the middle of the sermon. That caused the man at the window to interrupt, "Shout hit out, Preach. Cain't hear a word 'bove that thar hyst'ery." From another window came an "Amen!" And, when Dr. Miller invited all wishing to hear more about the road to heaven to gather up front where he would talk with them personally, there was a stampede. Better get the lowdown here. Education used to be the enemy. But—well, maybe they were getting soft in the head, thinking that maybe the enemy *was* ignorance...

The man was hard to figure out. Maybe that's what kept them coming. One thing was certain, he wouldn't take "No" for an answer. First man they'd met who was so all-fired determined—and had a remedy for every excuse they had for not bringing their families to church. No shoes, they told him, and he up and took the whole mountainside to Solomon's Sale. Bertie said later that she and Abe never done such a booming business. Of course, they had to depend on volume, she grumbled. The Valley women were downright huffy, called it false advertising to offer only shoes, so they just had to mark down all the stock.

Well-shod now, the men ran short on excuses. And this preacher was a bold one, coming at all hours of the day without warning. Made it right hard to keep a man's business to himself. Most had given up the stilling and bootlegging, but liquor—like guns—was a necessity, wasn't it?

Gradually the mountain men began to wonder about their lifestyles. If they were wrong in their thinking, they were in a terrible fix with the Lord. The presence of strangers would hex the flowers, they'd been told. Why, then, did the daffodils bloom more golden than Gabriel's horn this year? A body could almost hear them blast. And who wanted to be caught doing something that might infuriate the Almighty if the end was close?

The only thing wrong with all this, the Norths realized later, was that the Valley became dangerously satisfied. And the satisfied rose is one whose petals are about to fall...

The petals of their blind optimism dropped on a day when one would least expect it. The rains had dwindled to misty curtains which parted to show the sun's face. Hope for peace was gaining sturdiness—just melting away gradually, in True's mind, much like the snow. Enough to let the valleys make their annual promise of spring—apple buds pink (in what farmers called "popcorn stage") and ground almost ready for plowing, while up on the mountains wild lilacs trailed like purple waterfalls. The sun was so sensible, too, holding back its warmest rays, which would melt the snow too fast and overfeed the river, creeks, and streams. Yes, peace was a fragile thing.

Oh, it was good to be alive! Mrs. Miller, the sweet-faced, iron-gray-haired wife of the minister, was coming today. School would be out soon. But she wanted to get the feel of it for next year so Jerry could get back to his studies. And other good things were happening in True's life. Young Wil had told her he was going to finish the dissertation on time, timeliness being of utmost importance to the august body before whom he must read his work in what they called his "orals." Midgie had written that the Reverend Randy *was* staying on and had plans for organizing a church. She *thought* there was another reason, but time would tell. And then there was the flow of letters from Kearby to Aunt Chrissy and Clarry to Jerry. Both girls were ecstatically happy, as was Jerry. And Clarry was *safe*...

So when and how did it all begin? One moment True was arranging the bucketful of spring beauties with pussy-willows. The next moment there was chaos. She hadn't so much as noticed the shift of the wind—its breath now too warm and dry, sucking away the sound of approaching hooves or voices of the riders.

"Trouble, Teacher—*bad* trouble." Little Josie's small voice held fear but no hint of danger. The child probably referred to the wind, which True now heard for the first time. The dread Chinook! Apprehension rose inside her. Her thoughts were busy with plans for getting the children home early when the door burst open, scattering papers about the room in wild disarray.

Suddenly above the roar of the wind there were shouts and angry voices. *Oh, not now, children.* "Pick up the papers and close the door," she ordered in an attempt to restore order. But the shouts grew louder.

"Let go of m'sister, dirty bully! Teac-*cher*!"

"Git th' gals, that 'un—'n t'other side 'er—yuh little weasel, git them teeth outta m'leg yuh half-pint b______"

The word he used was unacceptable, and the voice was that of a man! True whirled, her vision blurring as she saw some of the children curled into little balls for protection beneath their desks... others forming a human screen around the horrifying scene of three masked men trying to pin down two of the larger girls... and the remainder clinging to her skirt for protection. What on earth? *"Get out!"* she shouted wildly.

"Wanta be kilt—all of yuh—'n smell yore teacher's blood?" One of the men dragged the screaming girls away. The other aimed a gun at True. "Git goin'—got 'em both, Adamson's gal 'n yer sister as hostage!"

They rode east into the wind—*with the wrong girls*...

31

Warning—Unheeded

There was no time to warn Aunt Chrissy and Jerry. Time was of essence. The mountaineers must know the awful news. And, more importantly, they must know that "their kind" was not responsible. Else there would be civil war—and the fragile thread holding them together would snap. This True was thinking as she took the shortcut where the underbrush was thickest and blackberry vines tore at her long skirt and the laces of her boots as if to hold her back. Maybe the children would alert Mrs. Miller. She could take over in an emergency and—

But there was no more time for thinking. The tumultuous sound of rushing water told her she was nearing the stream. Fed by the river, it would be near flood-stage. And she must cross it by footlog. A quick survey told her that the high water had set the log swaying and that it was slippery from waves which washed against it with such force that they broke to course over the poorly anchored makeshift bridge. True looked away, hoping to overcome the seasickness she felt in the pit of her stomach.

But she couldn't afford the luxury of being sick. A moment's hesitation could mean loss of life! Not once did True think of her own life as she hoisted her skirt and set a tentative foot on the swaying log. It shifted warningly, but only dimly was she aware that she was in trouble. Closing her eyes momentarily, she let go of her skirt and balanced her weight by stretching both arms out the way she did when she, Young Wil, and Marty tried mastering the art of tightrope walking so many years before. Added to childhood memories was that of her more recent crossing. Déjà vu...

"Never look down!" True could almost hear Young Wil's warning. So, eyes wide open now, she fixed her gaze on the safe side of the log where she would set foot in only seconds if she kept her wits about her. The roar of the water said she was past midpoint. She was going to make it! And then a piece of bark let go of the parent trunk. There was no time to right herself. She was falling... falling... falling. The moment seemed to stretch into eternity.

God looks after fools, her husband was to tell her later. Surely He must have reached out and grabbed her, breaking the fall. Else how could she have landed with a violent jolt astride the log—almost senseless but safe? Her teeth ached. Her head swam dizzily. But somehow she must manage to pull her legs from the swirling water, which was getting higher. Soon the log would float away. She must *crawl.*

With superhuman strength, True jerked her petticoats free of the snags which had entangled them but perhaps saved her life. Cautiously, she pulled one leg at a time onto the slippery log and, in a dazed state, began to crawl and claw her way onto the opposite bank.

Surely the Lord told her to look back. And that glance over her shoulder gave her access to the most terrifying view of her life.

The children were crawling, one by one, behind her...

"Get back!" she tried to scream. But the teeth of the wind bit into each word, leaving no sound. She would have to direct them by hand.

Waving a hand frantically, True caught the eye of the first little girl. Who? She had no idea. The curtain of rain was blurring the picture, warping small faces grotesquely so that they were beyond recognition. How many were in this army? All the mountaineer children, undoubtedly.

She signaled them to crawl and pointed to her face. Bless their hearts! They understood and, like a trail of ants, they kept creeping toward her, eyes fixed on her face with complete confidence. She understood, understanding humbling her heart. How thankful she was that she had felt only yesterday to read them the story of "The Great Fisherman"—Peter—who must keep his eyes on Jesus to avoid sinking into the churning depths of the sea.

The log tilted crazily and, although True suppressed a scream, the faces focused on hers were calm and trusting. "Come on—that's it— stand up and jump, darling—*jump*—I'll catch you!"

The leader was close enough for True's words to penetrate. The tiny figure rose on unsteady legs and leaped. *Little Susie!* True held the frail body to her while directing the second child to jump.

"Run, both of you—run as fast as your legs will carry you! *Jump!*" she ordered the third and fourth children. "Go home quickly and tell your parents it was strangers—nobody from here—who kidnapped the girls!"

The procession seemed endless and the log was no longer visible. True had never prayed so hard. "*All* of them are coming—Lord, help me!"

At last it was over. The children scattered, dodging outcropping rocks, sliding down and getting up determinedly, never looking down to the valley floor. True lost all sense of direction in the gathering darkness. Somewhere she heard the welcome clang of a cowbell. They must be getting near to one of the cabins. She concentrated on her footing. "Uptilted," the folk who lived here described this part of the mountain. "Straight up" would have been more apt, True was thinking as her foot slipped and the wind did the rest. She fell, head striking something hard and solid...

She must have lost consciousness. Someone was wiping her face and speaking soothingly, but the words were garbled. "Children... told... said the doctors came... ready to care for... wounded." Jerry? Yes, the voice was stronger now. The words made sense.

It was too late, he said. Too late. The men went crazy. Ignored the message and, arming themselves, rode away. *They were going to kill every Appalachian in Slippery Elm. There would be a slaughter...*

32

The Legend of True North

Someday True would be called a vital, courageous woman in the annals of Oregon history. Even the pines would whisper her name as future generations told her story. She weighed and measured everything with those heaven-blue eyes, then tackled the job, big or little. Not a mean bone in her body, but spirited as a young pony—and often just as playful. Her young heart was molded from love, hope, and faith—and talk about endurance! Nobody ever figured, for instance, how she managed to get all those children across that flimsy footlog in time—Just before the whole contraption hurled itself down the raging torrent, angered at the delay. If ever a man had saved so many lives he'd have been awarded a medal.

But for now she felt like a failure through and through. How could she have imagined even in her wildest dreams that she could cut through the lineage of generations, take this one back to their fine heritage, build on it, renew their pride in a single year? They were so hungry in mind and spirit. And she could feed them! Hadn't she seen them bloom out, only to shrivel beneath the slightest pressure, renew their feuds, become actually violent over trivia? They had an iron will and, worse, seemed to take actual pleasure in finding a reason to keep their feuds alive. She had failed.

And she was so tired, so tired. It was hard to raise her head from the pillow to take the broth that Aunt Chrissy almost forced her to drink. Hard to move beneath the covers, but easy to remain in bed. Ordinarily, she thought foggily, she would have flatly refused to stay put when she was ordered to bed by Young Wil—

Young Wil! Reality was replacing the blind alleys through which she had passed. Where was he? What had happened? And for the first time, True pulled herself upright, fumbling for her robe.

Gently her aunt pushed her back. "Oh, my darling, you had us all so scared! But not too fast—easy—give yourself time."

Time? There was no time! That was the last she remembered clearly. What followed came back in fragments with voids between. Never mind the blow on her head . . . not when people were killing other people . . .

It *all* came back then. Jerry's bringing her to one of the cabins on the mountains. Men making a litter . . . bringing her home . . . so they weren't all gone? True must have spoken aloud, for Aunt Chrissy filled her in. "Remember Young Wil's departure, sweetheart?"

True nodded with a half-smile. "What a foolhardy thing to do, brat! Can't I trust you to stay out of trouble. This is a nasty blow, Uncle Wil. Give me a hand—I have to go, but, yes, you stay. We never know what'll happen. I'm glad you sent for the girls—*hold still!*"

"Wil North," True managed to mumble numbly, "you—are—bos-sy—"

She may have argued or pleaded—or had she dreamed that part? Either way, he was as convinced as she that one person could save the world. And now he was gone . . . but would she have it otherwise?

"School's dismissed," Aunt Chrissy went on to say. "The roof was blown off—and the children are in no condition to study. Kearby and Clarry are home—and you know why. It was a case of mistaken identity. The kidnappers could return—now, stay put—"

"I'm hungry! And then there are a million things I must do."

But first she must learn the facts. And they came from all sources. Faster than True would have believed possible.

The first night True sat up, a woolly blanket wrapped about her and her toes toasting before the widemouthed fireplace where a blazing fire cast friendly shadows leaping over the waxed furniture in the Big House parlor, a surprise guest came calling. At the loud, persistent knock, Kearby and Clarry scampered to the kitchen. Jerry rose, hesitated, and picked up Uncle Wil's hunting rifle.

"Not on your life!" Jerry's mother sprang forward and grabbed the gun. "We do *not* settle problems that way. *No violence.* You know that."

Jerry stood straight and tall. Then he decisively opened the latch.

Without prelude, a bulky, rain-soaked man burst into the room. True's shock was so great that her eyes could focus only on the puddles of muddy water forming around the enormous boots, worn so thin that two toes were visible. *Mr. Courtland, the man she had disarmed!*

"Ain't no social call, this," he said, nervously twisting his hat and glancing with combined awe and uneasiness around the cozy room. "I jest had t'tell of circumstances 'mongst our people. It's beholdin' I am t'yuh, Miz North. Yer one fine lady—and brave'rn them three whut walked through far—*fire*—in th' Good Book—not gittin' their feet burnt! Savin' m'baby, Little Susie, 'n all th' rest—depend on us t'be rewardin' y'all with 'nuther of them roasted pigs. God bless ye—" he wiped his eyes, almost overcome with emotion. "Guess I better be sittin'. Th' rest'll take a spell..."

His story began.

There was a great commotion as the men from Centerville cantered into Slippery Elm, which was all but deserted. Just beyond, a great group had congregated to see the outcome of a "dilly of a fight" which was a downright peculiar one. Two men had married twin sisters (cousins, of course, all being inbred). The women got caught in the rainstorm, one making it across the rain-swollen stream and the other stuck on the other side. Well, the husbands were waiting and the one closest to the river grabbed what he thought was his wife, but 'twas the twin. When the stream settled back to normal, the other man crossed to get his wife. Only problem was they got themselves the wrong women. That was history.

But this was now—in this storm. Seems like when they found out the difference the men decided they'd better get trading, might even have to offer "boot." Trouble was, the "confounded women" didn't want to change back, and the men were madder than hornets. The principle of the thing, you know. So they were all yelling like bats outta you-know-where. Now should they get shooting or act like their wives said? Could mean 'twas meant to be...

A preacher—kind of funny-like one—came. Randy Somebody. Must have been "Prim'tive," for he said they'd have to switch back. Had those men crying and saying they hadn't meant any harm—wanted to be baptized while the creek was high. Preacher had a hard time telling them they'd all be drowned. But they said 'twas fine. They'd die clean—

True found herself wanting to burst into laughter. No wonder the girls, who had summoned enough courage to peek around the door facing, were stifling snickers. But what had this to do with the critical situation between the two groups of Appalachian people? Chris Beth asked. "And you girls," she called over her shoulder without turning, "get the coffee boiling. Our guest must be chilled."

Oh, but it did have something to do with it! Mr. Courtland's weathered face crinkled into a smile. "God's way of lettin' tempers cool—'n do His mir'cle! Sudden-like there wuz a tug on this arm here—'n then on 'tother. 'N, bless Pete, thar they wuz—my gals—my *beau*-tee-fulest li'l gals in this ole worl'! Safer'n a pig in a poke!"

The big mountaineer took leave as unceremoniously as he had entered—refusing coffee and refusing to answer any more questions. Two of his boys had taken their sisters home. Now he must be with their mother.

There was no sleep at the Big House that night. Where was Young Wil? What had happened to cause the release of the two Courtland girls held captive? Who was responsible? True would feel better if Grandma Mollie were here, only to have Jerry blurt out, "She's with the men—insisted that the bereaved womenfolk would need comforting."

"With them?" True said dully. "You mean—why, I didn't even know O'Higgin went, and now you tell me this. Grandma Mollie in Slippery Elm," she repeated, unable to believe her ears. "Has everybody gone crazy?"

"Up there, yes, I'd be a-sayin' thet's accurate-like." There had been a prolonged silence as True's question hung between them. And now it was answered by Miss Mollie herself. "I let myself in th' back way. O'Higgin's tetherin' th' horse thataway. Like ourse'ves, th' nag gits winded—"

"Oh, Grandma Mollie!" When True sprang to where the big woman had sunk wearily into a rocker, she was followed immediately by the rest of the family, all chorusing, "Tell us—*tell* us!"

"Leave me Mollie-gal ketchin' a wee bit o'air!" O'Higgin boomed as he slammed the kitchen door against the wave of cold morning air.

"Yuh wanta tell hit—go ahead—after yuh stomp them muddy boots!" his wife ordered in her scrubbed-clean household voice. Of course, in the end, it was the two of them who gave the account as they saw it.

The Reverend Randy had himself a real problem, a bear by the tail, they said—even before the Centerville army came looking for trouble.

Early in the year as it was, 'twas time to store barrels of liquid spirits to mix with the other kind of Spirit that preachers always hoped to generate in their summer tent meetings. No real problem, mind you, amongst the Slippery Elm folks—Reverend Randy and Marty (oh, what a pair!) had just about dried that place out. Until the arrival of "that clan." Humph! Claiming that 'twas a necessary part of the revival—had to have communion, didn't they? Now Randy and Tillie refused to deal with the stuff, so they brought their own to peddle. Sold it, too, at a whopping profit, until Randy ordered them out—called them a tribe of Gypsies and worse, a "den of thieves." Mad to the core, they were all out to get Randy. But would you believe the mountain folks who came riding in to make trouble ended it? Leastwise, stalled it for awhile.

The rumor made the rounds somehow. And one big mortal just up and preached himself! " 'Tain't God's will we go shootin' preachers—guess that'd take us all to th' fiery pit yer so 'feared of yuh fled th' homeland! Whatta bunch of cowards 'n hypocrits—hellbound! Thet preacher's right! No wonder our child'urn's a disgrace, built of th' same dust as their parents—'n jest as dirty! Know why? *We made 'em thet way*!"

There was a mumbling amongst the crowd, then silence so thick you could serve it on a platter. Even the katydids hushed making music. Hearts began hammering like a cabin was being roofed. And then!

"Hit ain't right," another man yelled from the angry mob of uninvited guests. "Us wantin' t'lay down arms lack we do, 'cuz we're seekin' out a edju-*ca*-shun 'n wuz seein' th' light—'til yuh done this hor'ble thang—stealin' our innocent virgins—ye servants of th' devil!"

There was a terrible commotion then. *Terrible*. Everybody on the opposite side of the river drew their guns, then, appearing to think a minute, replaced them. But their protests were so loud that "that body of peacemakers—you know, th' wonderful kinfolks of Clarry's—heard and just boldly marched into all, singin' praises like th' katydids—" Miss Mollie began, only to be interrupted by her husband.

"Begory! They jest up 'n poured all thet rot-gut into the risen river, they did, they did! Howled like wildcats, eh, Mollie-gal? Th' owners, they be. Whilst some of them thet be pretenders of faith took on th' notion 'twould be a good time fer bein' 'baptized in th' spirit—down stream, that be!"

"Irish is a-tellin' hit straight—'ceptin' fer th' vital part! Turns out them Appalachians wuzn't responsible a-tall—"

"Right ye be, me lassie! Right ye be! But t'git back to me version, th' hypocrits wantin' t'be 'baptized in th' spirit' got theirselves one whoppin' surprise. Our folks up 'n whipped out guns—and me, I be wishin' fer me bagpipes t'celebrate—feelin' 'twas justified usin' weapons in sech case as this be—"

"Killin's never justified, O'Higgin!"

O'Higgin laughed and did a jig. "'Twarn't necessary. Them cowards jest dropped t'their knees 'n begged fer mercy—hard tellin' if they be a-pleadin' t'th' Almighty on 'is throne er them thet be on th' riverside!"

True shook her head. Unbelievable, all of it. But where was her husband? Yet what she must ask was: "If they didn't, who did? I mean, who took my students?"

"Oh, thet—" Grandma Mollie shrugged as if that were a minor part of the whole scenario. "Why, 'twas th' crooks seekin' Adamson's loot. Th' militia arrived, found 'em, 'n hauled 'em off t'court without takin' time t'tear down their ugly faces from th' post-office wall, 'n guess whut!"

She was about to say that the awful war had ended, that folks would go on to tell about the legend of True North...

33

"Starbright"

The next day dawned bright and clear—just right for turning the calendar to "April." True woke up early, feeling refreshed and completely restored. The morning star still lingered in the west when she stole out of the Big House and hurried to the cabin. She must clean house and have sourdough pancakes ready for mixing when Young Wil arrived. This was the day her husband would be home—her heart told her so. She unbraided her hair, brushed it vigorously, and then—allowing it to cascade down her back—knelt at the window still in her robe. "Good morning, Lord; there is so much to thank You for—and one of them is for hanging the stars in the sky—stars to light the night—and stars of hope—"

Again she looked at the star, its brilliance lighting the horizon. Who said one must pray with eyes closed? Hers were wide open, lighted with awe at God's handiwork. "Starlight, star bright—" she incorporated into her prayer, so lost in wonder that she failed to hear the little squeak of joy which the cabin door always gave when someone entered.

"'First star I see tonight'—and it's tangled into your hair."

The words were soft, tender, almost reverent. "Wil—*Wil*! Oh, my darling—my darling!"

True was in her husband's arms, held with such tenderness that it seemed almost a sacrilege when he kissed her ear and whispered, "What's for breakfast, my little heroine?"

Over pancakes, Young Wil rounded out the story, made it come alive for True. No need pretending, he grinned as he poured honey generously over a third helping—he was scared, just plain scared. He, Marty, the Valley folk who went along with O'Higgin, and the two ministers decided it was prudent not to interfere unless the situation got out of hand. Did they have a hand in the truce? Well—he guessed so—who could say? The outcome, of course, had to be an answer to prayers which flooded heaven. But who could have guessed *how* God would choose to go about it?

True laid down her fork. "I just never dreamed—are you aware of how much the two clans *hated* each other? It was a prime example of the irresistible force meeting head-on with the immovable object—if such a condition were possible."

"You don't believe that can happen, huh?" he grinned over his coffee cup.

"I doubt it. Some day that force would come up against something that proved it to be irresistible—or the immovable object would budge—I think. I'm not smart like you—so you tell *me*."

"Not smart? Ha! Women have always been our superiors. They just have the good sense to keep it to themselves. I quite agree with your logic, Mrs. North, but—let's suppose it *were* possible?"

True shook her heavy hair, pushing at a curl that kept falling over her right eye. She squinted in concentration, then turned palms up.

"Both would be consumed by friction."

"So," she said slowly, "that's how it happened—and they both realized they would be destroyed—here and in the hereafter—"

Young Wil looked longingly at the stack of brown sourdough pancakes. "Get thee behind me, Satan!" Then, wiping his mouth determinedly and refolding his napkin, he returned to the Appalachians. "Of course, they disliked giving in—kept chipping away at trivia—which church was *The Church*—amusing claims about Luther, Wesley, even John the Baptist (claiming he was a Primitive, of course!). But what clinched the deal was, of all people, that bold little foreman of the Double N! Billy Joe marched up and stood between the armies separated by a river and stubborn thinking.

"Now looky here, folks. D'yuh honest-to-Pete think th' first question our Maker's a-gonna ask is, 'Which denomination wuz yuh?' "

The Reverend Randy, taking advantage over the sudden silence, moved in to outline the plan, the *real* plan to salvation, raising his voice until it rang against the mountain. (The Slippery Elm folk needed a message of "th' ole-time religion" through the mouth of a "God-fearin' man whut wuzn't a-feared t'speak up.") Dr. Miller followed, wading right out into the threatening current of the water, and talked about living out that Plan. "Are you aware," the big man with the gentle voice asked, "that first and foremost we are to love God with all our hearts—the first commandment—and that *all* the others relate to man's love for his brother? Think about it," he pleaded.

Billy Joe, overcome with the limelight he had captured, wasn't about to lose it. "Ever hear of shootin' yer neighbor 'cuz yuh love 'im so much—did'ja, huh? Yuh gotta minister to 'em—thet's whut—'n thet means bustin' up them stills, so as not t'take advantage of another man's weakness like a bunch of buzzards—understan'? Otherwise, ye cain't go 'round askin' t'be baptized—thet'd be empty as some of yer thick skulls! Wanna git into heaven—huh?"

They understood.

Young Wil consulted his pocketwatch and whistled. "I'm late—"

"Late! Wil North, you've had no sleep for a week!"

He laughed. "Now who's being bossy? You, the *perfect* model—want to spoil your reputation?"

"*Perfect*? Who said *that*?"

"All of them—both sides! Poor Billy Joe's moment of glory was short-lived. All began babbling about how it was you who taught their children right from wrong and the children brought the ideas home. Come with me while I shave."

True lifted the heavy kettle, wondering if there was enough hot water. Fortunately there was. She hurried to the bedroom and poured the white china washbasin full. There was a burst of steam and immediately the mirror above the washstand was fogged over. Before blotting it clean, she looked at her blurred image, unable to recognize her reflection. *Who am I, Lord?* her heart whispered. *Just what do You expect of me?*

The moment passed. Seating herself on the slipper chair nearby, she asked a long series of questions, listening raptly while her husband filled her in between practiced strokes of the straight razor, making neat ravines through the mountains of white lather. Yes, of course, he saw Marty's family. Helped celebrate the March Hare's birthday, in fact. Midgie loved the tiny gold ring that True ordered through Meier and Frank's with "Chris" engraved inside along with his birthday. "She probably told you the details," Young Wil said, reaching sheepishly into his back pocket to pull out a crumpled envelope. And, yes, he had a chance to talk briefly with Tillie, though not long enough to find out the secret of that glow on her face. Anna-Lee had been in touch with Clarry.

"She wants the girl back and is perfectly capable of teaching her at home—they all prefer that, you know. There's a real change in Clarry—and I," he paused to wrap a hot towel around his face and mumble through it, "give you credit for that, too. She identified with the diary—says our generation is repeating the history recorded, and," removing the towel, he looked straight into her eyes, "that theirs will carry on in the same tradition. Now, don't ask where she fits in—I think you know. Just be prepared to use that fatal charm of yours on Chrissy—uh, *Aunt* Chrissy—one hill at a time. Now, no more questions—do I have a clean white shirt? Oh, all the hands send love, and of course an invitation to visit. And no begging's necessary," he grinned, buttoning the starched shirt that True had laid out wordlessly. "We'll go just as soon as this book and exam are finished, I promise. Button the top, sweetie."

True wanted to rush into his arms with a squeal of delight, but something bothered her about the way he kept talking as if to head off further questions. What was he withholding?

"All right, out with it!" she said suddenly. "Something's wrong."

She had expected him to remind her of the time. Instead, he sat down on the edge of the bed and motioned her to join him. "Yes—something *is* wrong, having nothing to do with the reconciliation—at least, not directly." He dropped his head into his hands. Alarmed, True placed a supporting arm about his slumped-over shoulders and waited.

"What I saw there made me sick. And I don't know how to handle it. If I explain the medical facts, they're sure to equate it with 'God's will,' predestination, or God's way of showing His wrath for their sins. Some of the problems we can solve with a health program such as you have going here. Education's slow, but it will get them there eventually. But meantime—well, help me figure out what to do."

They were going blind, almost all of them. Young Wil's voice choked with emotion. They called it "sore eyes" and washed them with salt water, which was like pouring oil on a spreading fire. The eyes burned worse. They clawed and tore at them because of the irritation—yes, there was a name for it, *trachoma,* according to Uncle Wil's medical book. And the prognosis was worse than what they endured now. Blurred vision first, then the eyeballs would dry up in their sockets—blindness. And (True was sure he almost gagged) then there was another kind of problem, with eyes rolling around in their skulls. This afflicted the newest generation. Unable to focus. Couldn't read. Could hardly see to feed themselves. Research showed that some, maybe all, of the problem was due to intermarriages practiced over a long history. Of course, there were other problems. Typhoid had begun cropping up. Fortunately, he had vaccine to begin an immunization program—but they needed three injections—and then there was lung fever, hookworm, and trichinosis from a heavy diet of pork—

One of Young Wil's fists struck the opposite palm with a *whang*!

Sickened, True tried to make her voice sound steady. "One hill at a time, darling—remember? Go back. I'll finish the school year and join you. Then we can get answers and help from the State Department of Health when you're called to Portland—"

"I've been summoned. The date is April fifteenth." His voice was flat with acceptance of failure. "And you can't leave—not now—"

"Things will work out, darling. We *won't* surrender. Let's pray!"

There was no progress in getting the roof on the school repaired. Men promised to help, but they had problems with damage at home. All this aroused Nate Goldsmith's ire so that his screams of rage would have done credit to a bull moose. The school remained without a roof.

Feeling depressed, True suggested to Chris Beth that they get an early start and pay Miss Mollie a call. It would be good for them all. Taken by surprise, the older woman gathered up her colorful scraps and rolled them into a bundle while trying with one hand to hoist the quilting frame to the ceiling. The result was a scattering of diamond-shaped scraps all over the floor of Turn-Around Inn's parlor.

"How lovely!" The guests hurried to give their hostess a hand. "Who will receive this—oh, *these*, two of them! A full-size and a wee one?"

"They're promised—leastwise, in my mind. A surprise, sort of."

True laughed. "Is the pattern a secret, too?"

Grandma Mollie relaxed. "Not on yer life—'tis 'Star Bright'!"

34

Volunteers for Jesus

Easter!

Never before had Centerville Church held such a crowd as was in attendance the following Sunday. Word had circulated that the mountaineers were coming en masse. And then there were the faithful of the Valley. In addition, there were newcomers—actually well-known, but strangers to the church. Probably out of curiosity, True whispered to Aunt Chrissy.

Well, they couldn't have chosen a better day, Aunt Chrissy was to whisper back, tears coursing down her cheeks . . .

Dr. Miller shook hands with them all as they entered, calling the regulars by name. "Punkie" Perkins, who claimed to be an atheist, was noted for being on the defensive. "What kind of doctor are yuh—treat animals er human bodies?"

"I treat men's souls," Dr. Miller answered with a smile.

A little flustered, Punkie muttered, "Well, yuh got'cher work cut out fer yuh here'bouts. Want me t'plead fer mercy?"

"God does." The gentle answer sent Punkie slinking into a corner.

That set the mood. The mountain folk, scrubbed, starched, and well-behaved, overheard and, with a look of pity at the man, marched with unexpected dignity to the very front pews.

Dr. Miller related the incident in Slippery Elm without emotion. "What they need more than cash contributions is love and understanding, and eventually some teaching *by people who understand.* What they need are recruits."

The closing song rang out:

> A volunteer for Jesus, a soldier true,
> Others have enlisted, why not you?

One could see the exhilaration in faces of the "Uplanders" as they stormed the pulpit. "Yuh ast fer recruits, yuh got 'em—learnin' t'read th' Good Book 'n cleanin' up th' mother-tongue, well as our sinful ways, Doc—'n who can be understandin' better'n us?"

Dr. Miller could not argue with that. Neither did he seem to doubt the good people's sincerity. A few low questions. A pumping of hands. Tears. And there were those who said Punkie Perkins crawled out the back window to escape being mobbed.

It was then that Jerry, followed by Kearby and Clarry (holding hands as if for strength) walked down the inclined aisle. "You asked for volunteers," Jerry's voice wavered only slightly. "Here are three. We've dreamed of faraway places—China, Africa—and talked about the needs in Slippery Elm. But that's a long way off. We just want to answer the call right now—then go back to school to prepare ourselves. 'Study to show thyself approved,' I think the Bible puts it—"

The minister was too overcome to do more than put his arms around them. That's when Chris Beth commenced to cry. Not that she cried alone.

The touching moment was shattered by Nate Goldsmith's bull-moose voice. "Now, how 'bout some volunteer *laborers*? None of this puts a roof on th' school." A few hands went up, but not enough to shake a roof. "Well," Nate looked at them pityingly, "'As ye sow, so shall ye reap.' Guess yuh'd ruther jest shut th' door in young faces—end th' year—"

The protests the little man expected failed to come. There was a shout of glee from the children instead, then another round of applause when O'Higgin suggested that the Valley ladies pack barrels of dried fruit, smoked meat, and usable clothing for the Centerville Appalachians to take to their

Slippery Elm brethren. "Hard it be, ye should be knowin', t'pray on a empty stummick—want I should pronounce the benediction?"

Dr. Miller nodded. The congregation joined hands. The benediction was powerful.

35

Some Went, Others Stayed

Clarry returned the diary to True the day she departed to finish the school year with Kearby. There were tears in her lovely eyes. "I am torn between three worlds," she said. "Kearby's world, this beautiful Valley—and, yes, uh—Jerry—and Anna-Lee Hancock, who is my family. But the diary helped. I am not the first to wonder which direction I must take—eventually—oh, what a beautiful Easter—"

There was a sudden blast of April-sweet air as the door was flung open to admit O'Higgin into the cabin. Had he knocked? Or eavesdropped?

"Th' top o'th' mornin' to ye, lassies!" he smiled with a doff of his hat, then picked right up on the conversation. "Decisions never be easy, me bonnie one. Think back on Christopher Columbus—think 'twas easy fer 'im t'set sail on a square ocean? Then th' Pilgrims, so we be worshipin' as we be choosin' —tho' sometimes I be needin' t'borrow me a school dictionary t'tell what brand o'faith most lay claim to. Be thet no matter—long as we love Jesus—oh, 'twas right proud o'ye I be yesterday, lass! Then there be me own ancestors—rest their souls—who be makin' th' greater contribution t'history, them what lef' when th' potato crops failed er them whut be stayin' t'build back? Who be th' quitter? None o'them," he answered himself. "All be hearin' th' voice o'God—jest like you, lass—jest like th' clan bustin' up on th' mountainside—some gonna be stayin' jest like True and her Young Wil—"

There was no chance for Clarry Hancock to reply, for Kearby had come to bid her goodbye. Chris Beth was with her to hurry them along, but even so they were delayed by an unexpected turn of events.

Clarry's serious mood disappeared with a dimpled grin, a reminder of how young she was. "Did you show True his picture?"

Kearby's face reddened. The glance she gave her mother from lowered eyelids was uneasy. Chris Beth met her daughter's eyes levelly.

"We have always been open, Kearby—all of us—as a family. I have no idea who *he* is and have no intention of prying—"

True walked over to embrace her cousin, whom she thought of as Baby Sister. "Who is the Mystery Man, sweetie? Want to share him?"

Kearby's lower lip trembled as if she were on the verge of tears. Clarry's regret at her question showed in her face. But, to the surprise of them all, Kearby lifted her chin, shoved a hand into an overstuffed bag, and, after fumbling for some time, pulled out the photograph of the young man. Young, yes, but older than these girls, one glance told True. The thin, bespectacled face held a certain charm. What was the look? Determination? Dedication? Whatever, it was appealing. And True said as much, praying that Aunt Chrissy would soft-pedal her concerns.

And she did. "Is this the young man you wrote about? Why haven't you brought him for a visit? The brother of a friend, you wrote?"

Little lights of joy flared in Kearby's face and the words tumbled out. Kevin was wonderful. Handsome in a mature way, enough older to make boys her age look silly. How much older? Nine years, maybe, and *so* brilliant and devoted to his college work—going to be a minister like Uncle Joe. Kearby was *so* glad Mother understood; she could tell by Aunt Vangie's diary that the sisters had seen so many kinds of love . . . Young Wil's for his teacher (Chris Beth) . . .

Mother's for Uncle Joe, then Daddy... and don't forget (triumphantly) that Young Wil was as much older than True as Kevin is my senior. "Of course, we have to make decisions... a long time from now..."

Wagons loaded ("lock, stock, 'n barrel," Nate described it), the mountaineers left just short of April fifteenth. Even in the excitement of the self-proclaimed "evangelists'" departure, the date set wheels turning in True's head. The date was significant... well, of *course* it was... the day Young Wil was scheduled to make his presentation before the august Board. And she could go! Why, the roofless school had proven a blessing—letting the mountaineers take their children and leave for Slippery Elm and allowing her to go with her husband!

A sea of faces swam around her... beautiful blond angels... and, in contrast, those with midnight hair and eyes (proof of a commingling of genes)... and those with carrot-red hair and a sprinkling of freckles marching across small noses. And then there was Buster—big, brutal Buster, who had learned to deal with life in his own way. Books were a waste of paper for the onetime bully, but he had powerful muscles and a will of iron. God could make use of more like him. If Buster could learn the value of obedience, anybody could. After all, no matter what one's "doctrine," wasn't obedience a key word? "I ain't never gonna be full of frivol a'gin, Teacher, all cuz of you loved me 'n learnt me Jesus kin put th' likes of me t'work. I dun made my paw see th' light." "Boy's right," his hardheaded, giant father (who once met life with balled-up fists) agreed. "Ain't a-gonna lay a hand on nobody 'ceptin' t'try healin' their souls. But yuh kin betcha life I'm a-gonna meet thet incestin' head-on—gonna bury hit, 'n be a pallbearer fer th' fun'ral!"

"Now, be rememberin'," O'Higgin blew his nose and began, "ther' be no disgrace in failure—"

Mr. Courtland saluted smartly. "Lessen ye blame it on somebody else!"

The children made a great production of saying good-bye, weeping, holding to True's skirts, and worshiping her with their eyes. True withheld her tears until they were out of sight. And then she wept bitterly, for a part of her heart was gone.

36

The Outside World

Once, at the top of the rise leading out of the Valley, True looked over her shoulder for one last look at the painted scene spread as far as the eye could see. Orchards in full bloom. Gardens lushly verdant with promise. And newly scarred land which—after removal of the conifer trees—became "black gold" to tillers of the rich, raw land. Every person she knew and loved took on substance in a new form, as if momentarily God gave her a peek into their very souls. "You would be proud of us, Angel Mother," she mused as if she sat alone in the buggy seat—"those who left to fulfill God's purpose, and those who remained behind for the same reason."

Young Wil pretended not to see her wipe away a tear. "And now, it's on to Portland!" True smiled. Then she laughed aloud. "Do you realize that we're going to get that honeymoon at last?"

The room felt stuffy. Her eyelids felt heavy, so heavy. Maybe she was coming down with—what was that horrible eye disease? True wondered vaguely if Young Wil had incorporated—*trachoma*, that was it—in his case studies. But listen, she must *listen*. Someone, a portly gentleman with a stern face, was introducing Young Wil. Their future lay at stake.

"Gentlemen," her husband was saying, "before presenting my paper, may I present my wife, True North, without whose help I would have been unable to conduct the live research. *True!*"

Taken by surprise, she stood. Aware only of a spattering of polite applause by the men, she concentrated on his opening statement: "We are caught in a decade of change. And, lest we move too fast—no matter what cries out from the human body for help—there must be research and case studies. Science alone is not enough, unless we test it. Medicine is like a limpet at midtide struggling to be at home on the land of the past and the sea of the future. Tenaciously and nostalgically, too often sentimentally, one foot desperately clinging to the anchor of certainty of home remedies while the other reaches for the unknown. Our glory lies in seeing ourselves as guardians—riding out the tide of untested trends. What have we in common in this hall today? We are doctors, under oath to treat the flesh and—according to my thesis—*the relationship between the mind and the body*. Call it Mental Health!"

The men listened respectfully. Then, they—like her—became so absorbed that her "studies," combined with her husband's observations, took on flesh, walking and talking up and down the aisles, crying out for help—and getting it. How? By conviction that someone listened... understood... and cared...

"Oh, darling, you were eloquent," True whispered shakily as hand-in-hand they left the men to caucus for what might be hours or days.

"I had *you*. I watched your eyes, pretending the committee cared as much—and, in a way, I guess they do. Time will tell. What we need is oxygen to clear our brains!"

"You mean noise to numb them—let's take a walk—and not think."

Eagerly they descended the stairs and were about to go out the front door when Young Wil stopped. "Oh, I need to see these people," he said, reading aloud: "STATE DEPARTMENT OF HEALTH AND WELFARE."

True understood and sat down on a bench against the wall. Then feeling suddenly weary, she closed her eyes—only to have them fly open at the sound of Michael St. John's "True North!" and then teasingly, "We have to stop meeting like this!"

True felt genuinely pleased to see him, and invited him to sit down. "Only for a moment," Michael said. "I guess we are both wondering what brought the other here."

True explained, and he was sympathetic. "I would spend no time worrying over the doctor's 'pass' or 'fail' chances. He's a bright man, True, and among the most dedicated. As for the needs of our mountain people, nobody is more aware than I. I wish," he said slowly, "that God had shaken my shoulders before He did—think of what I could have done back there in Atlanta for the deprived—"

"It is never too late, Michael. I am proud of you—but, tell me what you are doing here."

His face lighted up. "I'm working on getting a school in Slippery Elm—so much red tape—but I might as well make use of the pull I have with some of the powers that be. I know them all through my holdings in the railroads, which, as rumor has it, may come under government control. Then," he inhaled deeply, "I am giving thought to entering the political arena. Washington could use some tough but caring men. 'Congressman St. John'—how about that, huh?"

True smiled in encouragement but had no time to reply. The head of an austere woman who looked for all the world as if she had been sucking on a lemon popped out of the "DEPARTMENT OF EDUCATION" door. "Mr. Alexander will see you now—*only* you," she added with a forbidding look.

The old debonair Michael returned. He winked at True boldly, making sure that the man-tailored woman saw. "Where are you staying?" he called over his shoulder.

"We call it 'Honeymoon Hotel'—ours—"

A look of near-envy crossed his face. The woman remained at the door, her eyes narrowing in suspicion. For Michael, laughter, even in the face of uncertainty, came easy. True found herself joining him now. For that she was always grateful, as it was the last time she was to see him in person, although his face would smile triumphantly in *The Oregonian* the next election year. And his name would be engraved one day on the ST. JOHN SCHOOL in a town once called Slippery Elm.

Young Wil was smiling when he came back. The health department was going to send a committee to Slippery Elm to "investigate matters." That must surely translate into help, since nobody could fail to see the need.

But she said nothing, for no misgivings must spoil his mood. Why, her husband was whistling under his breath in a way she had not heard him do for what the mountain people would call a "coon's age." Unbidden, more of their colloquialisms swarmed back—"noisome" . . . "brutishism" . . . and such Biblical words as "verily, verily" . . . "hireling" . . . "at cock's crow" . . . "I say unto you" . . . "art" (for *are*). *Stop this,* True ordered her mind. But she realized then that the people she had grown to love and understand had perhaps come closer to the original language of the Bible than some of the other interpreters. What's more, they had left more than a speech pattern which would crop up unexpectedly now and then among descendants of the original Oregon settlers as the years went by. As for herself—well, they had done more than take away a part of her heart; they had left a part of theirs in return.

Young Wil was still whistling. Should he—in the city? It seemed almost inappropriate to express one's joy here. Well, proper or not, money couldn't purchase from her the thrill of seeing the exuberance in her husband's face. He looked downright little-boyish as he stopped at the building's exit and said, "'*Eloquent*'? Did I really do that well—or," hesitating uncertainly, "just how do you define the word?"

His speech, he must be talking about. Young Wil, who was always so sure of himself, should take to heart her adjective? True felt like whistling herself! "Eloquent?" (How *would* she define it? He just *was*!) "I guess," she said slowly, "eloquent is saying the just-right words—and no more."

"Oh, darling!" Young Wil grabbed her up and swung her around. "I'm going to buy you the prettiest dress in Portland!"

"Wil North," True gasped in embarrassment, "put me down! What will people think?"

"That we're in love!" he laughed triumphantly before setting True on her feet. "Everything's coming up roses—you've made me feel it!"

True was giddy with happiness. She might as well have been sipping liquid ambrosia from the peak of Mount Olympus. Oh, God was good!

Outside, True could only gasp at the scene spread before her. Where were all these people going in such a hurry—ladies sweeping grandly down the boardwalks with heads held so high True marveled that they didn't trip over their pointed-toe shoes? And look at those hats! Bedecked with flowers and ribbons, the brims were so large it was bewildering that the elegant ladies could avoid colliding with one another. Most had male escorts dressed in proper black (resembling undertakers to True). The men held their heads just as proudly. They were shod with glistening shoes and spats and carried canes without needing them!

Sighing, True cast one glance at the simple blue broadcloth suit she had bought on the "Better Dress" rack at Solomon's. Imagine her thinking that the brooch would look too ornate for Young Wil's presentation! "I'll take you up on that offer for a new dress," she said.

Not that he could hear her above the earsplitting noise. The metallic grind of trolley wheels against their tracks. The clopping of horses' feet against a hard-surface street. The screams of vendors. The backfiring of automobiles. And, above it all, the shrill whistles of seagoing vessels mingled with whistles of smoking manufacturing plants. Why, the very sun was blotted out of the sky periodically as something resembling standpipes belched out smoke. A veil of (True shivered at the word) Stygian darkness overhead.

It would be good to see light, even artificial, inside a store.

In an exclusive boutique True passed over the frilly finery, settling instead for a dark, up-to-date suit, but agreed with the saleslady that the rose-pink blouse was right. A hairdo? True looked at the elaborate coiffures of the boardwalk strollers and knew it was foolish to have a professional do her hair, only to cover it with a hat. So which? At Young Wil's urging, she decided on the hairstyling. Her reward was his gasp of admiration at the nest of golden curls on top, the back caught up smartly in a figure eight.

"One of those wagon-wheel things the other ladies wear would spoil it. But come with me—" So, he had been window shopping?

Smiling, he led her into a millinery shoppe next door. "Oh, so this is your lovely wife," the milliner said kindly, "and here is what your husband has in mind—three pink ruffles which fit snugly between the becoming curls and the stylish figure eight."

This time it was True who gasped. She was no longer the country mouse. Why not be frivolous—maybe even a bit dramatic? But, no, not the ostrich boa. Nothing else, thank you. True walked out of the shoppe holding herself in a stately manner, wondering (with an inner giggle) if she "swept" along instead of walking...

The beautiful honeymoon-week was magic-filled. Unaware that admiring glances followed wherever they went, Mr. and Mrs.—*no*, Dr. and Mrs.—Wilson North II strolled the boardwalk unfalteringly. They held hands seated in the privacy of an intimate alcove where a young man with a celluloid collar served them... attended theaters and operas in the afternoons... and strolled the beach barefoot at night... then attended a formal church service on Sunday—the only place, oddly, where they felt ignored and ill-at-ease. The congregation faced forward during the service and each other afterward, ignoring the strangers in their midst. Fellowship? A foreign word...

April twenty-second? True would remember the date forever. They were enjoying a leisurely breakfast in bed when the telegram arrived.

"Oh, no!" True's laughter filled the room, almost upsetting her coffee on the tray she balanced on her propped-up knees. "If that's the *family*—"

"It isn't." Young Wil had scanned the yellow sheet and begun to dress. "The committee has reached a decision. I must report *now*—"

He was pale and his hands shook, causing True's own heart to pick up tempo. She helped him adjust his tie and held out his coat. Too soon he was gone. For a year they had worked on a twin aim. Now he must stand before these men with rapier-sharp minds and hear their reaction to: 1. the problem; and 2. the solution.

The door swung open. Young Wil was back with his report. He grabbed True, still in her robe, and danced her around the room. "Did anybody ever tell you that you have the most beautiful eyes God ever used to complete a perfect face?"

"Wil North!" But the swing of his hands erased all solemnity. They went for the idea . . . bought the book and wanted another. *And* how soon could he assume duties as Chief-of-Staff at the big hospital under construction?

37

Crossroads

"It's almost May." Young Wil's statement pointed out the obvious. True knew, as he knew, that both of them had made small and meaningless conversation since boarding the train at Portland bound for Slippery Elm. Anything to avoid the decisions lying ahead.

Her husband tried again. "I hope," he said, running restless fingers through his thick hair, "we remembered gifts for everybody back home." They were at the crossroads and—

Question: *Where was home?*

True smoothed the folds of her old blue broadcloth. It seemed more appropriate to save her new purchases for some special occasion. "I think so. Diaries seemed appropriate for the girls—and Jerry, for some reason, has always wanted a feathered quill..."

A new pipe for Daddy Wil. Aunt Chrissy was right—he would never get away from chewing on the polished reed stem of his ancient corncob pipe, which often went unlighted. The newer ones, meerschaums, had celluloid stems. Aunt Chrissy would love the white India embroidered silk parasol with scalloped edges...and wait until Grandma Mollie saw the hardwood cabinet for her spices. *Spice!* The very word sent True's senses reeling...Miss Mollie's big kitchen with the monstrous cookstove, its warming closet always filling the air with the memorable fragrance of spice (which never quarreled somehow with the yeasty smell of rising sourdough). And then there were the seasonal smells—honeysuckle mingled with orchards-in-bloom in springtime, jam-ready grapes ripening in the summer sun, and the fingers of fragrance that reached out from every cranny when she baked the great, clove-stuck hams. True inhaled deeply, realizing that she was seeing the rails ahead through a blur. They never should have left—

Quickly, Young Wil picked up the conversation. "O'Higgin will love the *Song-Leaders' Manual* I found, all the new hymns included. He can read notes, you know—me, I'm a follower, but able to keep up by following his hair-raising baritone which shakes the rafters."

They summed up together then. A leather ledger (name embossed in gold) for Marty . . . an assortment of silk lilacs, daisy wreaths, and roses so real that one could almost smell them for Midgie, a dream-come-true . . . a hand-painted rocking horse for two-year-old Chris . . . a white ostrich feather fan for Mariah (on sale) . . . and, for Tillie and Reverend Randy, the most extravagant gifts of all. The delicate translucent-pink china cup with 22-karat gold on the fluted edge for Tillie's collection would be the most beautiful thing she had owned since leaving her Eastern "social-whirl" world in search of her niece, who would prove to be Marty's mother. She was starved for beauty. And, as for her dear friend, the minister, he needed a new Bible to replace the aging one from which he tried to teach. The leather-bound one, complete with colored maps and a comprehensive concordance, would thrill his soul and make it well worth the unbelievable price.

By now the Norths' cloud of concern had lifted and their excitement grew by the minute. They laughed over the other purchases—all practical. The ranch hands would be overjoyed with the burlap bags of new grain, the platform scale, the riveted cream cans, the improved dilution contraption for separating cream from the milk, and the new-style automatic rotary churn with a hand crank. *Oh, there went the whistle!*

True grabbed her paisley bag while Young Wil busied himself with the overhead luggage. "Where's the candy?" His words were garbled because he was holding the brim of his hat between his teeth.

the baggage car—horehound, peppermint sticks—
arling, *look* at the hills of home!"

er husband looked at her sharply, then realized that was not fully aware of her words; she was too engrossed in the view. How could she ever have thought of the landscape here as benign? The straight-up cliffs following the curve of the rushing river, less heavily forested than the Valley beyond the "hum," were beautiful in their own way. Roots of the giant oaks clung to the eroded cliffs—gnarled and inspiring in their fight for life—amid boulders that even now were shifting colors like a kaleidoscope, the patterns of light and shadow always changing. In the back country, clumps of leafless field lilies sprang up in unexpected beauty, and occasionally a person could find the near-extinct trillium among the wood violets in glades of sword fern. Strange that now even the savage-billed vultures sailing in search of the carcass of a baby lamb or calf had a certain charm—graceful in their near-still wings which flashed iridescent-purple against the sun. They were doing the work that nature intended. Scavengers though they were, the giant birds cleared the landscape, preventing disease. How life had changed True's outlook! She saw the balance of nature in a new way. A new balance, too, in people—all fulfilling God's purpose one way or another . . .

And it was quiet. So quiet. The city seemed far away. Just a restful silence that restored her soul—

And burst her eardrums! "Surprise! *Surprise*!" Surely a million voices chanted wildly, the echoes bouncing back from the canyon walls.

What on earth? Who—? *Who*? Just everybody she and Young Wil had ever known—both here and in the Valley! Aunt Chrissy . . . Daddy Wil . . . O'Higgin waving his shillelagh . . . Grandma Mollie waving her best silk handkerchief. True's eyes were unable to focus on them all, except that some inner instinct told her that all those for whom she and Young Wil had purchased gifts were *here*—and that Midgie and Marty (holding the March Hare) were elbowing their way through the crowd.

"Midgie—oh, Midgie darling—you're *pregnant*!" True gasped in surprise as her sister-in-law reached out in an effort to embrace her. "Talk about being 'great with child,'" she panted. "That's me—due for 'travail' any minute—when are you and Young Wil planning—" (a family? Yes, when?) . . .

Backslapping, hugging, everybody talking at once. Portland's noise could never rival *this*! And Tillie screaming above several heads, "I knew you'd come—I knew you'd make it for our wedding. I *knew* it!"

How on earth did little bowlegged Billy Joe, the Beetle, make it to Young Wil's side? "Midgie oughta be deliverin' 'bout th' same time as th' prize heifer! Guess she—th' boss's Missus—ain't a-gonna let a thang like thet keep 'er from holdin' the big blow-out—sez yuh done hit afore 'n kin do it a'gin—brang the girl-chile into th' world—"

Grandma Mollie shoved him aside. "Me? I'm a-gonna stan' up with th' bride 'n groom—Cousin Tillie 'n thet wonderful preacher-husband. Brangs back mem'ries—how I stood alongside yore precious mother a-holdin' Marty whilst Chris Beth took 'er vows—with our precious Vangie lookin' 'bout lack Midgie here—double weddin' lack yours—"

When she paused to blow her nose, O'Higgin interrupted, "Wonderful mon Cousin Tillie be takin'—wonderful mon—"

"*Man*," Miss Mollie corrected between blows of her nose.

Jerry exclaimed excitedly, "I'm hiking up through the Gap. They'll be here tomorrow—both factions of the Appalachians—but somebody ought to tell them we've arrived safely."

"And, besides, I can't wait," he might as well have added.

Tomorrow the children would be swinging to her skirts, all talking at once as the adults were doing now. True was glad that she and Young Wil had run what must have been all the candy stores in Portland in short supply. She was glad, too, that their choice of gifts for Tillie and Randy were their most elegant purchase. Just right for a bride and groom. And, how could she have chosen a more suitable outfit for a wedding? Not that she and Young Wil would be in the wedding party. The day belonged to an older generation, which was as it should be. The world needed to know that love was not reserved for youth, but that true love, blessed by the Spirit, endured timelessly, each year more precious than the one before. She wondered who would perform the ceremony—and then she saw Dr. Miller. Shovel in hand, he was helping dig the barbecue pit.

Oh, they had thought of everything! True felt she would burst with happiness. She was sure she could *hear* the vast acres of wheat growing... that the daisies which usually folded their white-petaled lashes at sunset wouldn't sleep a wink tonight... and that the May moon rising over the Gap truly *was* made of green cheese.

A small tug at her skirt told True she was not alone. In a nursery-rhyme mood, she swung little Chris up and around dizzily. His golden curls bounced, his laughter rang out merrily, and her own skirt billowed like an inverted mushroom. "As I was going to St. Ives..."

St. Ives! Why, that was it, of course. Michael, his life dedicated to service, undoubtedly would be led to build a church. It was no curse to be wealthy, but God expected good stewardship—money was not to be flaunted but shared to help others. Meantime, she and Young Wil would enjoy their moment of glory as "godparents"...

38

"Whither Thou Goest..."

It would be a night of pandemonium. Hammers would ring out as the ranch hands nailed together a platform for the ceremony and the Grand March musicale to follow. Cookstoves would gobble up wood faster than the men could split the stovewood. And the "good wives" would be doing everything a good woman was supposed to: baking... making last-minute nips and tucks in the handsome blue-over-white gown which only Mariah's clever fingers could adjust from a "stout women's size" pattern to a "young-matron" appearance (the nervous bride's only concern being that her wealth of long hair would be dry enough to crimp into a becoming style, the back being somewhat like True's—True *would* help?). And flowers... flowers everywhere... who took that cake frosting recipe? It was lying right here... "Men, stop that poundin'. Want this weddin' cake t'fall?... Child-*ren*, stop runnin' thro' th' archway else no cake fer yuh tomorrow!"

A week... wasn't that how long Young Wil had to decide? The Portland offer would be the greatest opportunity of his life—one of the three directions which they must decide between, True reviewed in her mind. And yet her heart knew a strange peace even when the options changed from three to four! Because she had made her decision already...

True's eyes scanned the crowd for her husband. There was a compelling urge to talk with him, say the things she'd been unable to find words for on the train. Her eyes met

Chris Beth's instead. Her aunt laid down her apron and shouldered her way to where True stood.

"You look lost, darling—missing your mate? I understand—you and I are only half-people without our Wils! They're talking together," she frowned, "a little too seriously for all this—"

Aunt Chrissy made an arc toward the enlarging group. In her hand was a stack of envelopes. "In the commotion, I forgot your mail."

True thanked her and began thumbing through the packet, not sure she knew what she was looking for. Was it the letter from William Prescott? If so, her subconscious was working overtime. The man was out of their lives. Totally and completely. Well, wasn't he?

In the subdued light of a low-burning lamp moments later she was ripping open his envelope and scanning the contents. He had survived the "murderous wilderness" (as others called the Great Smokies—those who predicted he would never come out alive). He loved the mountains and wondered how he could have ever left home, no matter what the reason. The enmity, for the most part, was gone, but remnants of doubt remained. There were those who advised him to be "a mite mo' keerful." Old rancors died hard, so he was compelled to work on forgiveness along with the three R's—there being no enlightened preacher. True, there hadn't been a "killing or a stilling" for a long while, but disease was taking the populace faster than the shotguns used to. Oh, the wasted potential... fine minds falling to ruin... healthy bodies of former generations wasting away, neglected. Were they really any better off? Fires that once raged were now a bed of ashes. "I guess," he wrote in near-conclusion, "I've done little more than sink an axe in a giant oak. But where helpers would once have been executed, the people now pray for them—only their belief in God is waning. If He doesn't answer prayer, what's the need of it all?"

True closed her eyes in an effort to withhold the tears. William Prescott had no right to do this to her! Casting his own burdens on her—or *were* they his own? Behind her eyelids flashed visions. Sights and sounds that were somehow familiar, reminders that God created it all and—in some strange way which she did not fully understand—put every man in charge of his brother.

She hovered too much, Young Wil had told her. But how did one escape? Again she saw them, heard them, *dreamed* them. As they were and as they ought to be. Hordes of worshipers in a large church . . . singing, shouting, even allowing for an even distribution of those with colored skins, heretofore "horsewhipped" if they came near . . . the mellow voices of a black choir whose only musical accompaniment lay outside the church, the soft melody of running water, swift and glistening, as pure as their souls . . . and then the evening-gloam . . . the sad-sweet calls of the whip-poorwills chaining themselves to the hearts of all who heard. For sure, "hit was a-gonna rain . . ." Beautiful Appalachia restored . . .

True did not hear Young Wil tiptoe into the room. "Oh, here you are, my love," he said, tactfully ignoring the letter in her hand. "I'm guessing you had to rest a bit. Small wonder—and to think! *Mañana* will be worse. Oh, the tumult . . . Lung and Tongue will bark their fool heads off . . . the March Hare will bark the shins of every guest with that 'Kiddie Kar' we have yet to present. Soooo, Young Doctor North prescribes a walk for his beloved patient—but not alone, *never alone*—"

It was the last two words that undid her, let the dammed-up wall of tears come in a cleansing flood. Too long, too long, she had held them back . . . the sea was so wide, her boat so small . . .

They walked in the silence of the moonlight, holding hands but not talking. At length Young Wil said quietly, "The letter was from Prescott, wasn't it? Wanting us to join him—help out?"

True nodded, so sure was she that this was what the unread ending amounted to. Waiting for no words, her husband said, "Has Jerry seen the letter?"

"Jerry?" she repeated dully.

"Your brother—remember?" Young Wil was teasing, actually teasing her. And already love was working its magic. The situation was no longer a problem, and peace came stealing back. Her feet, like her heart, were light—wanting to leap ahead without dread or fear.

"He will enjoy it. And have you thought of Kearby and her young man? I am looking at the future through a peephole and seeing it clearly," Young Wil continued as if inspired. "I know the signs—they're all there for the four of them—and four brilliant young minds could shake those mountains."

"A teacher, a preacher—*and* perhaps a doctor. Did Kearby tell you that she was interested in medicine? Well, so is Clarry somewhat—darling, if anything should happen—uh, to me—I want Clarry to have Angel Mother's brooch—if she's family—" True said out of context.

"I understand, but nothing's going to happen to you, my sweet. You have work to do, remember? Sooo, shall we talk about our future?"

"All night if you wish, Dr. North," True said gaily. "You have some decisions to make—me, I've made mine!"

His next words made her wonder if he heard. "You know, standing back there on the platform, as you cast your eyes to the hills, it seemed to me that we stood at the crossroads of our future which melded into all the problems of the world—"

"—and that windswept platform became an *everywhere*, all the people becoming one," she finished for him. "I know. And there we stood, wondering which road to take, never knowing where the others might have led. Crossroads are lonely. To endure—or to let go—"

Surely Angel Mother, who had devoted her short adult years to righting a wrong in her mind, must be agonizing for True—understanding because choices were so hard for the child-mother. Or was she rejoicing that her beloved Valley had become a seeding ground for missionaries produced in her own family? Oh, why should memories come alive *now*? The softness of her singing to the bees . . . telling Bible stories . . . sharing adventures of successes and failures of pioneer life . . . popping corn. Daring to dream. And, most of all, filling the firelit room with the silver tinkle of her laughter. Aunt Chrissy had been the one with the quiet resolve, the courage which Angel Mother wanted for True, her wish granted. But the love for all that was beautiful, the silvery laughter, and the dreaming had been the legacy of the flowerlike creature who gave True birth.

Flowerlike? Yes. But fragile she was not. Else why, when Mary Evangeline North wrote the final entry in her diary—a message of goodbye—had the very foundation of the family been shaken? Why had it taken so long for them to see that she was plucky, too, seeing them through every crisis in another way? Only it was sad—but God had known. And only He knew His plan for the daughter she adored and her young husband...

Oh, dear, now I am weeping again! Have I no control?

"Darling—what have I said? Oh, *forgive me*!" The words wrung from Young Wil were filled with remorse.

True raised her eyes, twin violets in the moonlight, and allowed him to dry her foolish tears with a big white handkerchief that smelled faintly of antiseptics. "Forgive *you*? I am the one who begs forgiveness. Time just turned backward, so indulge me—and remember, Wil North, that it is vain and foolish not to forgive!"

"Brat! Oh, you little *brat*! Sunshine and shadows, that's you, *you*. But I love it—all," he grinned his endearing grin, "except for the woman's way of winning. You know we men are pushovers—that to us the most powerful flow of water on earth is your tears."

"I wasn't expecting them, darling. It's just that I was thinking back over the years—*analyzing*, if you need a medical term—our wonderful family, thinking of how each is a part of the other, a powerful influence. It seemed so sweet, and yet so sad. There are several kinds of *sad*, you know."

He inhaled deeply. "Smell the clover? I think I understand. Fragrance is not its main purpose, but is a sweet added benefit. Forgot I was poetic, didn't you—or assumed that if I made a rhyme it would be about parts of the body?"

"Ummm—like the heart? So back to our thesis, Doctor. Ours is a choosing, I guess, like the clover. All the choices you face have important purposes, but you must decide what *your* purpose is—test it, see if you chose what is right for you, or if its added benefits are too appealing to resist. There! We're even! You didn't know that I hid a brain beneath my bonnet!"

"You know you're bright, so stop fishing for compliments, but—" Young Wil paused, and when he spoke again the teasing was gone, "I'm glad you mentioned the Blue Ridge. Don't let Prescott's letter upset you too much. The outlook is brighter than he knows, I think. The old 'pop-skull' stuff is just about a thing of the past—too many Revenue officers keeping watch for even the backsliders to risk bootlegging, and the townsfolk have either grown leery or no longer have a taste for the fiery drink. And there's hope for the economy, too, according to word I pick up at the medical conferences. Coal mines are opening—bringing new hope—"

"Which you and I never lost."

"Right, sweetheart." He took her hand but did not turn around. That meant their talk was unfinished. "As I see it, we will not be choosing between a land we love, an area where we are needed, and a job with a great future. I would say that they're somewhat the same. There's always need for love, understanding, service—so it boils down to what my most precious piece of property desires!"

"Wil North! I'm not *your property*—oh, yes, I am, darling—"

He squeezed her hand, the muscles tightening in intensity. "You have reached a decision, so help *me*."

He did hear.

"Yes—yes, I have." She dreaded the words. But they must be said. "It depends on when—or *if*—you plan a family. Children's needs would be the first consideration."

She had thought it would be easier. Why was her heart pounding?

Leaning down, Young Wil pressed his warm cheek against hers and the grip on her hand tightened even more. "I leave that to you," he said, but his voice was husky. "Frankly, it's a novel idea, I confess—I guess there has been too little time to give it proper thought."

"I—I thought all men wanted a son?"

"To carry on the family name?" He chuckled. "Marty seems to be doing well enough in that area. And there's Jerry. Or did you suppose me to be so egotistical that I must make it my lifework to make sure that my genes are handed from this generation to the next—or, perish the thought, that I must create in my own image?"

True giggled. "In a mixed-up family like ours, none of that seems important. And, as for your last question, well, God has done that for you—created in *His* image."

There was silence. They walked on, and True noted that the grass was growing damp with dew. They should be getting back. Even the slant of the moon said so. There was Tillie's hair to do. And yet, as warm, intimate, and revealing as their talk had been, something was left unsaid. It hung between them, unfinished.

"I guess I need to confess something," True said slowly, "since it was I who brought up the matter of a family. So I confess that I have given it little thought—oh, not that I am opposed—you know how I adore Chris. He is a part of us. It's like joint custody—we never *own* our children, do we? It was so with my seeing Midgie through her pregnancy, your ushering him into the world, and," True laughed, "my trying to take care of him, only to have him snatched away by Marty!"

"Marty and Midgie needed a child to hold the marriage together. We have no such need—and, in most cases, I would declare that to be a wrong reason for bringing a child into the world. Their case seems different—as I guess all cases are. Generalizing is dangerous."

True agreed with him, then, with a rush of words, said that she felt less need to create than to love and serve those already created. *All* of them. All over the world! Most parents *wanted* to love but simply didn't know how. They, too, needed her—

"Mother Eve."

Young Wil spoke the words tenderly, softly, not spoiling their implication that she was greatly blest. It was True who spoke at length.

"I have always felt that if it is God's plan, He will send us children by the dozens—and that will be fine. We need not concern ourselves. And even then I would want to help others—learn to love—"

"Mother Eve," he said again. "And your preference on my job?"

"I didn't say preference. I said I had reached a *decision*."

"Well?" True fancied he was not breathing.

"I have decided that we must listen—listen with our hearts—else we may miss the still, small voice of God."

"Sooo," his voice shook ever so slightly as if he wrestled to regain control, "we herewith put it all in His hands—and go forth to enjoy the wedding feast?"

"Exactly."

"But—who can say where God will lead? What about *you*?"

As if by signal, they stopped and faced each other. This was the moment which counted. But True was prepared. "... whither thou goest ..."

She could say no more, and neither could he. But the way he embraced her spoke of a reverence unknown by the human tongue, a *knowing* which said: "God will walk with us wherever the road. If we stay, He will stay. God needs help in good conditions and in bad. And who are the winners? Those who listen and follow."

True was halfway to heaven already—here in her husband's arms, and there among the throbbing stars. A wellspring of laughter, born of joy, bubbled up inside her. She drew back slightly.

"Darling," she said solemnly, "I just couldn't have been a Mother Eve."

"And why not, prithee?"

"I could never have thought up a name like *Hippopotamus*!"

Together they laughed. Joyously. Triumphantly. And the hopeful hills sent back their laughter, its echo reaching "far beyond the heavens" ...

Leaving in the human heart a love everlasting ...
And the strength to endure ...
For: "Happy is he whose hope is in the Lord."